HONORABLY ENGAGED

ALSO BY KASEY STOCKTON

Regency Romance

The Jewels of Halstead Manor

The Lady of Larkspur Vale

The Widow of Falbrooke Court

The Recluse of Wolfeton House

The Smuggler of Camden Cove

Properly Kissed

Sensibly Wed

Pleasantly Pursued

Love in the Bargain

All is Mary and Bright

A Noble Inheritance

Myths of Moraigh Trilogy

Journey to Bongary Spring

Through the Fairy Tree

The Enemy Across the Loch

Contemporary Romance

Cotswolds Holiday

I'm Not Charlotte Lucas

Christmas in the City Series

HONORABLY ENGAGED

KASEY STOCKTON

GOLDEN OWL
PRESS

Copyright © 2023 by Kasey Stockton
Cover design by Seventhstar Art

First edition: April 2023
Golden Owl Press

Library of Congress Control Number: 2023906082
ISBN 978-1-952429-34-7
Fort Worth, TX

For Jane Austen & her beloved Mr. Darcy

CHAPTER I

MARIANNE

London, 1818

S *tuff and nonsense, Mari,* I scolded, smoothing the ten pound banknote on my lap. Light snuck through the foggy carriage window and shone on the scrolling ink, Bank of England stamped across the top. *Mr. Marbury has no cause to refuse you.*

My nerves danced over the impending confrontation. It awaited me on the other side of the burgundy-painted door to the publisher's office, but I had yet to so much as leave the safety and peace of my carriage. Eyes glued to the insulting slip of paper in my hands—a mere *ten pounds*—I ignored the sounds of traffic on the busy road. Hooves clopping, creaking leather, rolling wheels. I had one opportunity to make my wishes known, and I would not blunder it.

"Have you changed your mind, miss?" Keene asked, looking up with hopeful, round eyes from her seat opposite me. My maid had been against this outing from the beginning.

1

"No." I folded the paper neatly on its time-worn creases and slipped the ten pounds back into my reticule, pulling the drawstrings tight once again. "But you needn't join me. Wait here." I pushed the door open and alighted on my own. I did many things on my own, and there was no one in *this* part of town to censure me.

"But—"

"Wait here," I said again, turning to face my anxious maid. "I will return shortly."

I closed the door with a snap, then pulled the blue lace veil over my face. I might have some confidence in my ability to remain anonymous in this part of London, but I was no fool. My reputation was still of some import.

For now.

The bell over the door rang, announcing my arrival, and a man looked up from his desk which was set against the wall. He was young and thin and looked very much the secretary he likely was. "Can I help you, ma'am?" came his nasally voice.

"I require an audience with Mr. Marbury, if you please."

"Have you an appointment?"

Secretary, indeed. "No. But he will see me." I hoped. *Confidence, Mari.*

The man stood, a delayed display of chivalry. "Whom might I say is calling?"

"A woman he will very much wish to speak to."

The secretary looked uneasy. Was my veil off-putting? Or merely my sex?

"Inquire with Mr. Marbury, if you do not believe me," I challenged.

The man scurried away, likely to do just that. I squashed the temptation to fiddle with the cord of my reticule. Mother had taught me how to behave like a lady, and I had done a faultless job of it thus far, current situation notwithstanding.

I had a feeling my request would not be granted, but fortunately for me, the secretary had lit the path directly to the man I sought. I followed him down the short corridor and paused before a door, the gold plaque reading *Mr. Marbury, Publisher.*

Wouldn't one need to *publish* books to own that title? It was nearly enough of a joke to incite laughter, but I suppressed the inclination.

The door gave way easily, revealing the slender secretary standing before an overlarge oak desk, a portly man resting opposite with side-whiskers long enough to rival those of my cat.

"Mr. Marbury." I scrounged every bit of false confidence I could manufacture and stepped into the room. "It is of the utmost importance that I speak with you."

Mr. Marbury looked from me to the secretary, his ruddy cheeks visible beneath his twitching whiskers. "You've not made an appointment, madam."

"Not for lack of trying." I sent him a brief smile and took the seat opposite his desk, pulling my gloves off one finger at a time. Unnecessary, perhaps, but I hoped it would give him to understand that I didn't intend to leave until I spoke to him.

A look passed over his face. Resignation? The secretary gave up, retreating into the corridor. I waited until the door clicked closed behind him before I laid my gloves in my lap and lifted my veil to rest over my bonnet.

"We do not deal in periodicals, madam."

It would appear he did not recognize me. I supposed three years could do much to mature a young woman's face, but it stung all the same. Had I been dismissed from his mind as easily as my manuscript had? "I am well aware. You hardly deal in novels."

This set his back up. He leaned against his chair, his mouth turned down in a frown. It was the same expression he'd worn after our initial introduction, when I had come into his office for the first time and he had discovered the author of the manuscript he'd purchased through written correspondence—M.H.—was a woman.

I had no need of forming an enemy today. It was time to curtail my tongue.

He pulled a long-chained watch from his waistcoat pocket and checked the time. "I have a meeting shortly with a client who scheduled an *appointment*. Please state your business."

In other words: proceed with haste. Very well. I could do that. I would not bother replying to his barb, however, for I would have been more than happy to schedule an appointment if he'd replied to my letter. Finding time away from my mama for clandestine meetings was difficult to plan ahead of time, though, so it had worked to my benefit. Outings she would wholly disapprove of were more easily arranged in the moment.

I fixed him with the most forthright gaze I could. I already had the disadvantage of being a woman. Now that my future hung in the balance, I hoped he would at least listen to me, though he seemed more likely to shutter his ears. "You own the rights to my novel and have yet to do anything with it. I would like to purchase it back." I pulled the ten pound note from my reticule and smoothed it on the desk before me. "I am willing to pay the sum which was paid to me, along with another five pounds for your time." It pained me to do so, but I pulled out a second banknote and added it to the first.

Mr. Marbury looked from me to the banknotes, his eyes narrowing. "M.H."

"Yes." I would not proceed to provide my entire name, Marianne Hutton, but he was correct in guessing which novel of mine was gathering a layer of dust on his shelf. I held his gaze, channeling my father during a game of chess. "Will this agreement suit?"

He ran a pudgy hand over his chin. "No."

"Pardon?"

"No. I will not sell the rights back to you, Mrs. M.H."

Never before had I felt like a salmon, but currently it was a struggle to keep my mouth closed.

"I purchased the manuscript legally," he continued, "and it is mine to do with as I see fit."

My story was only fit for a dark cabinet? He did not think so when I had initially sent it to him. "You've had the manuscript in your possession for nearly three years, sir. If you will not publish the novel, then I shall find someone else to do so."

"I am afraid that is out of the question."

"Out of the—good heavens. Why? You cannot mean to imply that you retain the intention of publishing it?" Despite Mr. Marbury's proven incompetence, my chest inflated with the merest wisp of hope.

"At present, no. I haven't a minute to spare on another project. I am fully engaged with another author. A man who will be here any moment, and you are sitting in his seat."

Occupied by another author who was making enough money to require Mr. Marbury's full attention, of course. Another author whose book was published shortly after mine was meant to be. My chest thickened with dislike. "You speak of Mr. Dalton Henry, I assume?"

The man did not admit as much, but his further frustration gave him away. I pulled the banknotes from his desk and folded them again, tucking them into my reticule with distaste. Lowering my veil to hide my face, I stood, then pulled my gloves on with deliberate slowness.

I despised the man who had stolen my publishing slot and publisher's attention. The temptation to tarry and snatch a peek of the guilty party was large. Dalton Henry was likely a short man, slender and pale from his time indoors penning novels about ancient battles and feuds. My nose wrinkled in distaste. Nothing about this office was appealing. Not the man who ran it or the men he worked with.

"If that is all?" Mr. Marbury said, trying to push me out the door.

"If fifteen pounds is not sufficient, then what is?"

He breathed out an impatient sigh. "As I previously stated, I still plan to publish the novel."

"Eventually."

"Yes," he agreed.

"But that is not good enough for me, sir." *Eventually* would not provide me with an income to support myself. *Eventually* would not put my story on the shelves of book shops and lending libraries. *Eventually* would not free me from my stifling, confining Society life.

The idea of being forced to sew samplers or perform for Mama's dinner guests one day longer than necessary was enough to raise the tide of restless dread within me. I had worked hard over recent years to be the perfect daughter. I'd asked for nothing, and I'd been devoutly obedient. Now I had a plan, and Mr. Marbury with his long whiskers and hard eyes was standing in the way of that.

"Fifty pounds," I said. I didn't have fifty pounds, but that was beside the point. Papa could possibly be persuaded to lend it to me.

His graying eyebrows shot up. "No."

"One hundred pounds." I swallowed. Now I had truly lost my wits. But I would make the money back if the book was published elsewhere, surely.

The air was charged, and I could see the consideration passing over Mr. Marbury's face. My hands clenched into tense fists. I was close. He had opened his mouth to speak when the bell rang, indicating someone had entered the building through their front door. Mr. Marbury snapped his lips closed, shaking his head a little as though to clear it. "No."

I'd been close to having my manuscript returned to me. I could tell. So close.

"My client is here, madam. If you would be so kind as to allow me to show you to the door."

His client, the adventure author. Dalton Henry, ruining something for me yet again.

"If you change your mind—"

His hand went to my back, gently leading me into the corridor. "I will not change my mind."

I stepped from his reach, lifting my nose in the air to proceed before him with the breeding and refinement befitting my station, much as my mother had taught me to do, even though I was leaving my very soul in Mr. Marbury's clutches. He might have rejected my offer, but this was not the end of things. I would come up with a large enough sum to tempt him further and return with the banknotes to prove it was a viable offer.

Two men stood at the secretary's desk in the entryway. I noticed with a start that while one man was certainly narrow and fell on the paler side of the complexion spectrum—the secretary—the other man was his opposite in every way. Broad-shouldered and tall, with brown curly hair in a semblance of disarray, despite clear efforts on the part of the man to tame his wild locks. He held his hat in one hand and a stack of paper in the other. *This* was the author Dalton Henry? Not short, not pale, and in no way a man who seemed to write about adventure merely because he could not experience it on his own. This gentleman's easy stance and formidable bearing spoke of status and prestige. His sense of comfort in his own sphere was proof he'd seen something of the world.

If his sense of importance was a result of his success as an author, he would fall even lower in my esteem. Oddly, I wished that wasn't the case.

"Ah, Mr. Henry." Mr. Marbury's simpering soured my stomach. "If you'll give me but a moment, I am nearly ready to meet with you."

Mr. Henry turned to face his publisher. The moment our eyes

7

met, my stomach sank clear to the wood-planked floor. Despite the veil covering my face, his eyes lit with recognition, and I stifled the unladylike curse dancing on my tongue.

This was not Dalton Henry, author and complete stranger. No, *this* was Henry Bradwell, gentleman and long-time friend of my family.

Oh, drat. I was in a real quandary now.

CHAPTER 2
HENRY

M r. Marbury could hardly blame me for struggling to pay attention to his monologue while I was still recovering from the shock of seeing Marianne Hutton in his entryway, alone and wearing something of a disguise. I considered myself a generally intelligent man, but my mind failed to alight on a single reason for her presence that would not bode ill for me. What was her business here? Where was her maid or footman or mother? Furthermore, was my secret no longer intact?

"Mr. Henry?"

It never ceased to feel strange, being addressed by the pseudonym I had adopted for my novels. I was merely Henry or Bradwell to all but my publisher, and I had wanted it to remain that way. Would Miss Hutton tell everyone the truth? Would news of my secret reach my mother?

"Mr. Henry?" Mr. Marbury said again, his patience growing thinner.

I straightened in my seat. "Forgive me. My mind has run away. You were saying?"

"We cannot compete with the romantic novels. *Pride and Prej-*

udice. *Sense and Sensibility.* They have long had a monopoly on sales, and it would behoove us to alter our direction to better appeal to all readers."

"All readers?"

"As it stands, you tell a story fit for men alone."

Of course I did. That was my intention. But Mr. Marbury's raised eyebrows indicated he wanted something different. "You would like for it to also be fit for women?"

"Indeed." He leaned forward in his chair. "Many novels tell of adventure and love simultaneously. Can you not do the same?"

No. My stories could not. I didn't know the first thing about writing a love story. Good gads, he wanted an entire rewrite, did he not? My gaze flicked to the finished manuscript sitting on the desk between us. "You imply my *next* novel shall—"

"Not your next, Mr. Henry. This one." He tapped it with a thick finger. "We cannot hope to gain the sales we desire without appealing to the general population."

"That will take time."

"You may have it. It shouldn't be too much trouble. Just add a woman for your man to fall in love with."

Just add a character. As though it was as simple as placing an additional pear on one's plate or layering a second blanket over one's bed. The sheer work ahead of me was daunting. To say nothing of the fact that I did not know how to write a woman for my character to fall in love with. That was not something I had experience with.

There was a woman I'd considered romantically, once, but she had married my brother and now I no longer held her in a romantic regard. Which was the way I liked it. Steady. Safe. Secure.

Utterly devoid of feminine sensibilities.

"I am not sure I can do it, Mr. Marbury."

His smile slipped. "I'm afraid I need you to."

The threat loomed heavily in those words. Make the changes, or he wouldn't publish my book. He had to be bluffing. He would not sit on a manuscript that had the potential to bring him money, would he? His expression said otherwise, though. I supposed the least I could do now was try. "I will give it my best efforts."

"Very good, Mr. Henry. Quite capital."

I stood, anxious to be on my way. I would need to devise some excuse to drop in on the Huttons unannounced. I couldn't very well call on Marianne and request her company for a ride or a walk without inciting rumors, but I needed to speak to her. Nay, not speak. *Beg* her to forget she ever saw me in a publishing house.

Sliding my hat over my wayward curls, I took up my manuscript again. "You will have my answer within six months."

"Your answer?"

"About whether or not I am capable," I explained.

Mr. Marbury looked uneasy for the first time since I entered his office. "Three months. You should know by then if it is possible."

I nodded once. "Very well. Good day, sir."

Three months for an entire rewrite with an added character and a fresh romantic storyline? Marbury had gone mad.

The cool spring air met me when I burst outside, searching the street for a coach to hire. It had been ages since I'd gone to the Huttons' house, and I wasn't sure I could even recall where it was, which meant returning home for the address first. My limbs were achy and buzzing like a swarm of honeybees. What if Miss Hutton had already announced to the whole of her family that I was—

"Mr. Bradwell?"

11

I spun, coming face-to-face with the very woman I'd been hoping to search out. She was shorter than I recalled, her dark hair pinned up and tucked beneath her bonnet. Her brown eyes snapped, crackling like a freshly built fire and no less bright for the veil that covered them. "Marianne Hutton."

Her lips pressed into a flat line. "So it is true. You *are* Dalton—"

"No," I said, though we both knew it was a blatant lie. I glanced around us, but no one seemed to be paying us any mind. "Don't speak of it here, if you please. Is there somewhere we can speak privately?"

She looked at me shrewdly. I had known this woman for my entire life—our mothers were dear friends—but I had not seen her often, and I did not know her well. The truth was that Marianne Hutton was a veritable stranger, but in all our years of acquaintance, I'd never thought of her as anything other than soft-spoken and well-mannered. Never before had she acted so blatantly annoyed.

She gestured to the street. "My carriage is just over there, and my maid is waiting inside. I can convey you home if you'd like."

Was it entirely proper? Even with the presence of her maid, I wondered if her mother would not like it. But she did not seem concerned with propriety, and I needed privacy to beg for her silence. "That would be most agreeable, thank you."

Miss Hutton led the way to her carriage. "Tell Clayton where you'd like to go."

I opened the door for her, but she did not take my proffered hand, instead climbing in on her own, clutching her skirt to avoid tripping. I gave my direction to the coachman and followed Miss Hutton into the carriage, taking the seat opposite her and the nervous-looking maid. When the door was closed, she lifted her veil and untied her bonnet strings, sliding the hat from her head. She gave it to her maid, who retrieved a different bonnet from the hat box on her lap—sans veil—and Miss Hutton tied it into place, securing the bow to the left of her chin.

She truly was lovely—in every way except her attitude. Her straight nose was wrinkled while she settled in her seat and looked at me as if I was scented with manure.

I happened to know I smelled rather nice, so the cause for her distaste was unclear.

"You wished to speak privately?" she asked, the carriage rocking while it pulled onto the road and joined the traffic.

My gaze flicked to her maid.

"Keene is the soul of discretion. She can be trusted."

No servants could be trusted, but I would not argue that point. What choice did I have? "No one knows, Miss Hutton."

She looked puzzled, her shoulders swaying slightly with the motion of the carriage, before her brow cleared. "You refer to the pseudonym."

"Indeed. No one knows."

"Not your family?"

"Not even them."

"You wish for it to remain that way."

"I do." I pinched the edges of my portfolio, holding her brown eyes. "I trust I can rely on your discretion."

Miss Hutton leaned back against the squabs, a comfort settling over her. Was she relieved? How odd. "How long have you been with Marbury?"

"Just over three years."

"As I thought," she muttered.

"I beg your pardon?"

"You want me to keep your secret, which is rather fortuitous. I need a favor."

Keene looked at Miss Hutton with trepidation. "You cannot mean to press this further?" she asked timidly.

"I will do what I must." Settling her gaze on me again, Miss

Hutton looked more determined than any person had a right to. It was intimidating, if I was being honest. I feared for what she was about to ask of me. "You would agree that you have significant clout with Mr. Marbury, yes?"

"No." If I had, I would not be reworking my novel to include a romance.

She frowned. "We can agree to disagree on that score. Would you agree that your publisher wants to keep you happy?"

"Yes, that is a fair assessment."

"Would you say he listens to you?" she asked.

Did he? "I suppose so."

"Then I promise to keep your secret if you agree to help move my novel toward publication."

I choked, sputtering a cough. "That is what you were doing in there? Trying to publish a novel?" Quiet, soft-spoken Miss Hutton had written a book and proceeded to meet with a publisher on her own? Without her father or another man to support her?

"Not exactly. I was attempting to retrieve my manuscript from Mr. Marbury, and he refused me. If he will not sell back the rights to my novel, then he could be persuaded to publish it." She looked at the window, and I could tell this was a great difficulty for her.

"He has paid you for it already?"

"Yes." She leveled me with a gaze. "Three years ago."

I didn't notice the carriage come to a stop, surprised as I was by her admission. The pointed way in which she stated it could not hide her irritation at me, or the significance she allowed three years to hold. Did she blame me for her novel remaining unpublished? Surely she recognized I had nothing to do with it. Marbury made those decisions.

I could not argue that it was far too long to wait. I would be at the end of my patience, were I in her position. But the point that weighed upon me now was Marbury's role in this—it was abundantly clear that he *was* willing to sit on a manuscript. That certainly raised my desire to find success with my rewriting endeavors, and quickly.

"What do you need from me, then?" I asked.

"I want you to use your influence to move my book to publication. Mr. Marbury refused to sell back the rights, but at the rate he is moving, my book will never see the light of day."

There must be some reason he had yet to publish a novel he had paid for. I could speak to the man, but she was asking for something well outside my power. "I cannot make any promises."

She gave a little shrug. "You can make some effort, though?"

"If I do this, you'll keep my secret?"

She looked at me. "Yes."

My body tensed. I was not in general a social man, and sitting for so long in the company of a woman I did not know well, despite our families' long-standing friendship, was taxing. Addressing the matter of her novel with Marbury would be taxing, as well. But the effort would be worth prolonging my anonymity. "How shall I reach you after I've spoken to him?"

"Will you be attending any social functions in the upcoming week?"

"I suppose now I have no choice, if we are to communicate casually." The idea of Society balls, parties, or dinners was repulsive to me. I often attended them while in the country to appease my mother, but she was not here with us now, and there was no one to force my hand. My brothers would certainly find it odd if I suddenly showed an interest in the *ton*, but as they were not here either, it hardly signified. Besides, what other choice did I have?

"It is a benefit that our mothers have remained friends for so many years, Mr. Bradwell. It will not be seen as strange to seek one another out for a conversation."

A footman opened the door and looked at me expectantly.

We'd reached my townhouse, by the look of it. The ride had gone more quickly than I had realized, and still I had questions for Miss Hutton. This woman had written a book and sold it to a publisher, and I had assumed she cared for nothing above new music for the pianoforte or a finished embroidery project.

"What is the nature of your novel, Miss Hutton?"

"Romance." Her lips flickered in a tired smile. "If Marbury does not wish to proceed, I will find someone else who will. I don't pretend to find my own story incredible. It is certainly no *Persuasion*. But I do think it could bring a smile to many faces were it given the opportunity."

"Your dedication is impressive."

"Because I am a woman? Would my dedication be less impressive were I a man?"

Yes. That was absolutely what I had thought. Most women of my acquaintance would not chase anything of this nature. They would seethe privately in their frustration and lament their ill fortune. "I am impressed you are pursuing something you care so deeply about."

"I hope not to be forced to pursue it for much longer."

And she was relying on me to make it so. "Until we meet again." I stepped out of the carriage and gave her a bow, returning my hat to my head.

"Oh, Mr. Bradwell? Mr. Marbury is unaware of my full name. My manuscript is under the name M.H."

"Understood." The footman closed the door, hopped on the back of the carriage, and they were off. I stood on the street, watching her leave. A small tendril of unease curled through my body. I was not entirely safe yet. What if I was unable to make any headway with Mr. Marbury? Would Miss Hutton still be willing to aid in my anonymity? She had not seemed a spiteful woman, but I did not know the nature of her character beyond the fact that she held me in some way responsible for her lack of publication. My palms grew damp against the portfolio containing my manuscript, imagining how I would face my family if word got out. Indeed, how would I face Society as a whole?

I shook my head and mounted my steps. This would all be managed. One thing at a time.

CHAPTER 3

MARIANNE

My father's library was often a refuge for me, and the four days since seeing Mr. Bradwell had necessitated its use frequently. Waiting for word from the man turned out to be excessively tiring. I could not reconcile Henry Bradwell as the author of such well-loved novels. Papa owned a "Dalton Henry" book, but I had never opened it. Spite, perhaps? My frustration at being passed over for that man while my book languished on Marbury's shelves was no secret.

Well, it was a secret to the entirety of the world, but not something I hid from myself.

Julia poked her head through the doorway, her fichu slightly askew from the toddler resting on her hip, his chubby hand gripping her neckline. "I thought I would find you in here. Have you a minute?"

"I have many." I stood and reached both arms toward my nephew, who came to me willingly. I retook my seat, bouncing Frederick on my knee. "How have you been sleeping?"

"Better, a little." She lowered herself on the chair and leaned back in unladylike repose. "I wish he would go with Nanny, but he wants none other than me, and *never* at a decent hour."

"Nightmares do not play to the whims of mothers."

"No," Julia said, opening her eyes to reiterate her point. "They do not."

"Kitty?" Frederick asked, heedless of being the center of our conversation.

I stood, balancing him on my hip, and scanned the shelves until my gaze fell on a mass of gray striped fur. "Over there," I whispered, pointing up. "Do you see Mr. Darcy?"

"Kitty!" Frederick wiggled until I let him down, and he toddled toward the bookcase where my cat was taking a nap. He reached both hands in the air and jumped, as though he would be able to leap the six feet to the feline's hiding place.

"He'll be at that for hours," Julia said, yawning. "I do hope your cat doesn't wake up soon."

I lowered myself in the chair again, tucking my feet beneath me. "How is Mr. Walding?"

"Far away," Julia pouted. "There was flooding in Dorset, and he has gone to assess the damage to our home and see to the tenants. I do not expect him to return for some time."

"I shall pray he faces minimal repairs."

"Have you given any thought to acquiring a Mr. Walding of your own?"

"You want me to acquire your husband?"

"Don't be daft," she said. Only two years my senior, my sister and I had always been close. She had married Mr. Walding five years ago, though, changing our relationship somewhat. While I had long been marrying age, I had not followed her path to immediate matrimony. Now at three-and-twenty, I was a veritable spinster in my mother's eyes.

"My spinsterhood is not for lack of *trying* to find a husband."

Julia laughed. "You are young, Mari. You cannot claim spinsterhood quite yet."

"I doubt Mama shares that opinion."

Pity flashed in Julia's eyes. "She only wants you to be happy."

Happiness was writing. It was crafting a story and experiencing growth through the characters. It was not incessantly playing the part of hostess or worrying about seating arrangements and candle orders and who was going to pay the butcher. I wanted love and children and a home of my own, but I did not want to be a housekeeper.

Which was why I had not fully removed the possibility of never marrying at all. A tidy income from my novels and a cottage in the country would suit me better than hosting parties for the rest of my days. Until I raised the courage to discuss this option with my parents, I would continue to do my best to be their nearly-perfect daughter.

"Mr. Jacobson was nice," Julia said carefully. "Handsome and polite. He never once stepped on your toes whilst dancing or forced you to fetch your own refreshment."

"He was polite, but he had aspirations in politics."

Julia stared at me. "When did we begin to dislike politicians?"

"Never. But being a politician's wife would be uncomfortable."

She seemed to consider this. "It would require a taste for being a hostess. I know how much you dislike that possibility."

"Kitty!" Frederick yelled, continuing to jump. Mr. Darcy lounged atop his books, never opening an eye.

"Captain Neal?" Julia asked.

He had been attentive lately, and he was handsome enough with his sandy-brown hair and ruggedly crooked nose, but that was where his virtues ceased. "Navy man. I refuse to live on a ship."

"Unfair dislike of the ocean," she noted. "Mr. Ferrars?" she challenged.

"Too many sisters. Their family is constantly visiting one another."

"I did not realize we held a dislike for sisters as well."

I shot her a wry grimace. "That is not the issue."

"So you *would* like to marry. You simply do not wish for a husband who would require that you to do all the things a wife is typically called upon to do?"

"That phrasing is unfair." Though, in a sense, I supposed she was correct.

She widened her eyes innocently. "I am only trying to understand."

"Why? Do you want for me to wed soon and provide Frederick with little cousins?"

"That, and Mama asked if I understood your hesitation in selecting a husband. You have a good deal of eligible suitors—as you have the last few Seasons—yet you are disinterested in all of them. You are fortunate to have such indulgent parents who allow you to choose your own husband. I have many friends who would not have been permitted to carry on in this manner."

Of course. She was gathering information to pass on to Mama. "That was sneaky, Julia."

"It would have been sneaky if I never admitted my purpose in pursuing this conversation. Mama fails to understand why you did not accept Mr. Jacobson, and she wishes you would appear more interested in Captain Neal. She is nearly at her wit's end trying to find a husband to appease you. *Fussy girl*, she said."

"Fussy?" My eyes sought the ceiling, hoping to find patience in the panels up there.

"Adam is married and living contentedly in Kent. I am married and content. You are the only child left. If something was to happen to Mama and Papa, what would become of you?"

"I would take a governess position for my sweet little nephew."

"You know well that you would not need the requirement of an occupation to live with us, but that is beside the point. Once you are married and have a home of your own, Mama will cease to worry for your future."

It had never been told so plainly to me before. I could understand the appeal of having all of one's children comfortably situated. It also now made sense why my mother had thrown so many balls, dinners, and house parties at our country estate. I had wondered if she found me incapable of selecting a husband on my own. It was something of a relief to realize her motivations were less offensive.

My fingers toyed with a fraying thread on the chair's upholstery. "Perhaps the reason I have yet to find a husband is because the gentlemen Mama chooses for me are partial to social events. The idea of remaining in London and being a hostess for the rest of my life is exhausting."

She looked up in thought. "Can you not find a quiet man in the country, then? Mr. Walding and I do attend dinners or an intimate ball on occasion, but it is not so much as one would expect for Town."

"I suppose I could." Had I not already been doing so? I was obedient, giving my attention to every eligible gentleman Mama directed toward me until I deemed whether their lifestyle fit my tastes. More than often it did not.

I peered at Julia. Her heart-shaped face was trained on me, shadows pooling beneath her eyes. Her son had kept her awake so often of late that she was exhausted, which I understood, but it was beginning to take a toll. I supposed she would not trade sleep for Frederick, though. Some things were worth sacrificing for.

"Why have you not told Mama of your opinions? She might have altered her search had she known of your strong dislike for entertaining."

That was a valid question. "Is it not a daughter's duty to be obedient? Mama selected Mr. Walding for you, and I do not know another couple more suited to one another. She did the same for Adam and Harriet, and they are a love match as well."

"I want you to have that same love." Julia's eyes grew wistful. "It is chiefest among the feelings."

"Perhaps one day I will." Though my faith in finding that man under my mother's direction was dwindling. Thus my plan to obtain an income and move to a cottage in the country was growing more appealing. Perhaps living a quiet life would find me a man who wished to share in it, instead of hoping to discover him at one of London's stuffy events.

Julia remained for another hour. I helped Frederick coax Mr. Darcy down from his perch. We spoiled the cat with affection to make it worth his while, and they left us in the early afternoon.

Mama found me in the library, her bonnet dangling from her hands. "Shall we go for a walk? The park will be lovely at this time of day."

She only wants me to be taken care of, I reminded myself. Her overbearing matchmaking attempts were purely because she loved me. I pasted a smile on my face. "I should enjoy that, but if we see Mr. Jacobson, we must move the other direction."

"Oh, very well," Mama said, resigned.

St. James's Park was busier than I anticipated. The chilly wind made me grateful for my thick spencer jacket and the sunlight peering between naked tree branches.

"Mrs. Ormiston is throwing a dinner party next week," Mama said, "and I am told she intends to invite an earl."

"I have no aspirations of marrying into a title."

"I know. But perhaps you'll like him?"

I would not crush her dream so fully at present. Mama wished for me to make a concerted effort at courting this Season. Julia's conversation had lingered and tempted me to do so, but even if my mind had opened a little further on the matter, I did not wish to engage a man who so wholly espoused that which I disliked.

I would rather seek someone who far preferred a quiet night. Reading by the fire or playing a game of chess was much more to my taste. Someone I could discuss books with or—

"The Bradwell men!"

I jerked my head up to see Henry Bradwell walking alongside his brothers. He certainly espoused bookish behavior, and I would not be surprised if he preferred a quiet night in over a plethora of social functions. But our relationship was professional at present, and I would not set my bonnet at a man who was the reason my book had not yet been published.

Mother directed our path straight toward them. I smiled when she exchanged pleasantries with James Bradwell. It was too bad I could not pull Mr. Henry Bradwell aside now and question him about whether he'd had success with my manuscript or not.

"Will you also attend the ball, Miss Hutton?" Mr. Henry Bradwell asked, taking me by surprise. His eyes were bent on me, and his mouth was trained in a faint smile. It was a pleasant mouth, attractive in the sunlight. I shook the thought. Which ball were they speaking of? Ah yes, Miss Northcott's.

I met his gaze, trying to read his emotion. Was he telling me anything with his eyes? Nothing I could discern. "I intend to, yes."

"Then might I be so bold as to request you save a set for me? I care not which."

Dratted man. Could he not have refrained from singling me out so? I looked at Mama, disappointed to find her eagerly watching the exchange. There was nothing for it now. I wanted the information Mr. Bradwell would provide me. "I would be delighted to."

I took Mama's arm and we bid farewell before turning back into the park.

"Henry Bradwell is very handsome."

Oh heavens. "I am certain he meant nothing by that."

Mama's smirk proved she did not agree with me. "A man does not arrange a dance in advance without intent."

She was not wrong about that. She was misinterpreting the nature of Mr. Bradwell's intent, though. I was tempted to tell her of our arrangement, but telling her would also inform her of my book, and I was not prepared for that. I had also promised to keep Mr. Bradwell's secret.

"Why did I not consider him before?" Mama muttered, pulling me through the crowded walkway toward our home.

Dread gathered in my stomach. "What do you mean?"

"Henry Bradwell. He is a gentleman. I have adored his mother since we were girls together. He has a comfortable living. It is . . . a brilliant match, quite honestly."

"More brilliant than an earl?" I asked, a little uneasy.

She shot me an unamused smile. "You are not interested in an earl."

No, I was not. But I was not interested in Henry Bradwell, the stealer of publishers' affections, either.

CHAPTER 4

HENRY

Thea Northcott—very recently engaged to my brother, Benedict—radiated brightly as she greeted her guests and twirled about the dance floor in her intended's arms. Her joy was nearly palpable, and she made it difficult not to share in her happiness. Her ball had been a success, though I could not help my disappointment at the lack of Huttons so far. My eyes had swept the crowd since the first dance started, running constantly over the people in attendance, searching for Miss Hutton's dark hair and sharp, intelligent eyes among them.

James approached, looking at me with a shrewd eye. "You seem more distracted than usual this evening. Searching for someone in particular?"

"You are hunting for information, brother."

"It is warranted. You are acting out of the ordinary."

That was true. I would need to find a way to distract him so he did not watch my interactions with Miss Hutton so closely. "Where is my sister-in-law?" I looked over his shoulder but didn't see Felicity anywhere. "Surely she is looking for you."

"You cannot put me off forever. I will know what is going on between you and the Hutton girl. You cannot ask a woman to dance in advance without bringing it to my attention, you know." James seemed to hesitate before leaning closer and lowering his voice. "There is nothing wrong with setting your cap at a woman. If you find an interest in Miss Hutton, then I am glad of it."

Was my unattached situation a burden on James? "Careful, or you will soon sound like Mother."

"I have experienced the satisfaction of love, and I want the same for you."

"Now you certainly sound like Mother."

"There are worse things, I think," James said.

"I hate to disappoint you, but I do not have romantic designs on Miss Hutton. I already told you—it is strictly business between us."

James scrunched his nose. "Marriage can sometimes be a matter of business, but I had hoped that would not be the case for you."

Marriage? He could not be in earnest. "Perhaps someday a woman will catch my eye—"

My words lodged in my throat when my gaze set upon Miss Hutton across the room. She looked about, as if searching for someone—me, I guessed—and this sudden opportunity to admire her unawares would not be wasted. She wore a long gown of sage green, her rich brown hair swept up to highlight her slender neck. She was really beautiful, something I had noticed earlier but failed to pay much attention to when I was busy worrying about the state of my secret.

Her gaze danced over me before stuttering to a halt. The weight of her attention was heavier than I expected, and try as I might, I could not pull myself away from returning her frank stare.

"Or perhaps," James said, "one woman already has."

I sent him a scowl. He chuckled and walked away.

It was time to claim my dance.

I felt oddly shy, yet equally eager to hear from her. "Good evening, Mrs. Hutton. Miss Hutton." I bowed to each of them. "Mr. Hutton does not join you this evening?"

"He has already found the card room."

I bent my elbow and offered it to Miss Hutton. "Might I claim my set?"

"That would be agreeable." She placed her hand on the crook of my elbow and I led her toward the center of the ballroom, where a set was forming in two long lines. We took our places opposite each other, and I realized it would not be a good dance for those who wished to engage in private conversation.

Miss Hutton looked down the row of eager dancers and back at me, seeming to draw a similar conclusion.

"The room is quite stuffy already," she said.

"There is a small terrace open for fresh air, but it does not permit much space." It was superior to this dance, though, for our purposes.

The dance began, and we were no longer able to speak. We moved through the motions, neither of us willing to risk being overheard.

"Were you able to speak to our mutual friend?" she eventually asked.

My lips split in a soft smile. "Indeed, though I am afraid I do not bring a fair report."

"Drat." She'd spoken under her breath, but I heard it all the same. We moved through the remainder of the dance like clams at the whim of the ocean currents. When it came to an end, I offered my arm again. "Shall we investigate the terrace?"

"That would certainly be preferable to another dance in which we cannot speak openly," she muttered.

The terrace was indeed small, but as the new dance was forming, it was also empty save for a pair of ladies with their heads bent together on the other end. I led Miss Hutton to the farthest place opposite them and turned to lean against the stone balustrade, crossing my arms over my chest and keeping an eye out for anyone who had the same idea of escaping outside.

"Marbury?" she prompted.

"I spoke with him yesterday, but our meeting did not go well. He is inclined to hold onto your manuscript until he is ready to publish it. He does not want to go to the expense of gambling with your book until he has seen a larger profit from others, but he anticipates doing so within the next few years."

"*Years?*" She sagged against the balustrade beside me, her shoulder pressing lightly against my own.

"Forgive my impertinence, but might I ask why you are so desperate for the book to be published now? What is the reason for your haste?"

"Would you be satisfied if your book sat on Mr. Marbury's shelf for three years?"

"Not in the least."

She seemed content with my reply. "Not that it is of any great consequence, I suppose. It was hard enough finding someone who would publish a woman's work to begin with. Though even the man who paid me refuses to do much of anything with my book. At times I am tempted to give up, but I'm afraid I am too stubborn for that."

I straightened. "Give up? Because of such minor difficulties?"

"It is easy for you to call them minor when I am certain your book was published by the first person you approached."

"The second, actually." I would not tell her that both had made an offer for the manuscript. "It hardly matters, though, when Marbury wants to change my stories now."

"How so?"

"Apparently my sales cannot compare to that of *Pride and Prejudice*. Marbury would like me to add romance."

She laughed, and the melody of it swirled in my chest. A self-deprecating smile curled my lips. "Yes, it is quite humorous."

"What do you intend to do?"

"Attempt it. He's left me with little choice. Though I bent my mind to the task yesterday and was quite unsuccessful." I scrubbed a hand over my face. "I do not know the first thing about romance."

Miss Hutton pushed up from the balustrade, her movement away leaving my arm cold. "What if we helped each other?"

"What do you propose?"

"We each have something the other needs. I can help you with your romantic writing and you can help me publish my book."

Had she not been listening? Marbury was not ready to budge. "I attempted that already, and it was all for naught."

"It is a lost cause with *Mr. Marbury* for the time being, I grant you that. I have another story that is nearly finished. I could complete it, and you could help me find a new publisher for it— one that will not wait years. They are more likely to listen to you, as you're a man. My initials do not give my sex away."

"In turn, you will assist me with the romantic relationship in my story?"

"It is a mutually beneficial arrangement."

"I can see that." I looked through the open French doors at the people swirling about the ballroom, my family among them. What would they think if I suddenly spent a good deal of time with this woman? What would Society think as a whole?

It was best to discuss this potential setback now. "My brother was suspicious after I asked you to reserve a set for me. My family has begun to make assumptions about the nature of our relationship."

"As have mine." She gave a frustrated huff. "My mother was certainly overjoyed by it."

"James was the same. It almost tempts me to propose just to make him happy."

"I had a similar thought," she muttered.

"You aren't courting anyone, then?"

"My mother has been attempting to find me a suitable husband for the last few years, but so far none of them have been right for me."

I was curious what criteria she had for a partner. She was beautiful, quiet, clearly clever if she could write an entire novel. "What does Miss Hutton look for in a man?"

"He must be handsome, willing to dance, and possessed of *at least* 10,000 a year."

Shock rippled through me. "That is very . . . particular of you."

"I suppose you have not read *Pride and Prejudice*."

"I'm afraid not. Is that . . . oh. You were referencing a character, I suppose?"

"Mr. Darcy of Pemberley."

For some reason, that made me like her more. "You are in love with a fictional man?"

Her soft smile was charming. "Not in love, no. I merely hold a strong affection for him." She peered up at me, brushing a stray curl away from her eye, and my heart gave a strange pulse. "If we choose to work together, how do you think we can contrive to be alone often enough to discuss our novels?"

An idea floated through my mind, but I was unsure if it was born of temptation or the genuine answer to our dilemma.

"What are you thinking?" she asked. A small line formed between her eyebrows, one I wanted to smooth away.

I held her gaze. "What if I pretended to court you?"

Marianne

Was Mr. Bradwell mad? I blinked at him, but his expression didn't shift.

"What do you mean by *pretend?*" He'd swiftly made it clear with that word that he had no interest in actual courtship. It was at once a disappointment, and I did my best to cover up the sting that remained.

"I will act as if my intention is to court you: take you to the theater, for outings in the park, or rides about London in my brother's curricle. I can call on you at home. These will give us ample opportunities for quiet conversation."

His description sent a wave of butterflies through my stomach that I tried to subdue. It wouldn't be real. "And our families?"

"They will be thrilled, of course."

"Until we decide we don't suit." Or so I guessed. Our false courtship would need to be dissolved at some point.

"In which case you will end our arrangement, and I will run off to my hunting lodge in the north to lick my wounds."

"And all of London will find me unmarriageable."

He tucked his chin in surprise. "That cannot be."

"You know as well as I do that a woman does not break a courtship without carrying a stain with her."

"I suppose I cannot argue that." He looked toward the open doors, the orange glow from the nearby torchlights warming his face. "It was a foolish plan."

Was it foolish? There was no way to avoid raising Mama's matrimonial hopes if I wanted to spend time with Mr. Bradwell, and I truly thought we could have a mutually beneficial arrangement. Besides, aside from one another, there was no one else in our lives that knew of our writing. For now, at least, Mr. Bradwell was all I had.

Another couple came out to the terrace for a reprieve, and I could hear the second song in our set winding down. It was nearly time to return to Mama's side, but I wasn't eager to leave this conversation. Or was it the man I was conversing with I did not want to step away from? I needed to find a way to squash the little budding attraction growing in my chest. He was handsome, but I'd never been especially vulnerable to a man's good looks. Not even when he was possessed of striking blue eyes or unruly, curly hair, so rich and brown.

I shook the thought. If Mr. Bradwell desired a false courtship, it would only complicate things if I allowed my feelings to become real.

"It is an excellent plan, Mr. Bradwell." I lowered my voice to avoid being overheard. "If you agree to court me long enough to help me find a publisher, I will be able to provide for myself, and it will hardly matter at that point if I am deemed unmarriageable."

"It could take a good deal of time. A courtship of such length will have bigger repercussions when it is ended."

"It is a risk I am willing to take." In truth, the idea of receiving help to communicate with publishers trumped all other things. My father would never help me—he would not think it appropriate for a woman to publish a novel—and my brother was of a similar mind. My brother-in-law could perhaps be persuaded to do so, but he could not keep a secret to save his life. After three years of producing novels under a false name, it was very clear that Mr. Bradwell could keep a secret.

"When shall we begin?" I asked, trying not to sound too eager.

"My brother has recently become engaged, and we will be traveling to Cumberland for the wedding. I would not be surprised if he asks us to leave as soon as tomorrow."

"That is agreeable. I could use some time to complete my novel."

"Then shall we wait to begin our courtship until I return? I will call on you after my brother's wedding and make my intentions known."

His words sent a thrill through me. It was not the first time a man had expressed his interest in courting me, but it was the first time I'd had a positive reaction. I suspected my eagerness had more to do with our authoring relationship than it did anything of a romantic nature.

I felt eager all the same. "I will wish you safe travels then."

He picked up my hand and placed a kiss on my bent knuckles.

"What was that for?" I asked.

"Practice?" His blue eyes bore into mine. "I was wondering if I could believably court a woman."

My eyebrows lifted. "Have you never done so before?"

"No, never." His face contorted into an unpretentious smile. "There is a reason I need assistance with the romance in my novel."

"Perhaps you should read some romantic novels while you are on your journey."

"Do you intend to educate me?"

"Yes. I shall tutor you in all things love." I grinned. "We will begin with Pride and Prejudice."

CHAPTER 5

MARIANNE

Six eternally long weeks had passed since the night Henry and I had come to our decision. I had made some progress in my novel, but not as much as I had hoped to in that time. In truth, the fault lay at my own feet. I could have been far more productive if I had read less. It had been difficult to prioritize my own manuscript when I was busy reading everything Dalton Henry had ever published.

It was with great dismay that I discovered what an excellent writer Mr. Bradwell was. I had been prepared to loathe him for eternity on principle, but such would be impossible now that I had an appreciation for his talent. He had sent a messenger to me with his manuscript before leaving for Cumberland, and after devouring that, it was a short road to his other books. His novels were interesting. They had the ability to sweep me into another world, leaving me satisfied and half in love with the fictional man who had gone on the adventure—though none had yet to trump Mr. Darcy in my esteem. It confused me that Mr. Marbury had requested an additional romantic storyline when Mr. Bradwell's novels were so satisfying exactly the way they were.

I picked up the top sheet of paper of my own manuscript and read over the last few lines I had written, but my mind was not attending. Sunlight poured through my bedroom window, and I contemplated sending a note to my sister to inquire if she would like to walk in the park with me. Fresh air often helped loosen my mind when it stalled at any point in my writing.

Mr. Darcy stepped between my ankles, his long gray fur tickling the soft skin of my bare feet. I leaned down and picked him up, settling him on my lap as he stretched lazily over my legs. I stroked his back, peering through my window to the street below. A two-seated carriage pulled up in front of our door and the driver hopped down from the seat, while a groom climbed down from the back of the carriage and went to hold the horses' heads.

From this vantage point, it was impossible to tell who the man was that now approached our door, but a quickening in my chest revealed who I hoped it was. "Stop that at once," I muttered to my heart. I schooled my expression into one of indifference and hurried down the stairs, clutching Mr. Darcy in my arms.

A gentleman stood at our front door beside Shaw, our butler. His back was toward me, but that did not hide his identity. His height and breadth of shoulders combined with the shock of brown curls on his head was revealing. He turned away from the butler and seemed pleased when his eyes fell upon me.

"Ah, Miss Hutton," Mr. Bradwell said. "Precisely whom I was hoping to see." Light from the long windows poured over him, his hat hanging from gloved fingers. "Might I tempt you with a drive in Hyde Park?"

"That would be most agreeable."

His gaze dropped to Mr. Darcy.

I tightened my hold on the cat. "Allow me a moment to fetch my bonnet, if you will."

"And shoes, perhaps?"

I glanced down at my bare toes peeking from beneath my gown, and my cheeks flushed. "Only a moment, sir."

It had been warm in my chamber and I'd removed my stockings to cool my feet. Now I felt ridiculous.

"Shaw, will you inform Papa of my intentions?"

He nodded, and I hastened upstairs. I made quick work of pulling on stockings and half-boots, locating my gloves and bonnet, and letting Mr. Darcy from my room with the hope he would hunt mice in the attic and earn his keep. But he was just as lofty and entitled as his namesake, and instead he turned down the stairs to find himself easy prey in the kitchen maids, who were forever plying him with milk and scraps of meat.

With Mr. Bradwell's manuscript tucked beneath my shawl and pinned to my side by my arm, I made my way somewhat awkwardly toward the stairs.

"You are going out?" Papa asked, startling me from behind.

I jumped and nearly dropped the papers, barely managing to keep them tightly pinned to my side. "Mr. Bradwell has invited me for a ride in the park. May I go?"

"I was hoping to steal you for a game of chess, but I suppose that can wait. Will I be able to tear you from your novel later this afternoon?"

"With great difficulty," I said.

Papa chuckled. "Your ability to read those books until their pages are falling out almost tempts me to give them a go."

"You can, you know. You might enjoy them."

"Enjoy them?" His eyebrows shot up, his head tilting in surprise. "I shall keep to my trusted men."

Because heaven forbid believing a woman could write something equally entertaining. I did not open my mouth for fear of saying something disrespectful, instead turning to join one of my father's trusted male authors downstairs. If only he knew Dalton Henry stood in our entryway, he would surely expire from pleasure.

If he knew I'd also written a novel, I could only imagine the apoplexy he would endure.

Mr. Bradwell opened the door for me, offering the use of his hand as he led me toward his curricle. The sun warmed us through, and the late spring day was awash with flowers and heat, edging into summer with a bounty of flora yet remaining.

"I have your manuscript here."

"Oh." He looked where I indicated it beneath my arm. "Leave it on the seat, perhaps?"

I looked at the narrow bench. "You wish for me to sit on your novel?"

"I think that will keep it from blowing away, and I can secure it when you leave again."

"Very well." I slid the portfolio of papers down and sat on it, my dress spreading just enough to cover the portfolio in its entirety. Strange, but it worked.

"Hyde Park?" I questioned, mentioning our destination. "Is your design for us to be seen together?"

"Yes. I thought boldly proclaiming my intention to be near you would help it not seem strange when I continue to seek your company."

His declaration had an odd way of making my stomach feel as though it had been turned into a hive, swarming with bees. *My intention to be near you. When I continue to seek your company.* Good heavens, I would soon need to make use of my fan if he continued to induce me to blush.

Mr. Bradwell peered down at me. "Are you well, Miss Hutton?"

"Perfectly." I cleared my throat. "My father read about your brother's engagement in the paper. Was the wedding to your mother's satisfaction?"

"Very much so. But discussing my trip to Chelton is not why I brought you out here." He maneuvered the conveyance expertly from the road to the promenade in the park, instructing the horses to slow their walk in order to fall into traffic smoothly.

I was a little startled by the shift in conversation. If I had any lingering hopes that Henry could possibly see me in a romantic light, he had snuffed them. He viewed me as a tutor, a colleague even. Not as a woman. "You want to begin your instruction immediately? I hardly think this is the proper place to educate you on matters of romance. What if we are overheard?"

"Then our eavesdroppers will believe we are harboring romantic feelings for one another."

Which was the plan, was it not? Why in heaven's name did I feel so disappointed by that answer? Regardless of my budding attraction to Henry, we had an agreement, and I was benefiting from it just as much as he was. "I suppose that is a good point. Can you tell me what you'd like to first know?"

"I had hoped you would be willing to read a sampling of the romantic scene I've come up with. If you experience my ineptitude, you will be better able to help me improve."

A scoff ripped from my throat. "I read the entirety of the manuscript you left for me, Mr. Bradwell." The one currently hiding beneath me. "There is nothing that needs changing in it."

He looked over quickly, seeming to forget that he was the sole person responsible for driving our carriage. The horses took his leniency in stride and quickened their speed, pulling around an open-air barouche in a jerky motion that forced me to grip the side of the bench with one hand and hold my bonnet down with the other.

Mr. Bradwell redirected his attention to the horses and slowed them once more, a redness mottling his cheeks. "Perhaps, given the nature of our current understanding, we can dispense with use of formal names, Miss Hutton." He seemed to better regain his equilibrium. I had not yet released the side of the carriage, though I lowered my hand from my bonnet. "Our families are of longstanding acquaintance, and the nature of our business leads me to believe we will soon become good friends. Besides, each time you call me Mr. Bradwell, I wish to look about for James."

"Does no one else call you that?"

"I don't have much occasion for it. In the military, I was simply Bradwell. My family calls me Henry. The mister is only for the most formal of relationships, I suppose."

"How odd."

"Odd, yes. Too casual for Society? Probably. If you are uncomfortable, we shall not dispense with—"

"I take no issue with it. But perhaps only when we are alone."

"As I hope the majority of our time spent together is alone, that is agreeable to me."

Again, a stomach swarming with the pleasant hum of honeybees. I knew the way in which Mr. Bradwell—no, *Henry*—meant it, but my body had not received the message yet. It must be on the penny post or idling with a lazy servant somewhere, because the message was taking far too long to reach me.

He screwed up his nose. "My publisher does not agree with you about the state of my manuscript. I've already rewritten part of the first volume to include the introduction of a young miss, but I fear I have written her all wrong."

"Bring me the pages. I will see what can be done for them."

"I have them with me now, folded and tucked into a book. I thought the lending of novels a good cover for passing papers. I had not realized we could use your shawl." He shot me a smile, and I tried not to squirm.

Since we could not send letters to one another without risking our reputations, I liked the idea of using books in the future. "Speaking of books—"

A horse and rider pulled to a stop beside us. "Good day, Mr. Bradwell," Mr. Gatley said, his white hair peeking out from beneath his hat. His cheeks were ruddy and his eyes were bright, clearly happy to see Henry this afternoon. His gaze slid to me and his happiness faltered momentarily, though he recovered quickly and doffed his hat in a brief bow. "Miss Hutton."

"Good day," Henry returned, slowing our curricle until we rested beside the rider.

I dipped my head, though Mr. Gatley seemed inclined to wish me elsewhere.

"I had it on good authority you had returned to Chelton," he said to Henry. "A marriage in the family, I hear?"

"Yes, my brother Benedict has wed Miss Dorothea Northcott. I've returned to London on my own. The rest of my family stayed in Cumberland."

"Pity. I would have liked to invite you all to dine. Perhaps you could be induced to join us for dinner, Mr. Bradwell? Tomorrow, if you have no other engagements."

Henry appeared startled by this invitation. "I do not have any other engagements."

Mr. Gatley looked pleased with himself. His cheeks rounded, eyes wrinkling, until they fell on me again. He straightened on his saddle, blustering. "Miss Hutton, your family would be most welcome to join us as well."

It was always something of a bore to be an afterthought. "I am not certain we are available tomorrow evening, but I thank you for the invitation. It was most kind of you."

We were shortly on our way again. Henry's brow furrowed. "I cannot think why Mr. Gatley has a sudden desire for my company. He was a friend of my father's, but our acquaintance has mostly been in passing. I cannot recall the last time I attended a dinner at the Gatley house."

"When was the last time you were in London for the Season?"

He wrinkled his forehead. "Quite a while, I suppose. But that does not explain his actions. Perhaps my brother, when he was in Town . . . but why would Gatley wish to invite *me* to dinner?"

"Can you truly not think of any reason?" I asked. It was as plain to me as the sunlight beating down on us. Henry's present ignorance could very well explain why he had yet to court a single woman in his life.

He looked at me blankly for a moment before the horses required his attention once more.

"Miss Gatley," I said. I knew the woman. She was petite, blonde, and on the hunt for a husband. It was her second Season, to my knowledge, but she'd had a string of beaus last year. Perhaps she was as fastidious in her search for a partner as I was.

"What about her?" Henry asked in adorable ignorance. His brow cleared. "Oh. You believe she is the reason Mr. Gatley has developed a sudden interest in me."

"Perhaps I am mistaken. Do you and Mr. Gatley share an enjoyment in reading? In studying? Or perhaps in military pursuits?"

"He knew my father from school, not the military. I cannot think of anything else we have in common." Henry looked pained. "I almost wish I was ignorant of his motivations."

"You still might be." Though I harbored little belief of that.

He brightened. "I suppose I will find out shortly. Do you think you might join us?"

"I am fairly certain *that* invitation was only delivered out of politeness. Mr. Gatley's disappointment in my presence at your side was the other half of my reason for assuming he would very much like you to court his daughter."

"Your logic is faultless, but I still hope you are incorrect."

"You could do far worse than Miss Gatley."

He sent me a nervous expression. "I am certain one dinner will effectively kill any ambitions Miss Gatley or her father might have of securing me as her husband. I am not prone to any sense of false modesty. There is a reason I have never before courted a woman."

We pulled out from the park, and I was glad to not have been interrupted again, but this meant we were returning home, and our time was limited.

"I can sense there is something you would like to ask me," Henry said.

I swallowed the questions burning on my tongue. Had he never been in love? Had a woman never caught his eye? Was there a reason he hadn't courted, and what was it? Was he already in love with someone? All of these things were inappropriate. I redirected the conversation to even ground. "Have you finished the assignment I gave you before you left London?"

"To read *Pride and Prejudice*?" Henry kept his gaze on the horses. "I did."

"And?"

"I have many thoughts. The chief of which is that my novels are quite different from it."

"Indeed. What else did you notice?"

"That it was not something I would choose to read of my own accord."

"Because the focus is the relationship between Elizabeth and Mr. Darcy?"

"Yes. I do not typically read or write stories of a romantic nature."

Mr. Marbury was going to regret asking Henry to change his manuscript so deeply.

"I wonder if you would like the author's more recent work, *Persuasion*, better."

"Hmm," he said, noncommittally. I had to stifle my smile. He certainly did not wish to read another novel by *A Lady*, and I would not force him to. "The benefit was that I was able to leave my copy of the novel with my sister-in-law, who is an avid reader and will love the story."

"I have the pleasure of calling Felicity a friend of mine. I am not surprised that she would enjoy that story. By the by, how have you managed to keep your novels a secret from your family for so long?"

"I am so often sequestered in the library that no one in my family questions it. I also spend a good deal of time alone at our hunting box. And again, no one questions it." He looked up in thought. "I suppose I adopted the personality of a bookish man so early and thoroughly that whether I spend my time writing or reading, I am left alone. It has not been difficult to conceal."

"If your family is so accepting, why have you bothered to conceal it?"

"I intend to tell them one day. I never anticipated my books being so well circulated." He grinned. "I have the benefit of a mother who hardly leaves the house and two brothers who do not read. I left them hints in my contrived author name, but thus far no one has figured it out."

"Dalton Henry. The Henry is clearly your Christian name. What is the Dalton?"

"My full name is Henry Dalton Bradwell."

I laughed. "I suppose you could not have been more clear than that."

"I could only have been more clear if I had used my full name."

We pulled up in front of my door and Henry's groom ran to hold the horses' heads.

I was startled at the realization that the groom had been sitting behind us for the duration of our ride. "Are you not worried about your servants telling your secrets or revealing your identity as the author of your books?"

"Some of them, yes. Presley here is nearly deaf. An unfortunate side effect of Waterloo." He spoke nearly dismissively, as if he attempted to make it sound as though it was not something of great note. But Henry had also served in the army during the battle of Waterloo, and I suspected the lightness of his tone covered a great well of feelings.

Henry stepped down from the curricle and rounded the vehicle to offer me his hand. He led me up to my front door, which Shaw opened for us. "I still hope to see you tomorrow night," Henry said, bowing over my hand.

"Tomorrow night?" Mama asked, appearing behind Shaw in the entryway. She absorbed the view of my fingers bent within Henry's hold, and her eyes gleamed.

I snatched my hand away quickly. "Mr. Gatley extended an invitation to dinner, but I am sure he only meant to be polite."

Mama gave a surprised laugh. "Why would he not wish for us to accept? Mrs. Gatley is one of my particular friends."

Nearly every matron in London was Mama's *particular* friend. That was the product of being such a kind and generous soul as she was and very talented at making friends.

Her lips pinched together. "I suppose it is a moot point, as we are otherwise engaged tomorrow night. We have already accepted the invitation to the Hamiltons' ball."

"That settles it. Good day, Mr. Bradwell. Thank you for your company."

"Oh, I nearly forgot. I had a novel I wanted to lend to you, Miss Hutton. If you'll wait but a moment, I will fetch it."

Henry returned to the curricle as my mother gave me a very telling look.

"It is only a book," I hissed quietly.

Henry returned and placed the leatherbound novel in my hands. "Good day." He lifted his hat, bowing to Mama and me before taking his leave. Shaw closed the door behind him and Mama grinned at me like I was a bowl of milk and she was my cat.

"I cannot abide being smiled at in such a way."

"This feels different from the others," she said quietly, her tone laced with hope. "Does it not?"

Thus far Henry had not acted any differently from any of my other suitors, so I could only imagine that the difference Mama felt was in the way I accepted his attention. I was accustomed to not taking gentlemen seriously, doing my best to keep them at a distance so as not to involve my heart too deeply if I learned they were men of some esteem, or had a general aptitude for socializing.

"He is only a friend who also enjoys reading and discussing novels. I am absolutely certain nothing more will come of it."

Mama's smile faltered a little, causing guilt to stir within me, but I suppressed the temptation to retract my words. Henry had made it clear that we were friends and friends alone. He was perhaps the first gentleman of my acquaintance whom I would like to pursue a courtship with, and the first who wanted to do so under false pretenses. I needed to subdue my growing *tendre* before it caused any issues—like ruining my chance to finally have a book published.

My dream of finding my novel on the shelf at Hatchards wouldn't come to fruition without his help, to say nothing for the independence it would give me.

I lifted the novel he had given me. "Now if you will excuse me, I shall go read this book."

Mama shooed me away. "Of course. Go read, darling. Mr. Bradwell will wish to discuss it with you, I assume, when we next see him." Her giddy, hopeful smile had returned.

It was a testament to how badly she wanted me to marry that she was now encouraging bluestocking habits. Just a Season or two ago the very idea would have been unthinkable.

This was already growing far more complicated than I had expected.

CHAPTER 6
HENRY

I did not understand women. Not their motives, desires, or what induced them to blink incessantly while lowering their chins. I presumed it was a form of coquetry. What I did not comprehend was the alleged appeal.

Miss Gatley performed just such measures of enticement at the dinner party. It was enough to put me off her forever. Had I known this dinner would be so intimate—Mr. and Mrs. Gatley, their daughter, and myself—I likely would have developed a reason for excusing my absence.

Marianne had been correct. There could be no other reason for this invitation than Mr. Gatley's ill-conceived notion that I might be a good match for his simpering child.

"Does your brother still keep a box in the opera house?" Miss Gatley asked.

How had she known of that? Perhaps James and Mr. Gatley had seen one another earlier in the Season, as I'd suspected. I pasted a patient smile on my face. "Indeed. I believe it was paid for through the end of May."

"How lovely!" Miss Gatley clapped her hands together, her

blonde curls bouncing. "I have always dreamed of watching the opera from a box."

The room grew as quiet as a forest at midnight. All three Gatleys looked at me expectantly. Good gads, how was I to get out of this? If I was going to suffer through the opera, it would be as a measure to spend time with Marianne.

That was it. Nothing else could induce me to go. The way Miss Gatley watched me now, paired with the silence in the room, made this an altogether impossible situation. Three sets of eyes blinked at me until I could no longer sit in the heavy silence.

"I had considered putting a party together with the Huttons," I finally said. "Perhaps you would like to join us? I must admit that it is not my favorite form of entertainment, so I do not attend often."

Mrs. Gatley nodded. "That would be most appreciated, Mr. Bradwell. How kind of you to think to include us."

I lifted my goblet and took a long swallow. The following hour passed in a similar manner, until I stood at the door to take my leave of them.

I had walked to the Gatley residence because my rented townhouse was near enough, but my feet slowed before I could so much as turn the corner toward home. The Hamilton townhouse was the opposite direction, and not too far as to make walking impossible. I had searched out the invitation earlier among the stack gathering dust on the entry table and refreshed the address—not for any reason in particular, but in case I found myself with time.

I now had time.

I was taking advantage of the final few months of the arrangements James had made for the Season—his box at the opera, the townhouse he'd rented, the Almack's vouchers he'd sought out for us. The scant weeks left of the Season did not seem like nearly long enough to receive the help I needed from Marianne, but I would make do with what I had.

Men patrolled the streets outside of the Hamilton residence, undoubtedly informed of what was likely to be a veritable crush so they could keep the traffic moving. Judging by the sounds of music and people spilling from the house, they had been correct in their assumptions. I mounted the stairs, looking for Mrs. Hamilton so I might pay my respects to the hostess. She appeared caught up in a conversation with a bevy of matrons just inside the ballroom, so I waited.

The dancing was in full swing, and I found my gaze tripping over the women gathered, searching until I spotted Marianne. It was unsurprising to find her dancing. Her cheeks were flushed and a smile curved her lips while she engaged in a country dance with a tall, gangly man.

My body tightened, my breath stalling like a fist had clung to my lungs and squeezed. She did not notice me, so involved was she in the steps of the dance and the joy of moving cheerfully about the floor to the jaunty music. She was radiant, light on her feet, and a general beacon. It was a complete mystery to me how she had yet to marry.

Almost as much of a mystery as her supposed appreciation of my books. I still could not reconcile that she would enjoy adventure stories such as mine. I had not written them for the sensible set to enjoy. I understood women could appreciate classics, Shakespeare, even children's stories that were often rife with adventure—but *my* books? Those were not written with women in mind, much as Marbury understood.

I wanted to speak to Marianne, but in a crush such as this, there was no word we could say that would not be overheard. I was certain the terrace would be far too crowded; the parlor—or wherever they'd tucked the refreshments—likewise.

The dance continued. I skirted the throngs of onlookers until approaching my hostess, now that her friends had disbanded somewhat, and bowing toward her. "Good evening, Mrs. Hamilton. It is a pleasure to see you."

She sank a little, her ostrich plume bobbing. "The pleasure is mine."

"You must be extraordinarily pleased with the success of your evening."

She failed to temper her smile, which revealed precisely how pleased she was. "Your addition is most welcome, for we are always glad to receive a Bradwell at our gatherings. How kind of you to honor us with your presence this evening, sir. I presume you intend to dance?"

Oh. I could not think quickly enough of a reason not to. I was perfectly capable, but it was not my choice of activity. "If there is a woman in need of a partner, I am certainly willing."

Her grin widened. The music drew to a close, and women were being escorted away from the dance floor. Mrs. Hamilton took my sleeve so I might not escape. When a young woman who I presumed to be her daughter approached us, she released my captive arm.

"You'll remember my daughter, Miss Cecily Hamilton, of course."

I did not. Had I met the girl before now? I bowed. "Of course. You look lovely this evening, Miss Hamilton."

She simpered, ducking her head before looking up at me through her lashes. Why did women do that? Certainly it did not make it easy for them to see their target.

Mrs. Hamilton waited expectantly, as did her daughter. Was there a pamphlet recently produced, instructing misses of marriageable age that in order to entice a gentleman to offer that which she desires—a box at the opera, a set of dances, to name a few—one must simply sit in uncomfortable silence until the gentleman is overcome with the need to escape and offers precisely what the young lady seeks? Or perhaps they spread the tactic amongst themselves. Thus far, it had worked twice this evening in a young lady's favor.

"May I take the next set, Miss Hamilton?"

She accepted, placing her dainty glove on my forearm and allowing me to lead her onto the floor. The couples were gathering in groups of four for a cotillion, and I looked for Marianne, that we might join her set, but didn't see her. Miss Hamilton and I took our places, smiling at the other couple and waiting for two more to join us.

"I heard a rumor not too long ago you had returned to Town," Miss Hamilton said. "I am pleased you chose to attend my ball so soon after traveling such a great distance. You must be fatigued."

"The road is long between Chelton and London, but it was worth the effort."

She beamed at this, and I looked away, searching for something to set my attention on so I could prevent giving Miss Hamilton any reason to believe I carried an interest in her. My gaze lifted to meet Marianne's, who now stood across from me beside another man of my acquaintance.

"Captain Neal," I said in some surprise. "I did not realize you were in London."

His smile stretched over straight teeth. Some men had all the luck. "With company such as this, how can I stay away? It is very good to see you again, Bradwell."

"And you." I dipped my head to him, then to Marianne. "Miss Hutton."

She returned the greeting. Her eyes were bright, her cheeks still pink from the exertion of her previous dance. She looked radiant.

The music required us to turn our attention to our dancing partners, but I could not help noticing for the remainder of the dance how closely Captain Neal's attention was pasted to Marianne. It was to be expected, of course, as he was meant to lead her through the steps, but it settled oddly in my stomach.

I hadn't danced often, and never with a woman in whom I had a romantic interest. Indeed, the only woman I had ever considered in the light of matrimony had married my brother, and I had quickly snuffed the flame of potential that had lightly simmered in my chest. That was history now, but even my feelings for Felicity had never extended to how my heart was beating at present, and how much I strongly disliked watching Marianne with Neal.

My consideration of Felicity had been interest. Intrigue. This was . . . jealousy? Had I been too premature in stating so boldly to Marianne our courtship should be completely falsified?

I missed my step, turning the wrong direction and failing to spin a young lady from one of the other couples beneath my arm. The rest of the dancers in our set were skilled enough to continue despite my mishap, and I shoved thoughts of Marianne and Captain Neal from my mind.

It was only one dance. Marianne hadn't given me any reason to believe she would add another man to her list of beaus. For all I was aware, Captain Neal had been a good friend of the Huttons as long as my family had—or some such reasonable, *brotherly* explanation.

Gads, man. There was no sense having such an introspective moment *now*.

We finished the remainder of the cotillion and moved to form a circle for a reel. Miss Hamilton did a fair job of trying to make conversation in the few moments we had to speak between the two dances, but I could not attend to her when Marianne continued to laugh at whatever inanities were spilling from Captain Neal's mouth.

This was ridiculous. I was no lovesick fool.

The end of the dance came eventually, and I escorted Miss Hamilton back to her mother, but not without watching Marianne the entire time. She was not nearby, and to my dismay, after depositing my dancing miss with her parents, I found that Captain Neal had not left the Huttons' side.

I made my way through the crowd, picking around groups of people and stopping only briefly to greet an acquaintance or reply to a question posed to me about my brothers and their recent nuptials. Marriage seemed to be foremost on everyone's minds: who was marriageable, who had recently been removed from the marriage market, and how to contrive a match.

Perhaps Marbury had not been ridiculous in his assumption that the general public desired more romance in their lives. If they did nothing but think of marriage, adding such to my novel would only please them, in theory.

The trouble was, I was positive I had made a mash of my attempt thus far, and I deeply wanted to know what Marianne thought of the pages I'd given her yesterday.

Mrs. Hutton, regal and polite as ever, was listening kindly to the captain as he described a recent storm he had suffered through. It took a great deal of effort not to sigh in long-suffering. Navy men were forever talking about their ships. Marianne would certainly see the tale for what it was—an attempt to secure her sympathies at his supposed brush with death. But upon closer inspection, Marianne did not wear the expression of one who could see Neal's true intentions. She was rapt with attention.

Blast. She was too intelligent to be taken in by one such as Neal.

Mrs. Hutton noticed me at last and her eyes lit. What typically sent me into a mode of vague concern with other matchmaking mamas instead ignited a fire of success. "Mr. Bradwell, we did not expect to see you this evening."

"I had not anticipated finding myself free."

"What a happy surprise this is." She gestured to Neal, who

was quite as tall as I was. "Are you acquainted with the captain?"

"I am." I dipped a greeting to him and looked to Marianne, who had thus far remained silent. "Would you give me the honor of your next set, Miss Hutton?"

She scrunched her nose slightly before smoothing her countenance. "I am afraid I have already promised the final set to another."

Just my luck.

"The benefit of arriving on time, eh?" Neal said, grinning like his joke was humorous. It was not.

I ignored him, looking to Marianne. "Then may I secure your time tomorrow afternoon? A walk in St. James's Park, perhaps?"

"Did it not look like rain to you, Bradwell?" Neal asked, affecting concern. "I do believe the incoming clouds were ominous."

"My walk here was uninhibited by moisture. I shall pray for a sunny afternoon, just as we had today." Sunny, warm, and absent of rain clouds.

"And I, as well," Marianne said. "I should enjoy that very much, Mr. Bradwell."

"Then it is settled. With that, I will bid you farewell." I bowed to them, and the women curtsied in turn. Neal and I exchanged pleasant farewells, but I suspected neither of us meant them. It appeared I had a rival for Miss Hutton's attention, and he a navy man. As I was of army stock, I was well-versed in strategy and devising tactics. I could hold my own in such a battle.

The door opened for me at the hand of a footman, and I stepped outside and swore.

Rain.

CHAPTER 7

MARIANNE

Captain Neal was just as attentive last night as he had been during the ball we'd attended last week, and the smattering of social engagements we had both found ourselves at in the previous months. He was kind and his stories interesting, but that was where my admiration ended. I did not wish to spend my life swinging from a hammock in a cramped ship's quarters for the foreseeable future.

Mama had different ideas of what was reasonable.

"You cannot discount the captain," she said at breakfast the following morning. "He is handsome, kind, of good standing within the navy, and will provide you a comfortable life."

"Comfortable is perhaps relative, Mama. I do not think I shall enjoy exchanging my bed for a hammock." He did have the benefit of not entertaining often, as he lived on a ship, but how would I write my novels when I was forever being jostled to and fro?

"Pish. Captains have natural beds, darling. I'm sure of it."

"You cannot call a bed natural if it rocks at the whims of an ocean—to say nothing for the very storms Captain Neal likes to describe to us in his anecdotes. Did you not hear Catherine

Downer speak at the garden party a few weeks ago about the trials her aunt faces married to a navy man? A wife of a captain must share his rations and sleeping quarters. She is not permitted her own." That did not sound pleasant to me.

Mama frowned at her eggs. "I approve of his dedication. All the while Mr. Jacobson was paying special attention to you those weeks ago, it did not deter Captain Neal in the least. He has not wavered in his consideration of you." She sipped from her cup. "I admit that after you rejected Mr. Jacobson's proposal, I did believe Captain Neal would come around more often. I cannot complain about a steadiness of character, though."

"It hardly matters how steady a character is when he is forced to divide his rations with a wife."

Mama made a noncommittal sound. "Mr. Bradwell does not have those same impairments. I believe he fought Napoleon, but his military career seems to be in the past."

Yes, but unbeknownst to my mother, Henry was not truly interested in acquiring my hand. He only wanted my brain, not for himself, but for the purpose of improving his novel. After reading the papers he had given me following our ride in Hyde Park, I could well see how he might need a little help.

I looked to the window and the water streaming down in rivulets.

"Trust a navy man to understand the weather," Mama muttered, following my gaze. "Perhaps you can invite Mr. Bradwell to remain for tea instead."

"If the sky has not cleared by the time he calls, I will do so."

The weather did not improve over the course of the day, and Henry arrived in our entryway with a gust of wind, his greatcoat dripping water on the tile floor. He was tall and broad, a little imposing in his rain-darkened coat. He must have felt my gaze, for he tilted his head up and found me looking at him over the upstairs banister, my gloveless hand resting on the smooth wooden railing.

"It is a little wet for the park," he said.

I smiled. "I thought the same thing. Would you like to join us for tea instead?"

He nodded. "I'd be delighted."

Shaw divested Henry of his coat and took it downstairs, undoubtedly to hang it by the fire to dry. Henry mounted the stairs to join me and Mama in the drawing room. I pulled on my gloves, securing them in place before he entered the room.

"What terrible weather we are having!" Mama said, gesturing for Henry to be seated.

He obeyed. "I cannot complain about the opportunity to visit with two lovely ladies, though I will agree that traveling in this rain is not a comfortable experience."

"Oh! Forgive my carelessness. You ought to have been deposited near the fire. Surely you are cold." Mama had a regal bearing, and she had always been attentive to her guests. It was an odd thing for her to have such an afterthought, which led me to believe it wasn't truly an afterthought at all. She looked up at me. "Marianne would be happy to sit closer to the fire, I am sure, so you may visit. I am afraid this handkerchief I am embroidering for Mr. Hutton has proved itself to be a most complicated pattern, requiring my full attention and as much sunlight as I can possibly have."

I glanced at Mama, but her affectation of an innocent woman was alarmingly genuine. She was a good actress, for I knew she did not struggle with her embroidery in general. Her priority was to find me a husband. Good heavens, Mama. This was far too obvious to ever be considered natural.

"I would like to sit nearer the fire," Henry said. "Which chairs shall I move, Miss Hutton?"

I would play along with Mama's ridiculous ruse because it served my purposes today, but I hated that she would believe herself successful in this sort of matchmaking. If she attempted it with anyone else, I would be forced to give the man a set down.

"Those would do nicely." I gestured to two padded chairs near the wall. Henry set to moving them right away, lifting each chair as though they weighed no more than a feather-filled pillow. I had pushed them before the fire a time or two and happened to know they were not as light as that.

I dropped my gaze to the carpet and took my seat, arranging my skirts over my knees. It would not do to be caught staring at the strain of muscle against his coat sleeves. Handsome arms had nothing to do with writing novels, so I would do well to separate the two in my mind.

Mama prepared a cup of tea for Henry as directed. She handed it to him before pouring mine. When we both had our tea, she took her work basket to the farthest seat possible and deposited herself there.

"Have you made any progress in the book I lent you?" he asked quietly.

"Yes."

His summer-sky gaze turned almost eager. "It would honor me if you would share your thoughts."

"I am of the same mind as you that the romantic relationship in the story could use a little more . . . finesse."

His eyebrows lifted. Perhaps it was my word choice that had surprised him. "In what way?"

I sipped my tea, then lowered the cup. "For example: a lady, in general, does not wish to be accosted by a stranger, however handsome and rugged he may appear."

His cup stilled before meeting his lips. "I had thought all ladies desired to be kissed."

I glanced to where Mama sat on her sofa, her needle and thread in hand. She was far enough away that I could speak very quietly and hope to not be entirely overheard, but I was certain her ear was trained on us. She would be doing her utmost to pick apart our conversation. I cleared my throat softly, searching for the words. "In general, yes. But even an adventurous pirate should show *some* decorum in regards to women, however fictional he might be. A subtle show of interest upon first meeting her will entice the lady without setting her back up."

"You mean to imply the pirate has been too strong in his initial attentions?"

"Indeed. If you found yourself interested in a woman, Mr. Bradwell, would *that* be your first course of action?"

He chuckled, watching the flames licking the interior of the hearth. "No. I would never impose myself on a lady in such a way." He lifted his blue gaze to meet mine. "But I am not a pirate."

"Perhaps not." Why had my throat gone dry? How very odd. I banished the sudden image of Henry at the helm of a ship from my mind and took another sip of my tea. "But while this story is about pirates and a woman in need of refuge and a family—or so I presume it will end that way—it is also intended to be consumed by ladies of England. Those are the ladies who will need to fall in love with your pirate as well."

Henry looked thoughtful. He rubbed his clean-shaven chin, finding a deep interest in the flames once again. "Perhaps the author hasn't the least idea how to make a lady fall in love with hi—with a pirate."

Mama's presence behind us made this delicate. I could not instruct Henry openly, of course. She would find it odd. "If only we could write him a letter in order to help him along."

Henry seemed to understand my meaning. "A letter would be very kind of us, for he could utilize our advice in his next story. How shall we compose it?" He leaned behind his chair to set his empty cup on the sofa's side table, then took my cup to do the same.

"As such: Dear Mr. Author, you have delighted us with your tale of a swashbuckling hero and the woman whom he saves from a lonely fate. It is our opinion that you could have made some changes to the hero's actions in order to make him more palatable to the general female population, and we have identified them as follows: first, the pirate needs to have a softness toward the woman, so she understands he is growing to care for her instead of wondering why he is so uncouth."

"Will that not take away from the pirate's reputation?"

"Not if she is the only person to see or notice the moments of softness. She will find herself drawn to discover why he only acts in that manner toward her, I imagine."

"Hmmm." Henry did not seem convinced.

"Another option, of course, is to give them a start where she finds him an irredeemable rake, then over the course of the story he performs such little kindnesses or special attention to her that she cannot help falling in love with him."

"In which case, he might be permitted to kiss her when she arrives on his ship in the first chapter."

My body tensed. "Indeed, though you will be forced to win the hearts of your readers again after such a foul action."

"You mean the author's readers?"

Had I not said as much? "Of course. I am merely growing incensed on behalf of the lonely woman. I cannot think clearly."

"Then let us move on to another subject. We can continue to compose our letter to the author at another time."

"I am not as fragile as that. I have another point I would like to make."

Henry leaned forward a little, and my attention dropped to the fraying thread on the edge of my armrest, my fingers smoothing it. "The action which you believe to be warranted at the start of their acquaintance would in fact be better saved for later, if only for the sheer purpose of allowing it the distinction it deserves. The kiss between two characters should not be rushed. It is the culmination of their feelings and ours, as the readers. We will find greater satisfaction if that particular action is given the consideration and, dare I say, *reverence* it deserves."

He peered at me thoughtfully. "I'd not thought of that before."

"We put such stock in that moment, do we not? When they come together. It seems silly to make light of it for the sake of entertainment."

"I agree with you on that score, Miss Hutton." He held my gaze. "I would never wish to make light of that which I too respect in all its bounds of propriety. Even for a daring pirate and his charge."

"Perhaps some pirates can be permitted to act the part of gentleman, and the ladies who read about them will be even more in love."

"Your perception is valuable. You see many things I have not considered."

"I am a lady, Mr. Bradwell. You are a man."

"That is exceedingly clear to me," he said softly.

My heart raced, the gentle tone differing so greatly from that which he typically used.

He shifted into a soft smile. "I think we have exhausted the topic of this author's failure to entice you to cheer on his hero."

"Perhaps we ought to compare it to *Pride and Prejudice*. You read the novel in its entirety, have you not?"

"I have. Mr. Darcy was not pleasant in the beginning, either."

"No. But he was a gentleman, even if he was full of pride. He was meant to be disliked, I feel. That author was successful in the transformation of Mr. Darcy's character, for who does not end the book fairly in love with him?"

Henry grinned. "I can say, with the greatest of truth, that I did not find myself in love with Mr. Darcy."

I laughed.

Henry's smile spread over his slightly uneven teeth, creating small lines beside his eyes that were endearing and handsome.

His smile felt intimate, drawing me in. When he lifted his gaze, his eyebrows followed suit. "It appears the sun has graced us with its presence."

"Shall we walk to the park?" Mama said, surprising me. I knew she was in the room with us, but her insertion into our conversation had been unexpected. "I will send Shaw to fetch your coat from the kitchen, Mr. Bradwell." She stood, bustling toward the door. Oh, she meant that she would seek him out *now*. She went into the corridor in search of our butler, leaving the door open.

"She must trust you excessively," I said. She had previously been the soul of propriety and discretion with my suitors. My mother had been the person who had discovered Henry's brother alone with Felicity in our library last year, and that situation ended in a wedding. Perhaps this trust was a sign she was becoming desperate. "Or she listened closely to our conversation and hoped that two people who were capable of discussing kissing would also be able to steal one in her absence."

His gaze dropped to my lips, lingering, making them burn from the attention.

My cheeks warmed. I'd meant it as a joke, but I was afraid it sounded far too serious. It was a heady thing to realize I would like very much for him to be the dashing pirate, stealing kisses without a care in the world. "But you are no pirate, Henry, and I am not a lonely woman in need of rescuing."

He straightened in his chair. "Of course not. You have a loving, supportive family, and many beaus dangling after you."

"Many? You exaggerate. I have *one*, and he is only a false beau, if you would kindly recall."

"I had not meant myself." His attention did not waver from my face. "I wonder if Captain Neal would be discouraged by your clear dismissal of his suit."

"He and I would not suit, so his discouragement would be welcome."

"My poor friend, to be so carelessly discarded." Henry watched my face for a reaction, it seemed. Despite his words, he did not appear to feel much sympathy for his *friend*.

"I could not abide living as a captain's wife. Life on a ship is not in the least desirable to me."

"Ah, but that is only one option."

"What do you mean?"

"You could set up a house on land, of course. Await his furloughs, raise your children in the country"—he lowered his voice—"write to your heart's content."

The picture he painted of a potential future robbed me of breath. It was everything I desired: a home away from Town, no requirement for hosting parties often, children of my own, the ability to write . . . good heavens, had I cast Captain Neal from my mind prematurely?

I had been fighting disappointment over the previous few days that Henry did not mean to court me in earnest. Perhaps he was correct, and I had a willing, appropriate gentleman who lingered over my hand and desired dancing with me, and—though more of a gratuity than a requirement—was handsome, as well.

"I have not considered Captain Neal before in that way. I suppose I must thank you for helping me see the potential where I had previously not found any."

A strange tightness fell over Henry's features. "After your help with my novel, Marianne, it is the very least I could do."

If I'd had any doubts before, that settled them. Henry did not see me in a romantic light.

Mama entered the room again. "Shall we?"

I straightened, doing my best to temper my disappointment. "We shall."

CHAPTER 8

HENRY

Foolish, foolish man. If I possessed even a whit of intelligence, I would not have pushed Marianne *toward* Neal. It was plain she did not count me as a suitor with how often she reminded me that our arrangement was a façade, but I couldn't deny the strange jealousy I'd felt last night watching her dance with other men.

Our walk in St. James's Park was pleasant, only stopping periodically to greet others who sought the weak sunlight after the rain had abated. When we made it back to the Hutton townhouse, Marianne lifted her hand to halt my exit. "Do not leave yet, if you please. I would like to return your novel."

I nodded, watching her follow her mother up the steps. I took the stairs at a slower pace, stepping through the doorway to wait for Marianne in the entryway. She had a lovely figure, and her taste was refined. For a woman not much younger than myself, I would still have expected the joviality of youth to cling to her. But Marianne was an aged soul in a young lady's body. She was wise, proven to me by the insight she exhibited when discussing novels.

Mrs. Hutton requested the attention of the butler and disappeared into the corridor as she spoke to him.

Marianne reappeared, coming sedately down the stairs, lifting the hem of her gown so as not to trip, my book in her other hand. "I have made some improvements where I could, but recall that they are merely suggestions."

I took the book from her outstretched hand. It was bulkier than I remembered. "How did you manage that? I did not leave much room between the lines."

"Sewing pins. You shall see." She smiled, and the effect was dazzling.

"When will I have the opportunity to see you again?" I found myself eager for her company before I had even left it.

"Mother is putting a card party together. I suspect your recent attention to me is her chief motivation for the event, so you can expect an invitation. I believe it will be on Tuesday next."

"Of course. I will keep my Tuesday clear. Now tell me, what are your thoughts on the opera? James secured a box, and I still have use of it for the next few weeks."

"I can be persuaded to enjoy it. Who does not appreciate a quality performance?"

"Many do not, I imagine. But I will settle on a date and send an invitation shortly. I believe the Gatleys will be joining us as well."

Her soft eyebrows pulled together. "Mr. Gatley will certainly not wish for my presence then. He cannot appreciate having a usurper among the party."

"Usurper?" I asked with some surprise.

"He must see me in that way if he has designs on making you his son-in-law."

The man certainly did harbor such a delusion as that. "He can design all he wishes. That is something that will never come to pass."

"Because you abhor marriage? Or are you simply convinced that you and Miss Gatley will not suit?"

"I am not ready to make any decisions of that nature. Marriage is not presently on my mind."

"Yet you are allowing Society to consider otherwise. Have you not wondered what the matrons will think when they see you courting me?"

I'd not believed it would have any great effect when we first devised our plan. "I assumed they would believe me to be smitten and respect that my attention has already been secured."

She chuckled and stepped closer, looking over her shoulder briefly as though making certain we were still alone. "That privilege is not afforded you until you have become engaged to a woman. While you are merely courting, you open yourself up to the advances of all the eligible young ladies of London."

She could not be correct, could she? Mr. Gatley had designs on increasing my acquaintance with his daughter, and Mrs. Hamilton had done the same with hers, but certainly neither of them had known of my arrangement with Marianne.

"I can see you are thinking over what I've said, and I can assure you that our ride in Hyde Park was enough to set the tongues wagging. Mr. Gatley, more than likely, had a different reason for singling you out, but your presence could have very well sparked the idea of your eligibility. You would be shocked to learn how fast news can travel among the mothers in Town."

"Shocked? Disturbed is perhaps more apt."

"Are you regretting our arrangement?" she asked.

I could not look into her worried brown eyes and regret anything yet. She had given me much to think about for improving my novel, and her company had been enjoyable thus far. If an association with Marianne brought a few matchmaking parents my direction, it would still be worth it to me. "No, I am not regretting it. I only hope it will not prove to be more of a headache than we'd anticipated."

"It will not," she said archly. "I fully anticipated the headache."

"In that case, I am glad to be the only ignorant sufferer." I bowed, tucking the book into my coat pocket. "Good day, Marianne."

"Good day, Henry."

There was a bit of a bounce in my step when I let myself down to the paving stones and turned toward my carriage. All jesting aside, when I had set out on this arrangement with Marianne, I'd had no idea how much I would enjoy it.

Or rather, *her*.

It was clear by the time I finished going over Marianne's notes—cleverly written and pinned over the places in my manuscript that needed revising—she knew what she was about. Her suggestions were mostly on the mark, and I appreciated her insights. I wished I'd had a friend with her expertise much earlier in my career, but I would content myself with having her now.

Three days had passed since our walk in the park. I had made good progress on my story thus far. I selected the next segment of pages, folded them neatly, and tucked them into a different book than the one I had pretended to lend her last time. In case her mother was keeping note of which novels I brought Marianne, I wanted to be certain not to raise any reason for alarm.

Felton, my valet, helped me dress, but I turned toward the shaving glass to tie my own cravat. "You have not left the house so often in years, sir. If you don't mind me saying so, we don't know what to think of this change."

"You need not think on it at all." I lifted my head so I could finish tying my cravat. "Certainly do not refine upon it too much. I have found an intellectual partner and she is doing a great deal to broaden my outlook on a variety of novels."

"Ah," he said in understanding. "Much like Mrs. Bradwell did when she came to Chelton."

"Yes, exactly like Felicity." It had been the very thing which had initially bonded me to my sister-in-law. Our discussions about the various novels we enjoyed were enthralling and interesting. I'd found a like soul in her, and she would always be one of my dearest friends.

"As for this new miss—"

"That will be enough from you," I said, turning to slide my arms into my coat. "You are worse than a gossiping mother."

"You wound me, sir."

"You are not so easily wounded, Felton," I muttered. I glanced at him once more on my way through the door, but he wasn't paying me any mind, gathering my discarded things and tidying the room. It was with minor jealousy that I'd watched Marianne speak freely of her writing in front of her maid. Could I trust Felton? The man had been with me since Father hired him as my batman in the army. We had been through much together.

Still, I worried that his tongue was too loose. A man who gossiped to you would often also gossip about you, and Felton was always too eager to share the latest tidbit he'd picked up downstairs.

No, the less people who knew my secret, the better.

I slipped a pair of opera glasses into one pocket and my novel stuffed with papers into another. If I could manage to sit beside Marianne, that would be most convenient, but if not, I would contrive a way to pass the book to her by the end of the evening. If Mrs. Hutton was to be depended upon, there would be ample opportunity to catch a quiet moment with her daughter. She'd thus far managed to keep every propriety while also allowing us time to speak in relative privacy. Cunning, brilliant woman.

My carriage pulled in front of the Hutton house. Our entire party was too large to fit into one vehicle, so we had planned to meet the Gatleys at the opera house. I'd swallowed my initial concern that the Gatleys would consider my lack of conveying them to the opera house an insult, but that was quickly squashed when I recalled their devices in forcing this invitation from my lips. It might be good to reiterate that my attention lay elsewhere.

The Hutton butler let me into the entryway, and a smattering of female voices somewhere on the floor above us caught my attention.

"I am only saying that you ought not to discount his attention quite yet."

"I haven't, Mama." That was Marianne. Her voice was becoming familiar, soothing my tensed neck. "It has recently been borne upon me that perhaps being the wife of a navy man would not be as horrible as I had imagined."

My stomach clenched, my neck bunching again. She was not speaking of me, as I'd originally assumed. She must be speaking of Neal.

"What of the divided rations?" Mrs. Hutton asked with amusement in her tone. "Has his attention made the prospect less distasteful to you?"

"Not at all. His attention had nothing to do with it." She paused a moment before continuing. "It was merely mentioned to me that I need not live on a ship at all. Many wives remain in England while their husbands are off in the military."

"I hadn't considered that."

"Neither have I, before now," Marianne said.

"Well, I only request you do not discount *anyone* quite yet."

Anyone, including me? I could only hope that was what she meant. It was not conceit that led me to believe Mrs. Hutton approved of me as a prospective husband. The hope in her eyes when she looked at me was proof enough.

"I do take your meaning, Mama. I have not discounted Mr. Bradwell either." Except she spoke in an odd tone, and I wondered why she altered her voice when speaking of me. Was I becoming a burden on her? That was a lowering thought.

"Here," Mrs. Hutton said. "Turn and let me help you with that." There was a bit of shuffling, the sound of fabric rustling, before she said, "All finished. Shall we go down and wait?"

I looked to the butler, but he stood against the wall, his face impassive. Did the Huttons know how clearly their voices could be overheard? I should have asked the butler to fetch the family. It was with a modicum of shame I realized I hadn't. But he shouldn't have needed to be asked, either.

The women came down the stairs together, and I lifted my gaze to meet Marianne's surprise at finding me waiting. Her dark hair was drawn away from her face, leaving it open to receive my admiration. She wore white gloves to the elbow and a white gown with silver shot through, making her appear as though she shone when the candlelight fell upon her, a train trailing the steps behind her. She was an angelic vision, the white a crisp contrast to her rich brown hair.

"Good evening." I bowed more formally than the occasion called for, but I found I needed a moment to compose my expression into one of neutrality.

"Shaw," Mrs. Hutton said, "will you please inform my husband we are ready to leave?"

He nodded and left the room.

"I've taken the liberty of reserving a table at the Clarendon following the opera," I said. "I hope you will join me for a refreshment."

Mrs. Hutton made a motion that jostled her daughter's arm. Had she *nudged* her?

"That was most kind of you," Marianne said, holding my

gaze. Was she trying to discover my purpose? If so, she would be disappointed—or perhaps relieved. I meant nothing more by securing the supper than to extend our evening together.

I cleared my throat. "I also brought you another novel, Miss Hutton, if it would please you to read it." A sudden, strange nervousness overcame me as I fished inside my coat pocket and pulled out the book, but when I lifted it, I found that Marianne's eyes were bright with—dare I say—excitement. Perhaps anticipation.

"How lovely, Mr. Bradwell." She extended her hand and took the book. "I look forward to our next debate."

"I do hope we will agree more about this one."

She laughed, the musical sound marching up my spine. "I can make you no promises, sir."

Mr. Hutton appeared and made his bows before we filed outside and climbed into the waiting carriage. Mr. and Mrs. Hutton sat together, so I slid in beside Marianne. It was not a small conveyance by any means, but neither was I a small man. My leg brushed hers as I settled into the seat. I moved it away, but when the carriage began rolling, rocking us gently with the motion, I could not help it from recurring. She did not seem the least disturbed by my touching her, so I allowed my leg to rest and pretended as though it did not affect me.

In general, I had never been one for seeking out female company. I had always carried a higher interest in intellectual pursuits than the petticoat line. When I had joined the army to follow in my father's footsteps, it had been in an attempt to please him, sacrificing my greater desire: university. When my father had died during the battle of Waterloo, I had been grateful for the moment we shared the day before, when he had pulled me aside and told me how proud I had made him—how proud he felt having a military son to carry on his legacy.

Waterloo changed everything. I promptly sold out.

Perhaps the part of me which recognized how I would be a

disappointment to my father, had he remained alive, kept me from avoiding that same fate with my mother. If I did not seek out a wife, I could not choose one who would fail to measure up in some way, as I seemed to do in other regards.

It was simply easier to keep to myself. Focus on my writing, my novels, the income that would provide for me.

But now I was feeling all manner of foreign things, and I could not identify if they were a product of throwing my cap at a woman or if they were because of Marianne in particular. Was this natural, to find myself thinking of her when I was away, or to discover that I was eager to extend our evening at a great expense to myself?

Her knee bumped mine again, and every particle of me was aware of how close she sat, the cloud of sweet perfume that clung to her, and the sharp intelligence she carried in her gaze.

"I brought my opera glass if anyone has need of it," I said, hoping to pull my attention away from our bumping knees.

"I believe Mama did as well," Marianne said.

Mrs. Hutton choked a little, but recovered herself quickly. "You would not wish to use mine, I fear. It is a tiny little thing, and not at all easy to see out of."

That was odd. "You are all more than welcome to share mine. Everyone shall have the chance to see the expressions on our singers' faces this evening."

Our carriage pulled to stop, and my groom opened the door for us. I climbed out and turned to offer Marianne my hand. She took it, and I enjoyed the feeling of her fingers wrapped in mine for a moment, pulling them closer to rest on my bent arm. When she left her hand there, I felt a surge of victory.

My affections were beginning to become engaged. This was not good at all.

CHAPTER 9

MARIANNE

Despite meeting with the Gatley family in the lobby and walking with them to our box for the evening, I somehow contrived to sit beside Henry. Or had he contrived to sit beside me? His seeming refusal to release my hand throughout our journey toward the box implied he wanted to keep me at his side. Was that because he desired my company, or merely to use me as a shield against the eager Miss Gatley?

My money was on the latter.

Mama sat on my other side, Papa beside her, and we were settled on the front row of two sets of chairs in Henry's box.

Lights flickered on and around the stage, highlighting the actors' faces as they sang forlornly to one another. The musicians were well-timed, the voices crisp and beautiful, ringing out through the gilded plasterwork room. Mama held her small opera glass to her eye like a tiny telescope. She tilted it this way and that, her mouth pinched in concentration.

"May I borrow that?" I was interested to see the woman's face and the details in her extravagant coiffure.

My mother seemed to hesitate before handing me the glass. I lifted it to my eye and startled when Henry's face filled the

77

small telescope, an unladylike sound of surprise ripping from my throat.

I lowered the telescope and looked at it, for while Henry appeared when I lifted the glass to my eye, he had not moved from the seat beside me. Mama's hand reached over to gently squeeze my leg.

She had expected that.

"Are you well?" Henry asked, leaning close and whispering, his voice tickling the small hairs near my ear.

A shiver went through my shoulders. "Yes."

I lifted the odd telescope again, slowly this time, and shifted it to see Henry's face once more. It was a strange device, and decidedly *not* an opera glass. It somehow managed to point toward the stage to give the illusion I was looking at the actors, but showed me the person seated beside me. I spun it slowly until it settled on Mama's face on my other side, and her innocence was far from genuine. She had some explaining to do later.

What possessed her to own such a device? And why did she feel the need to spy on anyone?

I centered the spy hole on Henry again. His expression was bland, his eyes flicking to the side repeatedly. Was he looking at me? I lowered the glass and leaned in to whisper to him. "Are you not enjoying the performance?"

"I am not averse to the opera in general, but tonight I cannot convince my mind to settle."

"You seem restless."

"Am I that obvious?"

I gestured gently to his foot, which bounced a little, and he immediately stilled it. It was impossible to see his expression without turning in my chair, but I could hear the soft chuckle reverberating from his chest.

"I've been caught out," he said. "I will do better for the remainder of the performance, I vow it." His gentle, teasing tone and the whisper meant only for me was not aiding my determination to remove Henry from my mind as a potential suitor. The man had proclaimed his desire to remain friends, and though I had not counted him among my particular friends until very recently, I thought I would like to keep him long after our ruse ended.

He was a man of great intellect, capable of discussing books and *willing* to do so with a woman—two large marks in his favor—and he was interesting. The butterflies he sent through my belly were only a minor inconvenience. They could be diminished with effort. Or perhaps replaced? Could Captain Neal be enticed to deliver a set of butterflies to my midsection? How did one go about developing the tiny flapping beasties, anyway?

I curled my fingers around the opera glass in my lap, doing my best to focus on the actors but unable to tear my gaze from Henry's restless knee. Was he anxious? I wanted to see his expression but could not risk turning to look at him again and drawing attention to my curiosity. The opera glass would do well enough.

When I had it situated in the proper position to see Henry's face, I was surprised to find him in a state of mild agitation, his gaze flicking from the stage to me again.

He looked at me for a long moment before leaning close, and my stomach clenched in anticipation.

"Anything of interest down there?" he asked.

I shifted the glass a little to see Miss Gatley, seated behind Henry. Her scowl was fierce and she was directing it at me, almost as though she was looking into the tiny mirror that captured her reflection and delivered it to my eye. I lowered the glass at once. "No, nothing of interest."

Henry straightened in his seat, and his active knee stalled.

"What has flustered you?" I whispered.

Miss Gatley leaned forward in her seat and tapped Henry on the shoulder with her fan.

He looked startled at first, but quickly covered the expression, turning in his seat to face her.

"We forgot our lorgnette at home." Her gaze shifted toward me, or so it felt, hot on my back.

I could not allow her to use this device and see how I had been *spying* during the course of the performance. She would spread that bit of gossip about London with zeal.

Henry looked to me, but I refused to meet his gaze. He cleared his throat. "Here, Miss Gatley." He fished in his coat pocket and pulled out a pair of glasses on a long, brass handle. "You may borrow mine."

I released my breath, relieved, and leaned back in my seat. I put the strange opera glass in my mother's hand and she took it, her cheeks pinking.

Henry did not allow me a respite. "Why do I feel like I saved you from an uncomfortable situation?"

"I have no idea what you refer to."

"Ah," he said. "We are to pretend, then?"

Could he see through me so easily? "There is no pretending."

"Is not our entire relationship pretending?"

I looked at him in surprise. He sent me a wink and directed his attention to the stage.

Miss Gatley leaned forward in her seat. "I am quite confused. Is the woman not meant to be in love with the man?"

Henry leaned back in his chair a little and explained the point of the plot that Miss Gatley had missed. Or had pretended to miss, if I had my guess. Her blonde curls bobbed as she paid special attention to Henry's explanation. The remainder of the first act continued in a similar manner, with Miss Gatley leaning forward to ask absurd questions which she might have just as easily directed to her mother or father, sitting on either side of her. The distracting nature of her flirtation devices was almost enough to tempt me to offer her my seat so Henry would no longer have to strain his neck.

Intermission came upon us, saving me from acting upon that impulse.

The party rose and filed from the box to leave in search of something to drink—or to boast about the man who escorted us, in Mrs. Gatley's and Mama's case, most likely. When we reached the corridor, I slowed my steps, taking Mama's hand and pulling on it softly. I waited until the rest of the party had gone on ahead of us.

She looked confused. "What is it?"

I lowered my voice. "Doing it much too brown, Mama."

"Whatever do you mean—"

"What in heaven's name was that device?"

She smiled, dropping her false confusion. "Mrs. Ormiston called it a jealousy glass. I told her of our opera plans last night, so she dropped it by this morning."

"For what purpose?"

"To watch the people beside or behind you. Whoever it is you are attempting to look at."

Well, I had figured that much out already. "Yes, but what did Mrs. Ormiston think you needed a jealousy glass for?"

"So I might see if Mr. Bradwell holds a particular interest for you. I did not care to let him see me watching, of course."

My stomach clenched. My mother was not a woman prone to dramatics, so this behavior was something of a surprise coming from her. "Mama," I said in a mildly rebuking tone. "Whatever has gotten into you?"

"I only wanted to ascertain his interest, darling."

His interest? Oh, dear. She was taking this courting much too seriously. "Do you not think his regular calls tell you enough?"

"Of course they are informative, but I cannot gauge the

depth of his interest when I am forever manufacturing ways to give you room to know his character."

"Perhaps you ought not concern yourself with creating opportunities for us to speak privately, then." Heavens, I did not mean that. Why did I say such a thing?

My mother narrowed her gaze slightly at me. "Are your affections engaged?"

Could she see through our façade? I glanced away. "It is too soon to know."

"There is nothing the matter with taking your time to discern the depth of your feelings. In fact, you may wish to spend time with both him and Captain Neal until you decide whom it is you care for most. Until you love one of them." She took both of my hands in hers and squeezed my fingers gently, a smile playing on her lips. "I am so pleased, Marianne."

Guilt filled me with a buzzing, warm energy up to my shoulders. I gave a small chuckle. "We should join the others."

"Right you are." She released my hands and strung her arm through mine, pulling me down the corridor toward the lobby where Papa and our party were waiting for us. When we stepped into the room and located our friends, Mama's grip on my arm tightened. "How fortunate we are," she whispered.

Captain Neal stood beside my father, speaking to him quietly. His gaze fell upon me and his eyes lit up. He was handsome, kind, got on well with my father, and my mother certainly approved. He was a hero, well respected in the navy. If married to him, I could live in the country, raise my children, and write to my heart's content.

Life with Captain Neal painted an utterly perfect picture. So why was my heart not beating any faster for him?

All the writing time in the world, I repeated to myself.

Drat. Still not beating any faster.

"Miss Hutton, you look lovely," Captain Neal said, bowing

over my hand. His sandy-colored hair was swept up off his fore-head, and his gray eyes locked on me as he straightened.

I curtseyed. Feelings could still develop. It was not as though I must love the man in the first few months of knowing him. "I did not realize we would have the pleasure of your company this evening, Captain."

"How fortunate I happened to fancy a night at the opera."

"Fortunate, indeed," Henry said dryly. He covered his evident displeasure with a smile. "Did we not speak of this just last night?"

Captain Neal affected an overly innocent expression, tilting his head to the side. "Did we? Now I needn't wonder who put the idea in my head." His gaze moved to me again with meaning.

Had he discovered from Henry that I would be attending the opera and pursued me? The thought sent something of a thrill through my chest. Thus far, Captain Neal had been attentive when we saw him in company, but he had not gone to great lengths to seek me out. I would not bother to look at Mama, for I was certain she was presently beaming.

"Have you come alone?" I asked.

"Indeed, I have. I hoped to feast my eyes on wholesome beauty." He looked at me. "And I have done just that."

Mr. Gatley cleared his throat. "We are for the Clarendon following the performance." Mr. Gatley looked between the captain and me. He seemed pleased, and I imagined he wanted me to be occupied so Miss Gatley would have more time with Henry. "Perhaps you will join us?"

Henry's expression tightened.

Captain Neal shook his head. "I could never impose."

"Nonsense," Henry said, pasting a smile on his face. "Your presence would be most gratifying."

"Then it is settled," Mama said. "Our party has grown."

"Not only for the Clarendon, perhaps," Miss Gatley suggested, her doll-like eyes rounding expectantly.

Henry nodded. "You will join us in the box, I hope."

Captain Neal did not remove his gaze from me when he replied. "I should enjoy that very much."

The remainder of the performance passed without my recognizing anything that occurred on the stage. I was too busy utilizing my mother's borrowed jealousy glass to watch the interactions between Henry and Miss Gatley, seated behind me.

Captain Neal had escorted me into the box, taking the seat beside mine and relegating Henry to the second row beside Miss Gatley. I'd caught Henry's eye when the interaction took place, and he'd winked at me. I only hoped Mama had not caught it as well.

Watching him through the opera glass was a lesson in truly pretending. I knew he did not have a genuine interest in Miss Gatley, but that did not stop me from feeling precisely what the jealousy glass intended when I saw them lean close and whisper together. I was overly curious about what passed between them so consistently. I had to shove my jealousy away and feign complete serenity.

The dinner at the Clarendon did not give me cause to feel my jealousy at a lesser degree. Henry was seated opposite me, beside Miss Gatley, Mr. Gatley on his other side. Captain Neal's presence evened our numbers perfectly, but his position next to me made it impossible to pay any mind to the conversation occurring across the table. When Miss Gatley threw her blonde curls gently in a demure laugh, I squeezed my fork hard enough to make my knuckles white.

I tore my attention away from them with an alarming degree

of difficulty. "What was it that inspired you to join the navy, Captain Neal?"

He lifted his glass to his lips and took a slow sip as though he contemplated his answer. "I have always been drawn to the sea. I took the career out of necessity, initially. My family is all gone, and when my father died, I had nowhere to go as a lad, so I took to the ocean. I grew to love life on a ship in a way I did not think I would."

"No family at all? Truly?" My heart broke a little for him.

"None," he said, shooting me a sad smile. "My mother died giving me life, and my father ten years later. It is my greatest wish to have a family of my own."

I could only imagine how deep a yearning he must feel for a wife, children, people to feel connected to. It would be an easier task to accomplish if he was not reliant on his ship's schedule. "Have you considered leaving the navy at all?"

"No. My blood now runs with seawater, I am afraid. I can abide a few months at a time on land, but I find myself eager to return to my ship before the end is up."

"Are you eager for it now?"

"At present, no. I have found something much more alluring than a ship to entice me to remain." His smile was perfectly clear.

I dropped my gaze and pushed my jelly about my plate a little with my fork, my cheeks growing warm. This man wanted a family more than I did, and my desire to have children of my own someday was strong. If nothing else, our goals certainly aligned.

He lowered his voice so he might not be overheard. "You will permit me to observe, Miss Hutton, that my suit has not been wholly rebuffed. I have thus allowed myself to believe it could perhaps be an acceptable course for me to continue."

Was he asking to court me? Good heavens, whatever did I

say to that? "I have previously been uncertain about the nature of your intentions, but I believe I understand them better now."

He looked pleased. "Let us say no more. I will do my best to continue to prove my worth to you, if you would be so kind as to accept my humble attention. I am not a young man, and my aims at coming to London are . . . focused."

Focused on matrimony, I assumed. It was a pretty speech. My heart thundered, though I could not identify whether it was from eager anticipation or an overwhelming sense of uncertainty. I felt both.

I searched for something to say to turn the tide of the conversation. "It is a pity that most of Society will be leaving for the country in a few short weeks."

"Do you count yourself among those who are choosing to find refuge in their great country manors?" he asked.

"My mother is usually eager to return to our estate in Cheshire by now, but she has not made any indication yet of our plans. How long do you intend to remain in London?"

"I have six more weeks before I must report to Plymouth." He gave me a lopsided smile. "It is not very long, but I think quite a great deal can be managed for those possessed of dedication."

In other words, if we tried hard enough, perhaps we could fall in love before he was due to return to his ship? I did not know if the deadline he imposed would entice or prohibit me from developing feelings for him, but my mind was certainly open to it.

"I could not help but overhear, Captain," Mama said, leaning nearer to me. "It is a pity we only have your company for six more weeks. How do you intend to spend your time?"

"I had hoped it would be in your presence, of course." He flashed a grin.

"That is just what I hoped to hear." My mother's feline smile was so unlike her that I began to grow slightly wary. What plan was she hatching, and which of her friends had given her the idea?

"Do not tease me, madam," he said playfully. "Do you intend to remain in London?"

"We do not," she said with no remorse. "I am in the midst of planning a house party at our home in Cheshire in a fortnight from now. I hope you will join us." She sat back in her seat a little to include the entire table and her invitation. "I hope you will *all* join us."

CHAPTER 10

HENRY

The surprise I felt at overhearing the invitation to the Huttons' house party was nothing compared to the shock on Marianne's face.

"A house party," Miss Gatley breathed, her blue eyes wide. "How exquisite."

"Do you think you will join?" Mr. Gatley asked me.

I wanted to look to his wife and inquire her opinion. There were many matchmaking mamas scattered across London, but this man was abnormally dedicated for a father.

I noticed many sets of eyes blinking at me. Not just the Gatleys, but Marianne and her mother watched me for a response, as well as the captain. The only person at this table who seemed not to care a whit whether I attended this house party was Mr. Hutton. His side whiskers quivered while he dug into his steak and ale pie, the jelly jiggling on his plate with every bite.

I wished I could devote myself to my meal so thoroughly to avoid the question. A house party meant more socializing than I was prepared for. My nature was not built for extended engagements, nor for a situation which required my attention for an entire week—or *two*—without any respite to be found in my own home.

I caught Marianne's gaze across the table and knew at once I would not reject an invitation that would mean spending more time with her. I had worried we wouldn't have enough time for discussion with summer coming upon us and so many families choosing to spend it in the countryside. A few additional weeks with her would be worth the discomfort of a house party, wouldn't they?

"Perhaps Mr. Bradwell has other engagements?" Captain Neal said.

He wished that was the case, no doubt. I forced myself to smile and hoped it looked more pleasant than a grimace. "No engagements that would preclude me from spending time with you all. I would be more than happy to join you, Mrs. Hutton. Thank you most kindly for the invitation."

"Such pretty manners," Mrs. Hutton said. "Your addition will be exceedingly welcome."

Marianne had regained her equilibrium, and her father had not seemed to pay any mind to the current conversation. It was an odd way to extend such an invitation, but knowing Mrs. Hutton, a formal invitation would not be too long in coming.

"Do you think you will attend?" I asked Mrs. Gatley

"Oh. I am not certain." She looked to her husband. "We were already invited—"

"Of course we shall." Mr. Gatley turned his attention to where Mr. Hutton was enjoying his wine. "I have heard wonderful things about your lake, sir."

Mr. Hutton smacked his lips slightly. "There is great sport to be had at Hutton House. The men are welcome to join me at the lake, of course. I think the respite of fishing will be much utilized."

I assumed Mr. Hutton would be just as absent in the country as he was in London.

If nothing else, this would be an opportunity for Marianne and me to continue our project together. With any luck, Mrs. Hutton would be as attentive in the country as she was in Town. The way I watched her look at Captain Neal left no mystery as to how she felt about him as a suitor for her daughter—hopeful. Somehow, I would have to reconcile myself with the fact that I was not the only man vying for Marianne's hand.

I had been correct, and a formal invitation followed the informal one only two days later. I was pleased that it was accompanied by a note, written in what I came to learn was Marianne's hand.

What an excellent opportunity for us to continue our dialogue on the interesting pirate story. I do hope you will respond favorably. I look forward to the next installment.
Yours, etc. M. Hutton

The book I'd lent to Marianne most recently had been returned with the invitation, my revised chapter tucked within its pages. I penned a quick acceptance to the house party, then took myself up to the study to devote my attention to this chapter, though my mind seemed to be lost elsewhere.

Sometimes the words flowed from my quill pen like an uninhibited river, coursing a path without heed of its surroundings. I could become so lost in a story I failed to eat. The only thing keeping me aware of my surroundings was the necessity of hiding my writing. Those moments rarely came outside of Sedwick Lodge, my family's hunting box.

The house had been my inheritance upon my father's death, along with a sum of money, but I had yet to move into it and fully claim it as my own. Knowing my father would be utterly disappointed in my failure to continue in a military career kept me from accepting the home as my own.

Instead, I wrote. Just as my creativity had the capacity to flow like a river, other times writing felt more like I had picked up a rock from that very same riverbed and was doing my best to wring water out of it. In other words: impossible.

The difficulty was that, regardless of which I seem to be experiencing, my desire to write never lessened.

Unfortunately, today had been more like a rock than a river.

I opened the pages of the book and withdrew the chapter Marianne had delivered earlier. Had she sent her maid to complete the task, or merely hoped whatever footman had been given the job would not open the novel and discover my pages for himself? Given her discretion, I imagined she had entrusted the task to her maid.

I read over Marianne's notes, pinned as they were over the top of my manuscript. There were a few I wanted to disregard, but for the most part knew I must accept. I highly valued her opinion.

I pulled out a fresh sheet of paper to begin my final rewrite of the chapter before moving onto the next, but one particular note caught my eye.

A lady will never refuse attention from a man she desires to be near. He can make her feel special by delivering heartfelt compliments, as you have so artfully done. He can also make her feel adored by sacrificing in some way as Mr. Darcy did in arranging Lydia's marriage to Mr. Wickham. Any sacrifice for the sake of the other person will do. If you choose to implement that in your story, it would be wise to choose the sacrifice now so you can prepare for it in the beginning of their relationship.

Sometimes I wondered at her wisdom. Was it the product of her own experience, or merely intuition because she was a woman? I ran my eyes over the last sentence and dropped my quill pen into the stand again. I could not write at present. I would much prefer to discuss what sorts of sacrifices Marianne had in mind.

I glanced at the clock on the mantel. Hmm. Much too late to call. Marianne had mentioned her engagements for the next few nights when I had spoken to her after the opera, but I could not recall if tonight was Lord Wenton's soiree or the Tomlinson rout.

A knock at the door pulled me from considering the merits of going out tonight. I stacked the manuscript papers and slid them into the top drawer of the desk. "Enter."

Felton stepped inside, a tray balanced on one hand.

"You've been relegated to delivering my dinner now, too?" I asked, moving aside a book to make room on the desk for my meal.

"I offered to complete this task, sir. It is an honor to provide you with your dinner."

"Overdoing it, Felton." I shook out the napkin provided on the tray and laid it over my lap. "What is it you need?"

He clutched his chest. "You wound—"

"Do not attempt flattery or the false sense of hurt pride. I may not have known you for a long time, but I know you well."

Felton grew unusually quiet. "Indeed, sir." He cleared his throat. "My brother has sent word that my father is not in good health."

I lifted my chin, catching his eye before he averted it toward the desk. He had been there when I last spoke to my father, waiting in the tent when I returned, and he had been there the next day when my father had died. "You must go to him."

"He is in Ipswitch, sir."

"You may be absent for as long as your father requires your attention, and your position will be waiting for you. Do you need funds?"

"I have plenty for my needs," he said with uncommon gentleness.

I stood, holding the napkin so it would not fall to the floor. "Can I aid you in any other way?"

"I do not know how long it shall take."

I gave him a self-deprecating smile. "My boots will certainly suffer in your absence, but I will make do."

Felton gave a curt nod, emotion not being his forté, and spun on his heel to leave.

"Felton," I said, drawing his attention back to me. "You'll recall I mourned the things left unsaid?"

"Indeed, sir."

I'd thought as much. While I had yet to bring Felton into my confidence—the man was still an unabashed gossip—I had lamented my failure to trust my father prior to his death. Felton had watched me grieve the man I lost and the opportunity to speak to him openly. I had wanted to tell him of my novels, yet had been too much afraid, instead allowing him to believe I'd had an interest in remaining in the military. Had I spoken the truth, perhaps I would feel differently now about my career. Perhaps I would not be so frightened to tell my mother or my brothers about my books.

"Do not wait to speak to your father of the things which are important to you. You will heartily regret it later if you do."

He looked at me for a long moment before bowing and slipping from the room. I retook my seat, lowering myself. It was a good thing, perhaps, that I could not recall which of the entertainments Marianne had agreed to attend tonight, for my melancholy mood prohibited me from being a good dance or card partner. I had a feeling it would also stand in the way of a decent literary conversation. My mind was now clouded with images of the past that I'd attempted to forget and the regrets that still powered my motives.

Buttery, flaky pie crust steamed on my plate and I dug my

fork into the dinner, releasing the rich aroma of stewed meat inside. Pages waited to be edited in the top drawer of the desk, but my mind could not attend to them now. By the time I finished my dinner, I had grown antsy for Marianne's conversation. I longed for her smile to fill the cracks and crevices of my shadowed chest with light.

Melancholy be hanged. I wanted to see her tonight.

The table in the front entryway of my townhouse held the salver with invitations, the number growing rapidly since my appearance with Marianne in the park that fateful day. I flipped through a handful of them, searching for the one which claimed today's date.

Ah, found it. The Tomlinson rout. I scanned the card and found, to my dismay, that it was a musicale. I had just half an hour until I would need to leave for the event. I made my way upstairs to change. Hopefully Marianne would welcome my presence and a bit of a conversation tonight.

"Going out?" Felton asked, responding to my bell pull.

"Yes. I have changed my mind."

"You? Or has the lovely Miss Hutton done so?" Felton smirked, disappearing into the dressing room to retrieve a new set of clothes for me.

When he returned, I gave him no quarter. "Unless Miss Hutton is shaped like my dinner, she could not have influenced me. The pie fully captured my attention."

"Of course, sir."

I slid out of my shirt and pulled a new one on. "Neither has she asked me to attend the event this evening."

"Of course, sir."

"Nor has she given me leave to imagine she would particularly welcome my company this evening."

"Of course—"

"Enough of that," I said, fastening my shirt closed.

Felton quietly held my waistcoat up, and I slid my arms into it. "Of course, sir."

My lips flattened in a wry smile while I fastened my buttons. "Am I truly so transparent?"

Felton grinned. "Of course, sir."

CHAPTER 11
HENRY

The Tomlinson house was narrow and tall. The drawing room had been cleared of all additional furniture and chairs set up in rows, most of which had been claimed by the time I arrived. I took a position standing against the wall in the back of the room and questioned the choices that had brought me to this point.

Socializing was a singularly exhausting activity for me. I considered it worthwhile when it meant the opportunity to speak to Marianne, but this was not what I'd hoped for. She was across the room and surrounded by others, her head tilted softly, listening to something her mother said to her. She wore a muted gown of soft lilac, but that did not take away from her radiance.

It was a folly of mine to not have arrived earlier, for from this vantage point I could easily see Captain Neal dancing attendance on her. Had the man escorted her here? That soured my stomach.

When I had agreed to feign a courtship with Marianne, I hadn't realized I would be fighting for her time or attention. It would not have bothered me had I known it from the outset, but it felt a great burden now. I would not concern myself with the nature of those feelings, though. Suffice it to say, I had once considered Captain Neal an interesting acquaintance, and now I could not stand sight of the man.

Odd, that. There was no accounting for my sudden dislike.

Mrs. Tomlinson stood at the front of the room and waited for the din to quiet, her gleaming eyes roaming over the occupants in the room with triumph. A seat remained empty in the back row, so I quietly took it.

"Thank you all for being here," Mrs. Tomlinson said, the feather upon her turban bobbing while she spoke. "Those of you who have agreed to perform have my sincere and heartfelt gratitude. I am eager to hear the numbers you have planned, for I'm certain it will be a feast for the ears." There was a light applause of agreement. "My daughter has agreed to be our first performer. Alice?"

Miss Tomlinson stood, taking her place daintily at the pianoforte centered ahead of the audience. Her feather matched that of her mother's and bobbed as she settled herself at the instrument. She began to play. The sound was lovely, the music just what every other accomplished young lady would deliver for us this evening, I was certain. What was this but an opportunity to parade the young ladies before eligible suitors and display their marriageable traits? I was generally fond of good music, but tonight I was once again antsy. It felt like a repeat of the opera. It was difficult to enjoy the music or the performances when my mind was taken up with Marianne.

I would much rather be in a quiet corner somewhere speaking to her.

The next few musical numbers were much the same. I could not repeat in what order or which young ladies performed, for they were all variations on the same theme. The night drew on. Half a dozen young women sang, played the pianoforte, or the harp.

"Miss Hutton will now delight us with a song," Mrs. Tomlinson said.

I sat up straighter. Marianne took the seat at the pianoforte and spread her music on the stand. Captain Neal rose to follow her. Hot jealousy swept through me like a gliding hawk.

She looked up at the audience, resting her fingers in a starting position, and I saw the moment she noticed me. Her gaze snagged, as if she was a loose thread and I was the offending nail that caught her. Color pinked her cheeks, lending her a charming humility, and her lashes lowered. She took a breath and began. Suddenly, listening to music was not quite as much of a chore.

This song was no different from the other pieces played this evening, but watching Marianne made the experience far more enjoyable—so long as I averted my gaze from the man turning pages for her.

When the song came to a close, Marianne gathered her music sheets and retook her seat, generously escorted by the captain. My hands clenched, and I actively rested them again. What had come over me? I was undoubtedly jealous, but I couldn't account for it. Marianne was beautiful, accomplished, well-read, unafraid of being seen as a bluestocking . . . she knew what she wanted, and she did not settle for less. She was—well, quite honestly, I believed I had found the perfect woman.

A woman who now gazed into Captain Neal's eyes with what appeared to be adoration.

The final few music performances passed quickly, and I rose along with the rest of the audience after clapping for the young women who had performed. A smattering of dishes had been prepared for refreshment in the parlor. I stood back, near the wall, and waited for most of the group to file from the room before crossing to the Hutton party and making my bows.

"Mr. Bradwell," Mrs. Hutton said, her eyes betraying her delight at finding me in attendance. "I did not realize we'd have the pleasure of your company this evening. What a treat for us all."

"Indeed," Marianne said. "I am glad to see you. Did you receive our invitation? I asked Keene to return your book when she delivered it."

Ah, so I had been correct, and she'd entrusted the errand to her maid. "I did, thank you. I shall scour my shelves for another to replace it."

"Not until we've discussed the last one, sir," she chided. "I am eager to hear your thoughts on the service rendered to the woman by her intended."

"How interesting," I said, unable to fight the small smile creeping onto my lips. Her artful way of referring to her notes but phrasing it as though it came from a novel was amusing. "I had wondered your opinions on that very thing."

"Goodness," Mrs. Hutton said, glancing from her daughter to me, then to Captain Neal. "You have quite intellectual conversations, do you not?"

Captain Neal chuckled good naturedly. "I can see I must read more if I have any hope of inspiring such a spirited greeting from Miss Hutton."

She smiled. "That is hardly the case, Captain. Your conversation is plenty stimulating."

"Indeed," I agreed. "It is difficult not to be taken with stories the likes of which you share. Your adventures surely equal that of the novels we read."

He gave me a briefly searching look. "This said humbly from a man who has seen more adventure than any man should care to, eh?"

He referred to my time under Wellington, fighting until we reached Waterloo. It was not a subject which I cared to speak of, so I gave a tight smile. "Can I procure you a glass of . . . whatever it is they are serving in the parlor, Miss Hutton?"

"Oh." She looked to Captain Neal. "I am afraid that errand has already been granted—"

"I will go," the captain said. "Mrs. Hutton, do you care to join me?"

What was he doing, actively giving me time alone with Marianne? He *did* know that was the ideal position to be in, did he not?

He led Mrs. Hutton from the room, and I offered Marianne my elbow for no other reason than to escort her further away from the people still sitting in chairs, lingering over their conversation.

"I did not know you appreciated music, Henry," Marianne said, pushing dark curls from her temple. "After the opera, I had assumed it was not in your taste."

"I do not mind the opera."

"Your bouncing knee said otherwise."

I cleared my throat. "That was out of the ordinary for me, I assure you."

She narrowed her gaze slightly. "I care not if you dislike music. You can tell me the truth."

"I promise you, that is not the case. It was the pressure of the evening that had bothered me at the opera—I'm not used to entertaining groups in such a way. Your playing tonight was simply lovely, Marianne. I found myself quite lost in it."

Her cheeks pinked again, the small spots of color giving me a rush of victory. I enjoyed inciting her to blush. "You are too kind."

"I am honest." I leaned slightly against the wall, Marianne standing beside me. "As are you, in your notes."

She cringed. "Too honest? I have not hurt your feelings, have I?"

"In telling me that my hero is a brute and you do not find him attractive? Not at all."

"In all fairness, I adored him when I first read your story, when the focus was on his quest and not wooing the orphan. I cannot like him in this new role."

"Then I am writing him incorrectly."

"Not necessarily. There are many women who might desire an uncouth, brash—"

"No, please, stop there. I understand." I ran my hand over my clean-shaven chin. "But how do I fix it?"

She hesitated.

I straightened, holding her gaze. "Speak the truth. If we do not have that, our arrangement has nothing."

Swallowing, Marianne gave a nod. "Can you not beg Mr. Marbury to reconsider his stance on adding romance to your novel?"

I understood at once. "Because I am only making my story worse by my edits?"

"No." She dropped her gaze and bit her lip, drawing my attention there and flooding it with pink color. When she lifted her eyes again, it was with resolution. "Yes. I cannot lie to you, not when we've agreed to help one another. It is silly that you've been asked to change that which is already so perfect."

Her praise filled my chest with warm exaltation and lifted my spirits. *Perfect?* She loved my story in the way it was originally written, and that was a compliment I could not easily forget. "You are too kind to me, Marianne. I do not know what I've done to deserve you."

Marianne

What *he'd* done to deserve *me*? The man was seeing far more in my advice than was warranted. All I had done was tell him his improvements were anything but, and I was willing to wager the book would succeed far greater if he ceased to attempt to change it.

"I have spoken to Marbury," he said regretfully. "He will not publish anything else. He wants—however misguided he might be—to compete with the author of *Pride and Prejudice*."

How did I tell a man that the story he was writing would never compete with such a thoroughly romantic tale? I pasted a smile on my face. "Then I suppose we must work harder."

"And faster," he said. "I will have the next chapter to you before Friday."

"This will be much more convenient when we've reached Cheshire."

He looked at me as if only now remembering the impending house party. His eyes were darker in the dim room, drawing me in like luscious pools in the night. His voice low, his efforts at not being overheard only making him sound deep and soothing. "How does your novel progress?"

"I am nearly finished," I said. "Only a few chapters yet remain until I reach the end. Then I will be able to devote all my time to aiding you once we reach Hutton House."

His smile was broad. "That must feel wonderful."

"It will when I am finished," I replied.

Henry nodded, understanding. A lock of his curly hair fell forward and I bit back the temptation to reach up and correct it for him. The strength of his attention kept me locked in place as it was. "Tell me about your traditions, Marianne. Will your mother keep us occupied for the entirety of our visit?"

"I'm afraid so. She has all manner of things planned to entertain her guests."

"So long as I am able to spend that time with you, I will be satisfied. Perhaps we can even read another novel and discuss it?"

"If only we had the time. You are keeping me quite busy on your own."

He looked slightly abashed. "Is it too much? I know you have your own story to consider."

"My own story is moving along at too slow a pace to be worth mentioning." Had my bitterness seeped into my words? I wanted the novel Mr. Marbury held hostage. This second one was not the same. Or perhaps it was the frustration of having a completed manuscript that had gone nowhere. Would the same happen with this second book?

Henry set his gaze on me. "What can I do to assist you?"

"Nothing." I shook off my concerns and tried to smile. This second novel *would* be published because I would have Henry's assistance this time. He'd already successfully had three novels move from manuscript to publication. He could do the same for mine. "I only need to find more time to devote to it."

"I could refrain from giving you more chapters. That will lessen the burden on your time."

"Your chapters are no burden, Henry. I quite enjoy them."

"Quite enjoy gnashing them to shreds, you mean?"

I could not help but grin. "You've asked for *romantic* assistance, sir. That is all I have done."

"You've done it well." He shifted, facing me more. "What sort of sacrifices did you have in mind for my pirate?"

Goodness. The way he looked at me so intently made the words dry on my tongue. I wanted the drink Captain Neal had gone to fetch, but equally wanted him to remain away so this conversation did not need to end. "Nothing, yet. I will think on it. Have you considered making him do small things to give the orphan a clue he might be interested in pursuing a relationship with her?"

"Small things?"

Guiding Henry in the art of romance was akin to teaching my father's hounds to lie still: it was something which did not come naturally to either of them.

"Yes, Henry, small things. Looking into her eyes for extended periods of time. Being caught watching her. Seeking her out."

He seemed to be considering my words.

"You could also have him perform a small act of service. Sneak away an extra biscuit for her or some such thing."

"An extra biscuit will prove his love?" Henry asked.

Exactly like Papa's hounds. "Proving he is thinking of her will give her an indication that he cares about her." I saw Captain Neal slip into the room again. "I will consider the matter further and provide you with a list of ideas."

"Thank you. If you'd like for me to read your—"

"Goodness, no," I breathed. "For a man who did not enjoy *Pride and Prejudice*, you certainly will not appreciate my story."

He looked dubious. "You could be underestimating yourself."

"I am not. I am purely predicting you will not have a taste for it."

"You've done nothing but intrigue me, Marianne."

"Then I'm afraid you will soon find yourself disappointed, for that was not my goal."

Captain Neal approached, handing me a glass. I thanked him and brought it to my lips, quenching my suddenly dry mouth with overly sweet orgeat.

Both men looked down at me, and I found myself wondering how I'd gone from having no serious suitors to possessing two: one whom I was attempting to fall in love with, and another who had no true interest in me, though I wished he did.

I smiled at them both before lowering my eyes and taking another sip to occupy me. This house party was going to be interesting, indeed.

CHAPTER 12

MARIANNE

The last week had passed in a flurry, and I was glad to now be out of London and in our comfortable estate in Cheshire. It wasn't a grand house by any means, but it was large enough to entertain a dozen friends or host a small ball. I stood on the terrace now, a warm breeze lifting the hem of my gown and fluttering comfortably over my skin. The red stone was bright in the sunlight and I inhaled the fresh country air.

Summer heat was already upon us, which had made the refuge to the open, rolling hills outside of our house a welcome change from London's stuffy drawing rooms and overcrowded soirees. It would be even more welcome when our guests arrived.

Which, to my good fortune, would be today. A child's squeal grabbed my attention, and I returned to the drawing room to find my nephew bent in half, his bottom in the air while he tried to fish something—or *someone*—from beneath the sofa.

"Kitty!" he called.

"I do not think Mr. Darcy is in a mood to socialize today, Frederick."

My nephew scrunched his brow in confusion. "Kitty?"

"He usually takes some days to reacquaint himself with the house after traveling. Perhaps we can go outside—"

"Kitty play!" Frederick called again, paying me no mind.

"Heavens, we need to teach you more words." I reached for my nephew, taking him in my arms and lifting his squirming body until I had his full attention, though his arm was still outstretched toward the sofa, as if he could not bear to give up his pursuit of my cat. "Shall we go outside, Frederick? We do not want to be too loud or your dear mama will wake, and she so desperately needs a nap."

"Out?" His little head tilted to the side, considering the treat.

"Kitty does not wish to play. Shall we go down to the lake and search for a duck?"

"Yes! Duck!" He wriggled with enthusiasm until I allowed him down, then ran for the door. I fetched his cap—which he immediately removed from his mop of brown hair and threw on the floor—then tied my bonnet in place and took his hand. Shaw picked up Frederick's hat to put it away.

The breeze chased us down the path toward Papa's lake. For the sake of not terrorizing the ducks, I hoped they were somewhere else. We walked along the edge of the water, and I held Frederick's hand lest he felt the need to jump in. He was a good boy, if a little wild. It was no wonder Julia was in a constant state of exhaustion, even with Nanny's help.

"Duck!" Frederick yelled, pointing to the other side of the lake. He pulled at my hand, but I tightened my grip. We were *not* swimming today.

"Yes, there is a duck," I said. "Oh, look. She has her ducklings!"

He yanked hard, but I did not relinquish my hold on his pudgy little hand.

"We must walk around the lake in order to see them, Frederick. We shall carefully stay on the path. If we are very gentle, perhaps we won't disturb them and cause them to run away."

The promise must have been enough for him, for he allowed me to lead him down the path skirting the perimeter of the lake. I wasn't sure he could quite understand me, but he must have sensed my willingness to show him the ducks so he could inspect them at closer range. Perhaps I should have waited until Nanny was available to come with us, but I thought I had a generally good sense when caring for Frederick.

When we reached the other side of the lake, the house was in view, along with the plume of dust that chased two carriages down the lane toward us.

They'd arrived. Well, *guests* had arrived. I wasn't sure who among my mother's friends occupied the carriages. Lord and Lady Moorington, the Gatleys, or the men. The uptick in my pulse proved whom I most wished to see, but I did not allow myself to feel anything other than a general excitement for the house party to begin. It was a dangerous thing to feel for a man who did not return one's feelings, and another to hope for feelings to grow where none existed.

I had two weeks to develop something for Captain Neal beyond a general attraction, and I was determined to do so.

Frederick pulled hard, his hand slipping free of mine, and ran down the edge of the slope toward the water, where the earth dropped off suddenly into the lake. The water was not deep, but neither was it a gentle transition from land to lake. If my nephew was to fall in, he would surely have difficulty remaining upright on the slick lakebed. Perhaps bringing him to see the ducks on this side of the water was not in the best taste. The mother duck took Frederick's approach with affront and scurried down the muddy bank into the water, her ducklings following her as she corralled them away from the impending danger of a small child.

"Here, duck!" Frederick called.

"The ducks do not wish to be held," I explained, hurrying down toward him. "They are like Mr. Darcy, and they will not permit you to pick them up."

He looked back at me, confusion on his tiny face.

I crouched low to be on the same level as him. "You are only meant to *look* at the ducks. Do you see the mother with her sweet babies?"

He nodded. "Hold duck?"

"Perhaps, but not today." They were swimming now, further out into the lake. "We cannot reach them."

The sounds of people exiting the carriages, of trunks being removed from the boot, of the commotion of servants, drew my attention toward the house. I could not hear much of what was occurring near the carriages, but I could see now the Gatleys had arrived, and it appeared they had brought Henry with them.

My stomach did a somersault, watching Henry step from the carriage and stretch subtly, leaning back to admire all of Hutton House. He did a slow turn, seeming to regard the entire property.

"Look, Frederick, our friends are here."

But when I faced my nephew, he was gone.

My heart raced, pounding in my chest when I registered the sound of a splash as Frederick lost his balance and teetered into the water, his small pudgy arm reaching out toward the birds as he fell.

A quick scream ripped from my throat. I could not think of anything but his little body falling beneath the water as I lifted my hem and jumped in. Water seeped through the layers of my gown, soaking me to just above the knee. I scooped Frederick from the water, his eyes wide as he coughed, his little arms clinging to me as I caught my breath. Water dripped from his body, drenching me to the skin and cooling me with the breeze.

I turned and faced the predicament of how to step back out of the lake. The ledge was just high enough to make it difficult while wearing a sodden gown and holding a fretful child. I lifted my foot, but the heavy skirt dragged. It wouldn't lift high enough for me to find purchase with my shoe.

Frederick wailed. The situation had evidently caught up to the child and he laid ventilation to the trauma of finding himself wet and recently submerged in a dreary lake.

"I know," I said. "That was frightening for the both of us." I gripped my hem and pulled it from the water, but the fabric was heavy and difficult to lift. Frederick threw his head back and wailed, ruining my balance. "You must keep still if you want me to remove us from this water, Frederick."

He did not heed me.

I trudged as close to the edge of the lake as I could and tried to set him on the ledge, but he clung to me like a barnacle. His cries did not lessen, but only seemed to be further exacerbated, his tiny fingers digging into the soft flesh of my arms.

"Frederick, you must—"

"Give him here."

I looked up to find Henry standing at the edge of the lake, his arms stretched toward me. His chest heaved. Had he run from the house? It was near enough, but the length of traveling around the lake to reach us could not have possibly been crossed in so short a time. Though he must have managed it, for here he was, exceedingly out of breath, worry edging his eyes.

"Go to Mr. Bradwell, Frederick." I lifted him higher. Henry leaned close and took him from my arms. Frederick fought the transition, but Henry walked a little away and deposited him on the ground before returning and reaching for me.

I slipped my hand into his and he held it securely. Gripping my skirt, I tugged it from the water and lifted my foot to the edge of the bank. I heaved up as Henry pulled me, stepping back. He yanked suddenly, tripping over Frederick and flying backward. We toppled to the ground, but Henry's arms went around me as we fell, cushioning me from the jarring landing.

"Oof," Henry said, as if the air knocked from his lungs.

I sprawled over him, his arms tight around my waist and my head resting against his solid chest. I could feel his heart beating wildly, and my neck heated. Frederick's screaming yanked me out of my Henry-induced trance. I shook my head, pushing up. He immediately released me, then helped me stand. My gown hung heavy near my feet, but I held it up and went to Frederick's side.

"Are you hurt?" I asked my nephew.

"Duck," he said, pointing toward the water, his mottled cheeks slick with tears. He certainly appeared unharmed.

"The ducks do not wish for a hug today."

"Perhaps they will another time," Henry said, no doubt attempting to be helpful. He looked at me, a strange light in his eyes, and I looked away. I would not analyze how much I'd enjoyed being wrapped in his arms, nor the shock that had since colored his countenance.

"Come, Frederick. We must clean you off." I took him by the hand. He hiccuped but came willingly.

Henry fell into step beside us, catching my eye. "This is your . . ."

"Goodness, introductions." I was flustered, unable to settle my gaze on any one thing for long. It was hard to focus when I had just been in his arms—however briefly. "Henry, this is my nephew, Frederick."

He leaned down a little. "Frederick, are you fond of animals?"

The boy looked up at Henry with mild curiosity. "Yes. Love kitty." He looked at the water with sorrow. "Duck."

"Ah yes. Two very fine specimens. What of horses?"

The small boy shook his head adamantly. "No horses."

"They are rather large for him," I explained.

"Deer?"

"From a distance, perhaps," I guessed.

"Birds?"

"Birds!" Frederick said.

"Fish?" Henry asked.

Frederick let go of my hand, his attention riveted by the stranger who was listing all of his favorite things. "Fish."

"Shall we do our best to find some fish tomorrow?" Henry asked.

"Duck!"

He appeared to be fighting a smile. "Yes, we will search for the ducks again. But perhaps you will be so good as to remain far away from the water."

A bit of fear entered Frederick's eyes, and he nodded. He was listening to Henry far better than he ever listened to me, and I wanted to know what sort of magic the man had over him. We made it to the house and up the front stone steps. I reached for Frederick's hand again, and he let me take it. "Shall we go find your mama?"

Shaw opened the door for us and gave our sodden, muddy clothes a second glance.

"Have the Gatleys been shown to their rooms?" I asked, wondering why they were nowhere to be seen.

"Indeed. Mrs. Hutton is up with them now."

"Frederick did his best to swim with the ducks," I explained. "Will you send Keene and Nanny up to my room?"

"Right away, miss."

I faced Henry. "And your man?"

"I did not travel with my valet. I will see to my clothes on my own."

Gracious. Did he know how? "I am certain Keene will be happy to assist you with whatever you need cleaned. Or my father's valet can be depended upon—"

"It is not necessary," Henry said, smiling. "I can manage well enough on my own."

Mud smeared his coat and trousers. I hoped he'd brought

enough clothing with him that this would not cause any great inconvenience.

Our butler seemed to absorb all of this. Perhaps he would see to Henry's cleaning needs. "If you will wait a moment, sir, I will fetch Mrs. Shaw to show you to your chamber."

"Of course," Henry agreed gallantly.

Shaw left to fetch the servants I'd asked for, and I pulled a sniffling Frederick up the stairs gently by the hand.

My sister appeared at the top of the stairs, her face pale, looking no more rested for the nap she'd just taken. "Goodness," Julia said, hurrying down the staircase. "What happened?"

"Frederick wanted to hold the ducks," I explained.

She gave me a look of surprise mixed with amusement. "And you thought to fish them out of the lake for him?"

I shot her a wry smile. "I fished *him* out of the lake after he fell in, and Mr. Bradwell helped me out when I could not make it on my own."

Julia seemed to notice Henry standing near the door. She lifted her eyebrows toward me, and heat bled into my cheeks again. I could not think of the moment we fell on the grass without my entire body warming in confusion.

Henry stepped forward to meet us on the stairs.

"Mr. Bradwell," she said. "I have not seen you in an age."

He dipped his head in a soft bow. "Your son is very entertaining."

She gave a laugh. "I believe that was a compliment, and I will take it."

"Will Mr. Walding be joining us?"

"I hope he will. He is managing estate business at present. We had flooding, and it caused a great deal of damage to some of the tenant houses."

"What a pity."

"Indeed." She tried to smile, but there was clear strain

behind it, matching the dullness in her eyes. She was not the chipper Julia I knew so well, though it was evident she was trying to be. "I am glad you've joined us, Mr. Bradwell. Papa could use the distraction of a few fishing friends so we might be spared excessive games of chess."

He grinned. "I am happy to be of service."

"Come now," I said, wanting to remove my sodden, smelly gown. "Nanny is being sent to my room for Frederick."

Julia gave Henry a searching look before agreeing and going up the stairs with me. She smirked when we reached the corridor and turned out of sight. "He is handsome."

"Whisper!" I admonished.

"He cannot hear us, surely."

"You never can tell what sounds will travel."

"So you deny it then?"

"Deny that sound can—"

"No, goose. That Henry Bradwell is handsome."

My cheeks warmed. "He is tolerable, I suppose."

Julia grinned, brightening her pale cheeks. "I knew it. You find him *exceedingly* handsome."

I did not argue with her further, because she was *exceedingly* correct.

CHAPTER 13

HENRY

Muddying my clothes upon first arriving at Hutton House had not been my intent, but alas, here I was with one coat, cravat, and pair of trousers utterly ruined. Despite my claims, I hadn't any idea how to clean mud from fabric. I'd always had Felton for that.

Dinner had come and gone, port had been shared among the gentlemen following dinner, and because Captain Neal had sent word that he would not arrive for another day, I had Marianne to myself in the drawing room. The soiled clothes were upstairs waiting to be cleaned, and I was waiting for the inspiration to determine how to manage them.

I crossed to where Marianne sat beside Lady Moorington on the sofa. "I was hoping to entice you to play a game of chess with me, Miss Hutton."

She gave me a look I failed to interpret. "I believe my mother has other plans for the evening."

Mrs. Hutton shook her head. "My plans can keep. We ought to save them for when more guests arrive."

"Guests?" Marianne asked. "Are we not only waiting for Captain Neal?"

"Daniel will join us in a few days," Lady Moorington said, a smile spreading over her lips. "No one is more surprised than I that my son accepted an invitation to an event I would be present at. I haven't seen him in an age."

"Neither have I," Marianne said. "Will Jane join us as well?"

I only knew Jane because she and her husband, Ewan, had visited us at Chelton last year. They had come shortly after my brother James married Felicity, Jane's cousin. Ewan was a Scotsman, and they lived in the lowlands somewhere.

"Unfortunately, no. Her attention is required at present to manage her babe."

"Of course," Marianne said. "How is she finding being a mother?"

Lady Moorington nodded. "She and Ewan are sweet parents. In fact, we are on our way to see them when we leave your home."

Lord Moorington settled in comfortably beside his wife. "Strapping young lad," he said.

I assumed he was referring to the baby.

"Shall we, then?" I asked.

Marianne stood, wiping her hands down her skirt. "Prepare to lose, sir. I have played many games of chess, and I am no amateur."

Mr. Hutton snorted from across the room, and Marianne shot him an amused smile.

"I take your father's reaction to mean that you might, in fact, be the opposite of what you claimed?"

"Oh, I have *played* many games of chess, but I cannot be bothered to improve my skill at all. I lose terribly every time."

"Then I will do my best to give you an enjoyable experience nonetheless."

We moved to a table set against the dark window, the chessboard inlaid on the table top in swirling white and black blocks of wood. Marianne took her seat and opened a drawer, removing the chess pieces and setting up the board on her side. I sat opposite her and followed suit.

"Have you had time to read my recent notes?" she asked, her voice quiet. "I left the book in your room when I learned which one my mother intended for you."

I tempered my surprise, leaving my focus on setting up my side of the board. "I did not see it."

"It should be on the writing table."

"I don't believe there is a writing table in my room." Or I did not recall seeing one. I tried to remember the furniture in the room, but it was sparse. A bed, a chest, a table with an ewer of water and a bowl. There was a chair, but no writing table.

"Perhaps you did not see it." She straightened her queen piece, then looked up at me. "Or perhaps I left the novel in Captain Neal's room."

"It is a good thing he will not arrive until tomorrow, then."

"I will sneak into the room and retrieve the book before I go to bed," she said conspiratorially, her focus still on her pieces. "Keene can deliver it to you."

"Splendid plan." I fought a smile. "Perhaps you should be writing adventure stories after all."

"Or a mystery?" she asked, raising her eyebrow.

"I would certainly take an interest in that story."

She looked down and moved one pawn. "I am not certain I could write anything without a heavy dose of romance, though, so perhaps you wouldn't be interested after all." There was a funny edge to her voice, and I didn't know what she meant by it.

"Because I am so inept on the matter?"

"No. You are not inept." The way her voice grew higher as she spoke gave away how little she believed that.

"How kind of you to try and spare my feelings." I moved a pawn as well, then folded my hands on the table in front of me.

"If I was capable in any way, though, I would not be begging you for help."

"Thank you for attempting to change our history, but it was I who first proposed an arrangement."

"And I who am most benefitting."

"To be fair, you cannot help me until I finish my manuscript." She took another pawn and moved it forward.

"Which would not be necessary if I had been successful in my first attempt to retrieve your manuscript."

She gave a small shrug. "We will both come out of this arrangement for the better, I hope."

"You will come out of this *house party* for the better, if the ratio of gentlemen to young ladies is an indication."

"Daniel Palmer is a rake, Henry," she whispered. "He was likely only invited for his poor mother's sake."

"If he was as bad as that, I cannot imagine anything would induce your mother to invite him to stay in a house with her unmarried daughter. To say nothing of the Gatleys."

"One can have unsavory habits without showing a want of decorum. I am confident he will be every inch the gentleman when his mother is around. He has long been an acquaintance of the family, so I doubt my parents feel any fear in his presence." She moved her piece, then lifted her gaze and grinned conspiratorially. "Or they did not expect him to accept the invitation, but extended it at the behest of his mother."

My money was on the latter. "How disappointing it is when one's strategy is foiled."

"I wouldn't be familiar with the concept. You undoubtedly have more experience in strategy than the rest of us."

"Save for perhaps Captain Neal."

Marianne nodded, watching my fingers as I chose a piece and slid it over on the board. She opened her mouth to speak, but closed it again. A battle waged in her expressions, and it only incited a curiosity in me to know what she was keeping to herself.

"What is it you are not saying?" I asked.

She folded her hands on the edge of the table and leaned forward slightly. "You do not speak of your time in the military. I would hate to ask you a question that would make you uncomfortable."

I was already there. Discomfort and my time in the army went hand in hand. I could not think of those years without thinking of my father or how I'd failed him. I swallowed against the heaviness in my throat. "I do not generally enjoy remembering those years, but you can ask me anything." The odd thing was that I meant it.

"Your father was renowned for his military career."

"Indeed, he was. It was why I chose to follow him. James was away at university and my younger brother, Benedict, was uninterested. My poor father was so disappointed in his unenthusiastic sons. We've had generations of military men."

"Did you attend university?"

"I intended to when I was finished with the army." I focused on the heavy black king piece, spinning it in place on the chessboard.

"What a sacrifice," she said quietly.

I looked up. "I felt that way at the time, but in reality, I was able to spend my father's final years with him. I sacrificed university, but I had that time. I cannot regret that."

"Even when it forced you to sacrifice something you wanted so deeply for something you were not suited to?"

My chest constricted while I considered how to answer her. I had always believed those years were worth sacrificing because I was able to spend them in my father's shadow, learning from him. Had he remained alive long enough to watch me sell out, perhaps things would have been different. If he'd remained alive, I might not have ever made the choice to leave the army, or I could have done so and disappointed him entirely. He was certainly disappointed, watching me from heaven now.

Her hand snuck across the table and rested on top of mine, causing me to draw still in every part of my body except my heart, which continued to beat with increasing speed. I clutched the king in my grip beneath the warmth of her skin and forced my gaze to meet hers.

"Forget I mentioned it." She smiled kindly. "I do not wish to make you uncomfortable."

"Trust me," I said, my voice hoarse. "You are doing no such thing." I gripped the king harder. "I've never spoken about this with another soul. It is a difficulty, but that does not mean it should be avoided. My father was a wonderful man, and I would not have done anything differently if I could go back and do it all over again." I gave her a tremulous smile. "Though in all honesty, if fate granted me that opportunity, I would attempt to convince my father to stay away from Waterloo. I'm not sure I would've had any great success in that endeavor, though."

"It is a blessing that we cannot return and change our past." She spoke with sensible conviction.

"Would you?"

She looked away. "I would not have sold Mr. Marbury my manuscript. Or I would have required him to sign a contract stating he would publish the book within a specified timeframe. But as I can do neither of those things now, I will not dwell on them." She gave a little shake of her head, but still did not remove her hand. Had she forgotten it was there?

I enjoyed the feeling of it. I wanted to turn my fingers so I could hold it, but I was afraid any movement would frighten her into retracting. I wanted to hold on to this feeling for as long as I could have it. It somehow managed to seep warmth through my skin and directly to my heart.

A smile curved her lips. "It is a great relief that we can make our characters do whatever we want them to do. Sometimes it feels as though we are the puppet masters, and they are our playthings."

I grinned. "Truly. It must be a sort of cathartic exercise to so wholly control something else without any repercussions."

"Thank you for trusting me, Henry." Her eyes flicked to where her parents were seated with Mrs. Gatley and Lord and Lady Moorington. "My conversations with you are always so rewarding. It is nice to feel like something other than a disappointment for a few minutes."

Disappointment? *Marianne?* "You cannot be in earnest. Your parents adore you."

"That is indisputable, but they are also frustrated—however much they try to hide it—that I remain unwed."

Ah, I saw what she meant. She was not living up to what her parents expected from her. I very much understood that. "Most parents worry until their daughters are happily settled. Your parents are probably only concerned for your future."

"They likely are. Which is why they invited two eligible bachelors to spend a fortnight with us, in the hopes there would be a good deal of courting at hand. You'll notice no one is paying us any mind at present." Her fingers moved gently over mine, and my heart beat fast. She added under her breath, "Though Mr. Gatley would surely be interrupting if he had joined us in the drawing room following dinner."

My mind stuttered to a stop, though that did not keep the amusement from displaying on my face. "You are in earnest then? Your relationship with the captain is not feigned?"

She pulled her hand away, moving a piece on the board, and I regretted my question. I was fairly certain she had skipped my turn, but I did not truly care. Neither of us were paying much attention to the chess game. "Yes, it is in earnest. I would not allow a gentleman to believe I was interested in pursuing a relationship if I was not. You are to thank for showing me the benefit of marrying someone such as Captain Neal."

"How kind of me," I said dryly. I heartily regretted ever mentioning anything positive about life with a navy captain.

She chuckled. "Do not sound so disappointed, sir. You will give me leave to disbelieve that the idea of my marrying someone else disappoints *you*."

But it did. I felt it keenly in my gut. What if I didn't want our courtship to be feigned anymore? What if I wanted it to be real? She was actively searching for a husband, and as far as I could tell, she was not in love with Captain Neal. Did that mean I still had a chance with Marianne? The way she looked up at me now produced a longing in my chest, hollow and aching to be filled with her. Her face turned up, her eyes wide, a careful expression on her brow that led me to believe she was holding her breath.

It was very like the way she had felt in my arms when I pulled her from the lake and tripped over her nephew. I could have held her for hours.

"Marianne, what would you say if I told you—"

The door to the drawing room opened, and Shaw stepped inside. "Captain Neal has arrived, ma'am."

"He's earlier than expected," Marianne said quietly.

"Has he been seen to?" Mrs. Hutton asked.

"The captain has been shown to his room and will take dinner on a tray."

"Does he plan to join us when he is finished eating?"

"Indeed," Shaw said. "Though he wishes to freshen up first."

"Of course," Mrs. Hutton said. "Thank you, Shaw."

The butler dipped his head and left, closing the door behind himself.

Captain Neal arriving meant everything had changed; I didn't have Marianne to myself anymore. Disappointment, indeed. I needed to find a way to speak with her privately throughout the course of the house party, and I had a feeling the task would require a great deal of creativity.

Marianne's face whipped toward me, her brown eyebrows lifted on her forehead. Concern flashed in her eyes.

"What is it?" I asked. Did she feel the shift in the house as I did?

"The book. Your most recent chapter, littered with *my* notes. They are in Captain Neal's room."

CHAPTER 14

MARIANNE

I was intimately familiar with the layout of the bedrooms where our guests were sleeping, and the room Mama had put Captain Neal in only possessed one chair—the one positioned at the small writing table. That meant Captain Neal would take his dinner seated at the table where the book waited. A book with a letter sitting primly on top that I had carelessly written to Henry.

Captain Neal was in that very room right now. Oh, blast. How could I have been so reckless?

My mistakes aside, I had promised to help Henry keep the secret of his authorship, and if Captain Neal found that letter and investigated the book, the secret would be no more. I stood quickly, bumping the chess table and causing some of the pieces to fall.

Henry took my hand. "Must we be concerned?"

"He will find my letter to you when he sits to eat his dinner."

He released my hand and leaned back in his chair. "What should we do?" he asked. "Should I pay him a visit?"

I was glad Henry understood the gravity of the situation. "I will fetch Keene. She'll know what to do."

"How will you escape this room without calling attention to your distress?"

"Miss Gatley was not required to attend because traveling had worn her out. I can say the same for me. Tending to my nephew today has tired me. It is time for me to retire for the evening." The opposite was true. My heart raced from Henry's conversation, the way he looked at me, whatever he had been about to say. But I could not think on that now. If I did not retrieve that letter and his pages soon, his secret would be out and he would have no cause to look at me kindly ever again.

"Good night, then, Marianne."

I crossed the room, forcing my steps to remain unhurried, and bent to whisper in my mother's ear. "I am for bed. I want to be rested for our guests tomorrow."

"Of course. Good night, dear."

I spread my smile among the guests before walking from the room and hurrying up the stairs toward my bedchamber. I tugged on the rope and waited, pacing to the window and back. *Foolish, thoughtless girl.*

Keene slipped inside the room and bobbed a curtsy.

"We have a crisis."

Her eyes rounded, and I would have found it comical in any other situation. I could not yet laugh though when the secrecy of Henry's authorship hung in the balance. "I left Mr. Bradwell's recent chapter in what I believed to be his room. Mrs. Shaw put him in a different room, and now Captain Neal is in there with Mr. Bradwell's manuscript pages and a letter written in my hand."

"A letter, ma'am?"

"Yes." I dropped my face in my hands. "I might have hinted in a letter to a gentleman that I was glad to spend time with him here. It was brazen and foolish, and I regret it most heartily right now, but if Captain Neal is to find it, I am in deep trouble. My very reputation is in peril."

Keene appeared as distressed as I felt. Brazen, indeed. "What should I do?" she asked.

"Can you retrieve it? Can you contrive a reason to enter a gentleman's room right now? I am afraid they'll bring his dinner tray to the writing desk and then all hope will be lost."

She screwed up her nose. "I can carry in hot water? Pretend I believed he requested it?"

"Would they not already have done that?"

"Of course. It will be a mistake on my part. I will pretend to be a foolish maid."

It was not the best plan, but it would do. "Yes. You do that." I lifted my hand, the plan forming as it left my mouth. "I will be casually passing his room when you knock at the door and make eye contact with him, and he will enter the corridor to greet me."

"So that he might be absent from the room in order for me to take the pages from the book."

"And the letter resting on top of it."

She turned for the door. "I shall fetch the water straight away."

"Hurry," I begged.

Keene scurried from the room, and I was certain she ran all the way downstairs to fill her bucket with warm water. I moved to the looking glass and checked my reflection, tucking a few loose curls into my coiffure, and pinching my cheeks to bring the color back into them.

By the time my maid returned, I was having an anxious fit of nerves. I followed her silently into the corridor, and we walked down to the other wing where the guest rooms for the gentlemen were located. I passed the room and waited for her to knock at the door. Small candle flames bounced in their holders, the light flickering against the walls and the white cap on

Keene's head. I tucked myself against the wall when Captain Neal's door opened.

"Yes?"

"Hot water, sir."

"I already have—"

I walked quickly at that point, and caught Captain Neal's eye, slowing my steps and pretending I didn't realize he would be standing there. I feigned surprise and prayed I was doing a believable job of it. "Captain Neal? I did not think you were arriving until tomorrow."

He was slightly disheveled but still wore his waist coat, his cravat missing. He was tall, his shoulders broad, and despite my feelings for Henry, I could not deny that the captain was a very attractive man. He smiled at me, seeming to forget about the maid standing before him with a pail of water. "Miss Hutton." He dipped his head. "I was able to take care of my business early and arrived ahead of schedule."

"How wonderful for us. I am glad you will be here for our morning ride. Do you enjoy riding, sir?"

He stepped forward, and Keene slipped past him quietly. I held my breath.

"I do, though I haven't brought any horses that would suit the purpose."

"My father has plenty for all of us. We must take our ride in the early hours of the morning, though, or he will surely steal you away for fishing or hunting, or some such thing that involves proving your prowess and providing us with dinner."

He chuckled. "A ride would be most excellent, even one so early. Of course—" He turned a little to look over his shoulder, and I panicked.

"But we mustn't stop there," I said hastily, drawing his attention back to me.

Intrigue flashed in his gray eyes and he set them on me again. "Oh? What else did you have in mind?"

What, indeed? "Breakfast? Shall we breakfast together before we ride? It will certainly bring me great joy to . . . eat . . . in your company." I did my best to subtly look behind him into the room, but I couldn't see the writing table or my maid from this perspective.

Admiration shone in his eyes. "Breakfast would be lovely."

"Wonderful. I will see you in the morning, Captain. I hope to find you well rested."

"Do you intend to take me on a bruising ride?"

"Only if you believe yourself capable."

He laughed a little louder. "I look forward to seeing you in the morning, Miss Hutton."

I dipped in a curtsy. "As do I." I turned, walking away and squeezing my eyes closed for a moment. I hoped Keene had finished her task and would be following shortly behind me.

By the time I reached my room, I was relieved to hear her just behind me. She held a bucket, but no book in her hands. I took her forearm and pulled her into my room, shutting the door behind me. "Did you find it?"

She set the empty bucket on the floor and pulled a stack of folded paper from her apron. I took the papers, pressing them to my stomach as my body flooded with relief. "Thank you. Did you happen to notice if they appeared disheveled? If they had been found?"

She looked away.

"Keene," I said, my tone holding the dismay that edged my hope. "Tell me."

"He opened the letter."

Blast. "This is not good."

"Will he know you wrote it for Mr. Bradwell?"

I sat on the edge of my bed and dropped my head into my hands. If only she could read. "Had I written Henry's name? I cannot recall. I do not believe I did."

"Do you remember what you wrote?"

131

"Hardly. It was a quick note, and I didn't sign my full name. But it won't be difficult to know who penned the letter."

She was quiet, hesitant. "You think Captain Neal might believe it was written to him?"

"He would. It was not directed to anyone in particular. At least, I think it was not." I threw my hand toward his room. "I went and invited him to breakfast and a ride because I could not think of any other way to prolong our conversation in the corridor. Surely that only reiterated that I wanted to spend time with the man."

"Is that not a good thing, miss?" Keene asked, confused. "Are you not wanting him to court you?"

I did, did I not? Except how I felt around the captain could not in any way compare to the feeling I had when I was holding Henry's hand.

I looked up and held my maid's gaze. "I think I am in a bit of a fix. The man I would like to spend time with has no real designs on me, and the man who seems willing to marry me does not inspire any particular feelings of love or affection yet."

"I imagine the second man is the one who received a note?"

"Indeed."

Keene's troubled expression did not bode well for me. "Would you like me to bring up a hot cup of chocolate?"

I smiled at her. She knew just what I craved in moments of distress. But my stomach was in turmoil. "I could not drink it now if I tried, but I thank you for the offer, Keene. I will retire early, I think."

She helped me ready for bed and banked the fire before leaving. I stood at my window and looked out through the dark glass at the half-moon overhead.

Oh drat. Whatever was I going to do?

I could not sleep, my mind wrestling with the idea of sneaking into Captain Neal's room to retrieve the letter Keene had left on his table. Perhaps if the man woke to find it missing, he would question whether it had been a reality or a dream. But if he was to wake during my sneaky adventure and find me in his room, all hope would be lost and my reputation with it.

I pulled on my purple dressing gown and fastened it at the neck. It had been hours since everyone had gone to sleep, and the quiet minutes passing only exacerbated my worry. Enough time had passed between me and my dinner now that I was growing ravenous. If nothing else, I could procure the hot cup of chocolate I had rejected earlier.

I lit my candle and carried it down the stairs, slipping into the servant's staircase and toward the kitchen.

A fire burned in the kitchen when I got there, and I pulled up short when I noticed a shadow jumping along the wall in the small stillroom. Someone was in there, and perhaps that someone would be able to tell me how to heat a pot of water.

"Pardon my intrusion," I said, poking my head through the doorway and freezing like a violet-colored icicle. Henry sat in breeches and a long, untucked shirt, bending over a bucket of water with a bar of lye in one hand and a pair of breeches gathered in his other.

"Oh!" I said, with some astonishment. "I did not expect to find you here."

He dropped the soap into the water and gave me a wry smile. "That was certainly my intention."

I crossed my arms over my chest and leaned one shoulder in the doorway. "Because you could not bear to be seen completing such a menial task?"

"Hardly. I waited until everyone was asleep so I would not be caught out at being utterly incompetent."

"No one will blame you for not knowing how to wash your own clothes, Henry."

133

The chagrin on his face was proof that I was wrong. He blamed himself heartily.

"Why did you not ask for help? Keene would be glad—"

"It was I who dismissed my servant so he could attend to a family matter, so it is I who will see to my affairs." He looked down at the soapy water in the bucket between his knees. "I would not wish to burden your servants further. I imagine they have a great deal to do in preparation for receiving additional guests this week."

Shame and confusion prickled at me. I had not considered the additional work we had already added to Keene's burden, only that she would not hesitate to do all I asked of her.

"I cannot tell whether it was thoughtfulness or pride that led you to this." I gestured to him, sitting above a bucket of water with a drenched pair of breeches hanging from his grip.

"Perhaps a bit of both." He dropped the clothing into the bucket. "To be honest, I have not the faintest idea what I am doing. Is this water meant to be cold or hot? It came cold from the pump, but the lye is not easy to work with, and I fear if I use this same method for all of my soiled garments, I might ruin my coat."

I took the coat and cravat from where they hung on the back of his chair. "Let me give these to Keene. If she does not have the time, she will find someone who does. I will tell her you are in no great rush to have them returned to you, so it will not be too great of an added burden."

His shoulders deflated a bit. "Very well. Thank her for me, if you please." He pulled his breeches from the bucket and wrung them out. "What brought you here in the middle of the night? Secret laundry of your own?"

"No. My reason is much more sophisticated. I'm hungry." I smiled. "I hoped to make a hot cup of chocolate, but one look at the kitchen reminded me how little I know in that department as well."

Henry wrung the breeches further, then shook them out and held them up. "It took me only a few minutes to come to that same conclusion about myself."

"Look at how helpless we are."

"I'm not entirely helpless in regards to your dilemma. I'm certain I can scavenge. You wanted drinking chocolate?"

"I had considered it, but that is entirely out of my knowledge or capabilities."

"It is fairly out of mine as well," he said, apologetically.

"Then I suppose tea will have to do." I left the stillroom and searched the kitchen for the tea box. I located it in the house-keeper's parlor, but when I tugged on the lid, it wouldn't budge. "Locked," I mumbled.

Henry followed me into the dark room. "Let me guess. Mrs. Shaw has the key?"

I turned and leaned against the armrest on the short sofa. "Yes, or my mother, neither of which I should like to wake in the middle of the night for tea." I chuckled. "To be honest, I'm not sure I would have been able to figure out how to light the stove."

He smiled. "*That* I can do. One does not traverse across the countryside with the army without learning how to start a fire. Even when one's father hires a batman for him."

I folded my arms over my chest. "You are welcome to prove your abilities, but without the key to the teabox, we'll have nothing more than hot water."

Lines formed on his forehead. "Shall I rummage in the larder? I can find something for you to eat."

"I can rummage for myself, Henry. But that is very kind of you to offer."

He hesitated for a second before speaking again. "Will you tell me what has kept you awake so long? I hope you aren't greatly troubled by the pages of my manuscript left in Neal's room."

We'd left our candles in the kitchen and thus had very little light to see by. Henry sounded concerned, but his face was swathed in shadow, his expression unreadable. The glint in his eyes proved he was looking at me, though. "Keene and I retrieved the manuscript pages but have no way of knowing whether Captain Neal found them first. I believe, based on what Keene described, that they went unnoticed. Your secret remains safe."

His shoulders visibly relaxed. "I cannot tell you what a relief that is. I am a private man, and the notion of everyone knowing I had penned those novels . . ." He gave a small shake. "If that is not troubling you, then I suspect there is more?"

"Yes." I swallowed. How did I tell this man I had written him a letter? It broke all manner of etiquette rules and placed both of our reputations in jeopardy. But had our entire relationship not done that very thing from the outset? Writing him a note to accompany his pages had felt natural, not at all like I was subjecting us to this danger.

Though, maybe *that* was the danger. Had I grown too comfortable with Henry? I'd written him notes to accompany his pages before, it was true, but none of them had been quite like this.

Henry took a careful step closer. "You are beginning to worry me."

"I have done something foolish," I whispered, bending my neck so I might attempt to look into his eyes.

"What is it?"

Pinching the end of my plait in my fingers, I toyed with the linen ribbon keeping it together. "When I left the book in your room, I also wrote a note."

"You've mentioned that, but it is not so terrible. You've done that every time."

"Yes. I have." How kind of him to point out my consistent failings at maintaining propriety. "This time, I did not tuck it into the book with the other pages. I sealed it with a wafer and left it on top of the novel." *Like a real letter.*

Henry was silent.

"I did not realize I would need to hide it," I said. "I was informed you would occupy that room, and I sealed the letter so your man would not peek at it, in case he could read."

"How thoughtful," he murmured. Was his mind bending to the dilemma of what to do now? "Neal found it, did he not? I assume that is the reason for your concern?"

"He did. The seal was broken."

"What was the nature of the letter?"

My heart pounded. "It was suggestive. It likely sounded eager for the house party so we could further our acquaintance. It was not an innocent note by any means."

Henry drew in a long breath, then stepped closer until I could make out his features slightly in the dark room. "Then you've given every reason for others to suspect an understanding."

"Precisely." I passed my fingers over my plait again. If Captain Neal shared the note with anyone, my reputation could be ruined. It was in his power now to make me a wanton woman.

"I suppose there is nothing else for it," Henry said, his low, serious voice washing over me. "I will marry you."

CHAPTER 15

HENRY

I had not imagined proposing marriage to Marianne in the housekeeper's parlor in the middle of the night—and certainly not in the dark. Where were our candles? But I would be lying if I tried to pretend I had not thought a time or two about how it would feel to say those words aloud. Her utter shock, however, was not what I had been expecting.

"Marriage?" she asked.

"What else is to be done? If Captain Neal found a letter that you wrote to me, then surely—"

"He does not know it was written to *you*. That is the trouble." She stepped back and rubbed her temples. "I signed it with my initials, but I did not direct it to you. Perhaps I was unconsciously worried this very thing would occur. Now Captain Neal must believe it was intended for him."

That changed things. Slick disappointment rushed through me. I rubbed a hand over my unshaven chin, feeling the beginnings of a scruffy beard. "Neal believes you wrote a clandestine note for him and left it in his room?"

"Indeed," she whispered.

My stomach clenched. "Neal believes you are eager for the opportunity to know *him* better."

"Which I should be. I mean, I *am*, of course." She rubbed her temples again. "But he surely believes I am the type of woman who would brazenly leave a note in a gentleman's bedchamber." She turned and dropped onto the small sofa, lowering her head to her hands. "If that abhors him, he could ruin me. If it pleases him, he'll believe I feel more than I do . . . oh, what am I to do?"

I skirted the sofa and took the seat beside her. I reached for her hand and pulled it away from her face, gently holding it in both of mine. If I harbored suspicions before that I might be developing something of a *tendré* for Marianne, the way I felt holding her hand confirmed those suspicions beyond doubt. Warmth seeped into my chest, spreading through me. "Did your maid not retrieve the letter when she retrieved my manuscript pages?"

"No. She saw that the wax had already been broken and left it there. Henry, it is even worse than that."

"How?" My stomach flipped at the ease in which she used my Christian name. Every time it slipped carelessly through her lips, I loved it even more.

She gave a watery chuckle. "The only way I could think to retrieve your manuscript pages was to send my maid into Captain Neal's room with hot water, but we needed a distraction so she could take the papers without him watching her."

"You provided that distraction?"

"I did. I waited outside his door and walked past when he opened it so I could entice him into conversation in the corridor and leave Keene free to take what she needed."

"How devious of you."

"Extremely. If all else fails in the marriage market, I could have a career as a Bow Street Runner."

I chuckled. "I do not think the uniform would suit you, Marianne. Despite how uncomfortable you might have felt distracting the captain, it does not seem so terrible."

"No. The terrible part was how eager I seemed to spend time with him. I invited him to take breakfast with me tomorrow and go for a ride following. It was nothing but a reiteration of the sentiments I supposedly proclaimed for him in that letter."

A hot slice of jealousy wound through my stomach as I imagined this unfolding in the corridor, the lights dim, how beautiful she had looked after dinner. I swallowed. "Are you looking forward to taking breakfast with him?"

"Not in the least."

"That's a vehement answer from someone who is supposedly courting the man."

"I am not *courting* him, exactly."

Had she not said only moments before she was looking forward to the opportunity to know him better? "His presence at your house party says differently."

"Yes. It says my mother wishes he might be in the running for her future son-in-law."

My hand tightened on hers. "And you, Marianne? How do you feel about the prospect of Captain Neal becoming your mother's future son-in-law?"

She chuckled softly. "I am not sure. In regards to him becoming my future husband, he certainly carries all the traits I find worthy."

"Such as?"

"He is kind, attentive, handsome. He will provide me with the opportunity to run my own house, raise my own children, and have the freedom to write while he is away."

Could *I* provide all of those things? "Will you tell him of your writing?"

"I suppose I must." She screwed up her face. "To be honest, though, I am not sure I wish to share that information with anyone."

"Then why is he here?" I asked gently.

She gave a soft scoff. "I must marry someone, Henry. I *want* to marry someone."

My throat grew dry. My recent words hung in the air between us. Was she thinking about my earlier declaration the same way I was? *I will marry you.* I had told her I could be her husband. If she agreed, all of this could be over, and the house party would become an opportunity to further my acquaintance with my future mother- and father-in-law. Instead, I had proposed it as a business arrangement, nothing more than an opportunity to pass chapters back and forth as I was writing and she was improving.

Would that be our life together? If we were to marry, would we be constantly writing our books and trading them with one another, helping each other to improve upon them? It sounded like a good deal of work, but for some reason, it also sounded utterly incredible.

I ran my thumbs over her knuckles one at a time, putting my focus there so I would not lose the nerve to speak. "If marrying the captain is what you wish then I will, of course, be in full support of you. But it will be a great sacrifice to me to lose your companionship and your clever letters."

"Why would my marrying Captain Neal end our friendship?" she asked. "Will you not wish to speak to me any longer?"

"When you're married, Marianne, it will no longer be appropriate. I cannot in good conscience write to you. I should not be doing it *now*."

"You do not do so now," she said simply. "I am the only one who has been inappropriate. I am sorry, Henry. I won't do it again."

"You needn't apologize to me. I enjoy your letters, as I've already said."

"It's a shame we cannot be brother and sister, then, and nothing about our relationship would ever need to change."

Brother and sister? Good gads, that was the last thing I wanted from her. But if that was how she felt about me, it certainly explained why my earlier declaration of marriage would be met with such discomfort, silence, and fear. How awful it would be to have someone propose marriage who one looked at as a *brother*. It made my stomach sour that she would see me in such a light.

"I have enough sisters now that my brothers are married. One of whom enjoys reading quite as much as you do."

"Felicity?" she asked, pulling her hand from mine. Did she feel the wall erect between us as well? "If she is such a devout reader, why have you not told her about your books yet?"

"I cannot tell Felicity without also admitting it to the rest of my family."

She pulled at the edge of her plait. "Such a supportive, loving family. I do not truly understand why you have yet to tell them." She narrowed her eyes slightly, as if attempting to make out my character.

"How could I? How can I tell them I left the army in pursuit of something so bookish? My brothers would not understand it. They cannot abide reading, and my selling out meant none of us would follow in my father's footsteps. Telling them this would disappoint them all." The words had flowed easily from my lips, chased into the dark room with zeal. I hadn't realized before how badly I'd wanted to share that fear, to speak it aloud.

"They think you are intending to return to the military someday?"

How did Marianne see through me? "If I inform them about my new career, then they will know that there is no chance of it at all. In a sense, the military line will end with me."

"Then you give your sons and nephews no credit at all. Can military pursuits not skip a generation?"

"I am sure they can, but it will not be the same." I shook my head and stood, running my hand through my disheveled hair. I noticed in that moment how unkempt I was, wearing nothing but breeches and a shirt. Our state of undress did not look well. If we were discovered, we would both be ruined. Marianne needed to go upstairs. We both needed to be in our rooms right now.

"You are agitated," she said, standing. "I did not mean to distress you, Henry. I only tried to understand."

"How can you understand when you did not know my father? His military career and his pride in the generations who had served before was his identity. He would never have been proud of my books. Not in the way he was honored to introduce me to anyone who cared to listen, to explain I was carrying on the Bradwell name in the military."

"That is too much pressure to put on your shoulders. You were not even an older son."

"The oldest son would have joined up after university, had he wanted to. I saved him from such a necessity."

"How selfless of you."

I scoffed. "Selfless would have been remaining in the military despite how much I hated it."

"You cannot put that upon yourself."

"It is a point of fact that if my father were alive, and I was no longer in the military, I would be an utter disappointment to him. My failure to rise in rank would be a disappointment. My dedication to writing and reading and literary pursuits would be a disappointment." Her eyes shone with compassion, and I leveled my voice. "I am not seeking your pity. I am merely stating facts."

"I cannot speak for your father, because I did not know him well, but I would like to think that after he healed from the disappointment of losing you in the military, he would be proud of the books you have written and the success you have found in your chosen career."

"So much success that my publisher is asking me to change

the way I write?" I could not continue this conversation. I needed to go to sleep. It appeared as though I had sought her pity, which was not at all what I wanted from her. My fears and the things which plagued me did not need to be discussed in the middle of the night in the housekeeper's parlor.

"You need to go to sleep," I said. "I need to do the same."

Her eyes snapped. "I am perfectly capable of determining when I ought to go to sleep, but I thank you for the concern."

"Of course you are. I only meant that this is not appropriate. If we were found—"

"It could be every bit as dangerous as if my letters to you were found? For our clandestine arrangement to be discovered, or the improper discussions we have about romance to be overheard?"

"Those are not improper," I said.

"My mother would very much disagree with you. If she knew our romantic discussions were not deepening our connection, but a true literary debate, she would not have permitted us to have so many of them."

"If her sole motivation is to find you a husband, it will surely please her when you take breakfast with the captain tomorrow."

"Yes. It shall."

"Good night, then," I said.

She walked from the room, taking her candle from the work-table in the center of the kitchen, then gathering my coat and cravat. "Good night, Henry."

"Wait," I said. When she reached the stairs, she turned back to face me. Candlelight bounced from her face, highlighting her cheekbones and the slope of her jaw line. She was so beautiful in full evening dress, her hair styled and color in her cheeks, but in this simple state, a dressing gown wound tightly around her and a long, brown plait falling over her shoulder, she looked no less lovely. "What *exactly* did you write in the letter?"

She swallowed, and I watched her throat move with the

motion. "Nothing more than I already told you. That I was looking forward to coming to know you better this week. That I had enjoyed our conversations and eagerly awaited more of them."

"Then permit me to tell you I was looking forward to the same, and very eagerly anticipating more time spent with you."

Marianne gazed at me for a moment before dipping her head in a slight curtsy. "Tomorrow, then? If you are awake, will you join us?"

I nodded, but I did not know what to think of the invitation. She had given me no cause to believe her truly enamored by the captain. Her distress when she believed he might assume she cared for him only proved that further, to say nothing of inviting me to join their ride. I couldn't very well give up an opportunity to spend time with her. "I will be there."

CHAPTER 16

MARIANNE

Breakfast, when taken between two gentlemen, was significantly less enjoyable than one might think. One would believe such handsome company could only have cause to improve the meal. I was finding the opposite to be true.

Instead, I didn't know which of them to speak to. I stared down at my plate, giving my roll a great deal of attention. "Have you found your rooms to be to your liking?"

"Yes—"

"Quite—"

They both grew silent again. "Captain Neal, you did not face much trouble on the road?"

"No trouble at all."

Silence, again.

I faced Henry. "Mr. Bradwell, you have a house in the north, do you not?"

"It is more of a hunting box. But I have appreciated the isolation it provides, so you will not hear me complaining of that."

"There is not much society to be had in the north?" Captain Neal inquired.

"There is, if one chooses to join it. But society is spread

much thinner than you'll find in Town, and as a single man who is not typically looking for an excess of social events, it suits me well."

"You must have many opportunities for riding, then," I said, glad to be out of the stilted silence.

"For writing?" Henry asked, looking sharply at me.

"*Riding.*" I enunciated better, feeling my cheeks warm. "Though I imagine the distance from your mother's house gives you ample opportunity to write letters to your family as well."

"Yes, I became very good at corresponding when I was on the Continent." He picked up his tea and took a long swallow.

"And you, Captain Neal? Are you a practiced correspondent?"

"In truth, I could be much better at both writing and riding. I do not practice either activity nearly enough."

"Then let us not delay for another minute." I pushed back my chair and stood, wiping my hands down the front of my deep green riding habit. My eyes were gritty, my exhaustion complete. I had only received a couple hours of sleep the night before, and I could feel it.

It had been impossible to fall asleep after that conversation with Henry, or after the marriage proposal that, in truth, was not really a marriage proposal at all.

I could not meet Henry's gaze without my cheeks pinking like a winter sunset. I was glad he had joined us today, but I had yet to settle upon how I truly felt after our conversation. Proposing marriage merely because he had thought my reputation was in jeopardy, and for no other reason, stung. When he'd said those words to me, I had been shocked into silence, but my body had reacted pleasantly. I had wanted to accept him, and the very idea, as well as the disappointment I'd felt when our conversation steered away from marriage, frightened me now.

I stepped away from the table as both men placed their napkins on their plates and followed me. Our groom, Nelson, waited outside with four saddled horses. Should I have invited Miss Gatley to join us? Perhaps now I appeared selfish, like I wanted to keep the gentlemen to myself.

Which was true, I supposed.

If Miss Gatley had come down for dinner last night or was awake for breakfast this morning, I would certainly have invited her.

I led Cinnamon to the mounting block and climbed the stone steps before settling myself in the saddle. We'd had a light rainfall that morning, it seemed, and I worried the ride would be muddy. Nelson and the gentlemen took their saddles, and we directed our horses away from the stables and the house. The hills rose behind Hutton House, and we traversed them, taking our time, climbing higher and higher while the sun steadily rose in the sky. Warm rays kissed my skin. I readjusted my hat to better allow the warmth to permeate my face, deciding to worry about the freckles later. Was there any better feeling than the warmth of the sun after a chill?

I glanced to where Henry rode beside me. The way he watched me now, his eyes trailing over my face as though they were the sunbeams washing over my skin, had a power all their own. They warmed my chest, filling me with the glow of the sun.

"You were in earnest when you implied you are an accomplished rider," Captain Neal said, stealing my attention.

"I only meant it in jest, Captain." In truth, we were not taking any particularly challenging trails.

He was slightly out of breath. "I have found it to be reality, however. It is very impressive, Miss Hutton. I think you do yourself a disservice to lessen your accomplishments. You should be proud of them."

"I have often thought the very same thing," Henry said. I knew he was not thinking of my riding.

"Goodness. You are both determined to put me to the blush.

All this talk of accomplishments is making me weary. Shall we race instead? The first person to reach the willow tree at the edge of the lake is the winner." I looked at each of them once before kicking Cinnamon into a run.

I had the advantage of knowing the terrain, so I fully expected to win. What I did not expect was for Henry to keep pace with me. His horse was a head behind mine, and we raced down the hill and over the green grass toward the lake. The sun glinted from the water and the warm breeze ran over me, invigorating in its freshness.

"You have given poor Neal the slip," Henry called.

"I have not! He is welcome to keep up." I pushed Cinnamon harder, pulling ahead of Henry as I circled around the lake. The house sat just on the other side, but I directed my horse away from it, making toward the tree nestled on the slope of the bank, its leaves trailing down to kiss the edge of the water.

"Well done!" Henry called, laughing. He pulled to a stop beside me, and we both slid down from our horses, our chests heaving. I grinned at him, unable to tear my gaze away. The smile he wore was so unlike anything I'd seen on him before. He was radiant. The fresh air and sunlight had done him well.

"The same to you, sir," I said. "You are an accomplished horseman."

"I've raced my brothers many times over the years," he countered. "I've had the practice."

I stepped out of the shade of the willow tree and searched the horizon for Captain Neal, but he was nowhere to be seen.

"He will find his way here," Henry assured me.

"But if he's lost—"

"Your groom is with him, Marianne. He cannot become lost."

That was a comforting notion. "He will think me the vainest of creatures for choosing to race, like I felt the need to prove my skill."

"Or he will be impressed by it."

I laughed. "What man is impressed when a woman outshines him? Don't all of you wish to be seen as superior?"

Henry's brown eyebrows rose, his chin tucking in surprise. "You do my sex a great disservice."

"How?"

"Some of us would not mind being beaten by a woman. Some of us are rather impressed when that situation occurs."

I shook my head, searching the hills again. I was glad to see Captain Neal appear on the other side of the lake, Nelson on his heels.

"I should know," Henry pressed. "I am feeling just such a thing now after being thoroughly beaten in a race."

My stomach flipped. "Heavens, sir," I said, chuckling lightly. "You cannot be in earnest. You act as though I beat you heartily when in fact you were directly beside me the entire time."

"You were difficult to keep up with, Marianne. Take the compliment."

"I would, had I felt I earned it."

Captain Neal came closer.

Henry stepped near enough that he could speak softly and not be overheard. "I am beginning to think your modesty is the only thing coming between me and some of *your* manuscript pages."

"Well done, Miss Hutton," Captain Neal called, coming to a stop not far from us and dismounting.

Henry took a step away from me, resting his hands idly behind his back.

"You assume I won," I said.

"Did you not?"

I laughed, but Henry did not join me.

Captain Neal's attention stayed on me. "Perhaps your man would be so good as to return our horses to the stables so I might tempt you into a sedate walk around the lake."

"That would be lovely," I said, looking to Nelson. The groom nodded.

"I will assist him," Henry said, his expression unreadable. Was he wary of giving the servants additional work again, or simply looking for an excuse to leave us? I tried to find the cause on his face, but he merely dipped his head to both of us and retook his saddle, taking Cinnamon's reins to lead her alongside him.

I watched him leave without a look back. What did that mean? Captain Neal bent his elbow, offering it to me. The skirt of my habit was too long on one side, but not nearly long enough to throw over my arm without exposing my legs. I bunched the fabric in my grip and lifted it high enough so it would not drag on the earth.

Taking Captain Neal's arm, I let him lead me toward the path skirting the edge of the water. The mid-morning sun was still shining brightly, but somehow the warmth felt a little like it had receded in the last few minutes. I looked at Henry over my shoulder, riding away and leading my horse, and wanted to be with him.

"You are very fond of your horse," Captain Neal said, drawing my attention forward.

My cheeks flooded with color. Was he kindly reminding me that my attention was meant to be on him at present? I was not good at courting. "I love her dearly," I said, glad it was the truth.

"Then it would be a great trial for you to be parted from her for an extended period of time."

"I manage well enough when we go to London for the Season every year, and that is at least a few months of separation. But I will admit I am heartily glad to be returned to her."

He nodded but said no more on the subject. It was a good time to tell him of my writing. If we were going to pursue a relationship, it would be the sort of thing a husband would need to know, of course. Though it was not something I intended to keep a secret forever as Henry has done, it was still a difficult thing to share. But I could not in good conscience allow a liaison to continue between myself and any man if he did not know that one day I would be a published author, that my name would be written—however disguised—on the front of a book. If that was the sort of thing to bring shame to Captain Neal the same way I imagined it would to my own father, then he needed to know before too long.

Only *how* did I tell him? It was frightening to make myself and my dreams vulnerable to anyone, let alone a man I was still coming to know.

Perhaps for now I would do my best to turn the conversation back in his direction. Just long enough to gather my courage.

"Have you any interests, Captain?" I readjusted my hold on my long skirt, careful not to let it drag in the mud. "Anything you enjoy doing when you are on leave?"

"Stargazing is a favorite pastime of mine," he said. "I enjoy it on the ship extensively. Searching for constellations and the like."

"You must have perfected it by now."

"Indeed. If the night sky is clear, I can show you some of them. We ought to be able to see Polaris and the Plough, and if we are fortunate, we might be able to make out Cassiopeia."

"That would be excellent. I have found the Plough on occasion, but I am afraid I do not have an eye for it."

He smiled kindly, the breeze ruffling his sandy-colored hair. "It is a good thing I do."

We passed the place where Frederick had fallen in the lake yesterday, and I tugged on Captain Neal's arm and adjusted my grip on my falling skirt once more. "Oh, look. Do you see the ducks hiding in the reeds there?"

"It is a wonder they do not take refuge in the willow," he said. "Much better coverage to be had beneath the branches."

"But rather less sunlight. Perhaps they enjoy the warmth when they are not hiding from us."

"Perhaps."

We rounded the lake, slowly skirting the water. Captain Neal told me about some of the men on his ship and the different ports he'd had the privilege of visiting. He shared about a recent storm that had almost knocked him from the deck and the fear it had instilled in his chest.

The mud grew slicker as we made our way down the path, and I gripped the captain's arm tighter when my footing became unsteady.

"Careful," he said.

"After yesterday, it would be just my luck were I to slip—" A squeal ripped from my throat when the toe of my boot slid backward and I flew head first into the muddy path.

"Miss Hutton," he called, reaching for me. "Have you hurt yourself?"

"Only my pride." I lifted my head from the sludge, my eyes making contact with fresh duck excrement. Good heavens, that was close.

Chirp! Chirp!

"Captain, do you hear that?" I pushed myself up, avoiding the excrement, and looked toward the reeds at the edge of the lake. A small, yellow duckling hopped in the grass, his chirp high.

"I do. Here, allow me—"

"No, wait." I waved him off and crawled toward the edge of the water, aware I looked somewhat crazed, or potentially just immature. I knelt in the soggy grass and reached for the duckling. He squealed, attempting to flee, but I managed to hold him, his soft, downy feathers so delicate in my palms. "I think he is lost. We must reunite him with his mother."

"Surely he can find her on his own. Animals have a sense for these things."

I looked at the captain over my shoulder, and his expression sent a jolt of surprise through me. He was looking at the fuzzy bird cupped in my hands and unable to hide his utter revulsion.

Blast. Was the man disgusted by the bird or by my behavior? "Are you not fond of birds, Captain?"

"I will not lie to you, Miss Hutton. The very idea of touching a wild animal brings me a great deal of displeasure."

Revulsion was more accurate.

"You needn't touch him." I tried to stand, but my blasted skirt was getting in the way.

"Allow me to assist you." Captain Neal approached, but hesitated as though he didn't know what to do. For a man who lived on a ship with mostly other men who were not—I imagined—the cleanest of specimens, his aversion to the dirt covering me and the bird in my hands was surprising.

"Do not trouble yourself." I tried to sound as though it was not a burden for him to leave me to my own devices. "I can find a way—"

"If you put down the bird, surely you can stand easier."

Where was Henry when I needed him? I drew a patient breath through my nose. "But then I might not be able to catch him again."

"Of course." Captain Neal sounded as though he did not understand why that would be a problem.

I looked to the stables, wishing Henry would appear.

"Shall I fetch help?" he asked.

"No, you needn't trouble yourself." That would be nothing short of ridiculous. Retrieving help so I might *stand*? I would find a way to accomplish the task on my own, or I would put the bird down and risk losing it. I looked to the house and thought of my little nephew in the nursery with Nanny. Captain Neal wanted an excuse to leave. I could see how uncomfortable he was. I looked up at him and gave him my best smile. "If you would return to the house and send for my nephew, Frederick, I would greatly appreciate it. He would love to hold this duckling."

"Of course. At once."

He made for the house with quick, wide steps, and I was left to find a way to stand in an inordinately long skirt with a squirming duckling in my hands. Gads, I needed help.

CHAPTER 17
HENRY

I stood in the entryway, divesting myself of my coat so Shaw could take it away to be cleaned. I'd given up avoiding extra work for the Hutton servants. I hoped Felton would return swiftly, but I also did not wish for his business to conclude too quickly, or that would imply his father had taken his final breath on this earth. I would simply need to leave the Hutton servants with some extra coins to speak my gratitude and make the additional work worth their time.

I cringed at the splatter along my coat tails. "The rain this morning left us with more mud than I anticipated."

"We shall see to it, sir." He took the mud-splattered coat while I slipped my gloves free.

The front door opened, and a harried-looking Captain Neal stepped inside, his eyes bouncing from me to the butler.

Marianne was nowhere to be seen, and her absence made my heart cease beating. Was she hurt? "What is it? Where is Marianne?"

He gave me a quick look before facing the butler. If he noticed my blunder in using her Christian name, he didn't mention it. "I was sent to fetch young Master Frederick. Evidently he would like to see a duck?"

Relief sluiced through me.

The butler nodded. "I will locate him at once, sir."

"Wait, Shaw." I crossed to him before he could disappear into the servants' staircase. "My coat, please?"

He handed it back to me and I slipped it over my shoulders, then pulled my gloves on as I waited for Frederick to be sent for.

Captain Neal hesitated, rubbing his chin as he paced the entryway. "Do you intend to lead Frederick to his aunt?" he asked.

"Yes. I can wait for the lad if you'd like to go now." It was only fair, after all. I had left them to their own devices already. Selfless of me, was it not?

"Thank you." He gave a dip of his head and turned toward the stairs, taking them up to the first floor bedchambers. I watched him go, surprised. Had he not intended to return to Marianne? That was an understatement. Had he *abandoned* her?

Frederick arrived shortly, a stout woman just behind him, her wrinkles and graying hair giving her position away. "Nanny?" I asked.

She gave a curt nod. "We were sent to find Miss Hutton."

"I will take you to her." It could not be too difficult to locate Marianne, surely.

We let ourselves outside, and Frederick pulled hard at his nanny's hand. "Duck!"

"Patience, Master Frederick." She struggled to keep him from yanking on her arm. "We will arrive soon enough."

But the lad didn't heed her.

"Frederick," I said sharply. He looked up at me, his eyes rounding. It was difficult not to smile at his sweet innocence, but I did my best to remain serious. "If you approach too quickly or too loudly, you will scare the ducks away. Do you recall what happened last time?"

He didn't appear to remember.

I softened my voice. "Let us go quietly so we do not scare the ducks."

"Duck," he repeated, though quieter this time. "I hold duck."

We continued to make our way toward the lake, and Nanny looked at me with approval.

Marianne was not difficult to find. Once we rounded the edge, we could see her sitting in the mud, a duckling cupped in her hands. She lifted her face toward us, and my heart gave a leap. Her smile was wide, the mud smeared over her cheekbone charming. She was so full of joy and exuberance and her brown eyes sparkled. When Frederick saw the duck in her hand and squealed, she did not so much as bat an eye in the face of his enthusiasm. If anything, it buoyed her further.

She spoke gently. "Come quietly, Frederick, or you will scare him."

In something of a miracle, Frederick did as he was bid. He approached his aunt carefully, squatting his short, chubby legs so he could take a closer look at the bird.

"If you are very gentle, you can hold him. Would you like that?"

The child nodded and held out his hands. Marianne lifted her arms slightly. "Would you like to sit on my lap, Frederick?"

He did so, and she placed the bird in his cupped hands.

The smile that spread over Frederick's lips matched his aunt's, both of their eyes cast down toward the bird nervously shaking in his hands. It gave a shudder, shaking out its little wings, and Frederick giggled.

My stomach gave an involuntary twist, as though I was receiving a small peek at what Marianne would look like as a mother. I liked what I saw very much.

"I think this duckling has become lost. Shall we reunite him with his mama?"

Frederick looked up at his aunt. "Mama?"

"Yes. The duckling probably wants his mama. Can you see her?"

They located her in the reeds further up the lake. Frederick attempted to stand, and I jumped forward to assist him. He refused to relinquish the bird, so I gripped him by the shoulders and lifted him from his aunt's lap. He took off waddling toward the mother duck as his nanny hurried after him.

I couldn't wipe the grin from my face. I reached for Marianne.

She looked at my hand, then both of her own. "I have been holding that bird for nearly twenty minutes now. Or longer."

"How kind of you." I failed to understand the implication of her statement, but judging by the way she said it, she had thought it held some significance.

Marianne looked at me again. "My hands are not clean."

Ah. Was she worried I would be disgusted by her holding a bird? I kept my hand stretched toward her. "That is the least of my worries."

Relief passed over her expression. She gathered the skirt of her habit to lift it from the mud and took my hand, allowing me to pull her up. She wobbled a little on her feet. "My foot is all pins and needles now."

"Stand here a moment, then. We do not want you falling in the lake again."

She looked over her shoulder to watch Frederick inch closer to the edge of the water where the mother duck was corralling her other ducklings.

"How do you know which duck he belongs to?" I asked.

"She is the only one with children I've seen." Marianne looked up at me, her eyes sparkling in the sunlight. "If nothing else, she can help the duckling find his mother."

"Hold still." I released her arm to bend down to the water and scoop some onto my fingers. It wasn't the cleanest water, but it would do. I straightened, shaking the excess off, then ran my thumb over the swipe of mud on her face. The moisture gathered and ran down her cheek in dirty rivulets, so I caught them with my dry hand and wiped all the mud away.

A blush rose up her neck and spotted her cheeks becomingly. "Thank you, Henry."

"I could not allow you to greet Mama Duck with such a mess on your face."

"Thoughtful, indeed."

I rinsed my hands in the lake and shook the water from them. Bending my arm, I offered it to Marianne. She curled her hand around my upper arm, her fingers digging into my muscle. I flexed it on impulse, then relaxed it immediately, my gaze shooting to see if she had noticed.

She glanced up at me, a smile playing on her lips. "Was that an attempt to prove your superior strength? I assure you, that isn't necessary."

"It was an impulse of the moment I heartily regret," I muttered.

She laughed, and the melody warmed me better than the sunlight had. "You should never regret demonstrating your strength, sir."

"Then I don't." Although, in truth, I felt a fool. We stood behind Nanny, who hovered over Frederick. He bent forward and released the duckling into the water with a splash. It took a minute for the tiny yellow bird to gather his bearings, but he swam a little until he had joined up with the rest of the ducklings following the mother.

Marianne grinned. "Reunited."

"That was selfless of you."

She dropped the long skirt of her habit with a splat. "Selfless would be not forcing another muddy garment on Keene. I think you will find me scrubbing the mud out of this tonight. Poor Keene does not deserve the mess I am bringing to her."

"If you do, and you ruin the habit in your ignorance, what shall you do then?"

"Wait to ride again until my mama can order a new one. What a ghastly thought."

"To order a new habit?"

"No." She wrinkled her nose. "To put off riding."

Laughter bubbled from my chest.

She stepped a little closer, and I could feel her shoulder pressing into my side. "Did you receive the chapter this morning? I was half tempted not to send it with Keene at all for fear it would somehow end up in the wrong hands."

"I did. Thank you. I have yet to look at your notes, though."

"Good heavens, enjoy them. They may well be the last ones I have the nerve to write."

It appeared the mixup with Captain Neal had bothered her more than I realized. "Was the captain particularly attentive this morning?"

"Indeed. Until I slipped in the mud, fell on my face, and soiled myself by holding a wild animal, at least." She let out a sigh. "I shall not judge his dislikes, for I cannot understand them. But I will admit I felt a little stranded."

An urge flushed through me to give the man a set down. He'd abandoned her? And what was that about soiling herself by holding a wild animal? Surely she could not be referring to the soft, downy duckling. "Forgive me if my absence caused you distress, Marianne. I was doing my best to give the captain time alone with you."

"Whatever for?"

I was momentarily lost for words. "So he might court you without impediment."

"I am beginning to think that effort is quite unnecessary."

My heart tripped, my breath growing ragged, though I tried to disguise it. Was it hope that bloomed now in my chest? That was an unreasonable response. This woman saw me as a *brother*. "Oh?"

"I wonder if he would be better suited to someone more biddable. Someone like Miss Gatley. What do you think?"

"It is not for me to say."

She gripped my sleeve tighter and laughed. "What an obnoxiously careful speech. Perhaps that will be my reply when you next ask for help on a chapter."

"That is hardly the same thing. Perhaps you should allow me to help *you* on a chapter."

"Because you are talented at romance?"

I tried not to let that comment sting. "Because I would love to read what you have written. I promise to refrain from giving my opinions if you think that will only make your story worse."

"Heavens, Henry. That is not at all what I meant. You will surely not make it worse, but it is frightening to make myself vulnerable in such a way."

I understood. Far too well, in fact, for I could not make myself vulnerable and tell her I had begun to feel things for her. Perhaps if she raised the gumption to give me some of her pages, I would raise the gumption to tell her my feelings toward her had changed.

We walked along the path at a more sedate pace than the nanny, who followed behind Frederick as he moved alongside the ducks.

I cleared my throat softly. "Marianne, do you think, once your mind is made, that it is unchangeable?"

"What do you mean?"

"I mean in regards to gentlemen. Do you feel that once you've made your mind up about a man, you cannot change it?"

Her brow furrowed. "I would like to say that is not the case, but how can I know? I thought I knew how I felt about Captain Neal, but his behavior surprised me today."

My breath caught, but I did not permit myself too much hope. "Was that behavior enough to put you off the man?"

"No. I will not fault his entire character from one perceived flaw. I cannot lie, though. It will greatly influence my feelings for him."

"And your feelings for me?"

She looked up sharply. "What do you mean by that?"

I tried to cover my nervous breathing with a soft smile. "We are friends, are we not? I wondered if that was subject to change. Have I done anything to influence you in that regard?"

Her confusion was adorable, but I wanted her to appear confident instead. "I cannot say."

"For fear of hurting my feelings?"

"Of course not. Oh, look." She released my arm and pointed at the water on the end of the lake. "There are more ducklings, after all. Do you think we gave our little friend to the right mother?"

I looked down at her, admiring her compassion. I missed the feel of her holding my arm. "Only time will tell."

CHAPTER 18

HENRY

The Huttons took an informal approach to seating at dinner. Despite having an earl in attendance, they allowed each person to select whom they would escort into the dining room and sit beside. I typically enjoyed that change, because it meant being able to sit beside a person of my choosing every night instead of sitting according to rank like some households enforced. But tonight I was wishing for a forced seating chart. I had been usurped, and Captain Neal had requested Marianne's company before I could ask to lead her to dinner. I resorted to conferring that request upon Miss Gatley, who proved to be a young, giggling sort of companion. The longer I spent listening to her, the more I craved Marianne's mature conversation.

Miss Gatley prattled on about the latest fashions and the lack of flounces on her gowns while we dug into our ham, boiled potatoes, and rolls. "But Mother would not allow an excess of flounces because she feared it would make me look like the sort of female who did not know her own mind."

"Extra . . . flounces?"

"Yes." She speared a potato and chewed it.

"I am afraid I do not understand."

"An excess of flounces is very much the style right now."

"Yes, I did understand that."

Miss Gatley looked at me with a furrowed brow, confusion fresh in the creases on her face.

"Is it not typical to style one's gowns after what is all the rage?" I asked.

Her shoulders relaxed a little. "Oh, I see. No, my mother did not want me to follow the style. She feared it would make me appear as though I follow others instead of making my own way."

What a strange way of looking at fashion. "I see. She thinks you ought to have your own style so a gentleman will believe you know your own mind." Though, even as she said it, she made it clear she was only listening to the whims of her mother. If she wanted gentlemen to believe her original, she should not tell them she was only being obedient.

"You would value a woman who knows her own mind," she said, a bite of bitterness to her tone I had not detected before.

"I am afraid I have never given much thought to styles in general."

She cut another potato. "I can see that."

I sipped from my goblet then, choking slightly on the mouthful of wine. It took great effort not to chuckle at her slight. Had the woman truly just told me I had no sense of style? I hesitated to speak, glancing down to my waistcoat. The bronze color was muted and classic. Or perhaps it was just an old fashion, and I called it classic so I could allow myself to believe I did not need to bother replacing it.

I glanced at Neal across the table. His cravat was stylishly formed, his waistcoat a dazzling blue. But his apparel didn't hold my attention very long when I noticed his table partner. Marianne appeared to be pleasantly lost in conversation with him. Had the captain redeemed himself in her opinion?

If only I could produce a duckling right now for her to hold.

Anything to put him off her. *Where was that blasted cat when I needed him?*

I tried to turn my attention back to Miss Gatley. I did not wish to be rude, and her snappish, clipped words meant she was already in a somewhat sour mood—little did I know why. "Did you enjoy yourself in London this year?"

"I did. It was enlightening."

Her speech seemed free, less retrained than usual, but also sour and snappish. I noticed her glance flicking to Captain Neal on occasion. Was she as disappointed as I had been about who had escorted whom to dinner this evening?

"Are you acquainted with the captain?" I asked.

"Hardly. I am aware of his good reputation, but I haven't had much opportunity to speak with him yet."

"We are somewhat acquainted, and what little I know of him has been good."

"Yes." She speared her meat with extra force. "Although I don't suppose the same can be said for everyone at this table."

The pointedness of her words made my blood turn to ice. She looked from her plate to me without any artifice in her eyes, and I swallowed the lump of apprehension. "I am afraid I do not know what you mean."

"Do you not?" She put down her fork and looked at me, waiting for an answer.

I picked up my goblet and took a sip of wine to postpone the necessity of answering her. Was she searching for gossip or implying she had some to share? Either way, I did not want to participate in such an uncomfortable conversation. Particularly not surrounded as we were now. "As far as I know, everyone in this room is above reproach. Did you hear of our fiasco with the duckling earlier today?"

"No. Well, I heard of it, but that is not what I refer to." She picked up her fork and knife to cut her potatoes into smaller bites. "I do not know if you were aware, but I took dinner in my room last night. Traveling always tires me excessively, so I retired early."

"I did. We missed you last night."

She didn't look convinced. Her focus remained on her plate, cutting her potato into smaller and smaller pieces. "I took a nap when we arrived, but evidently I slept too long, because after dinner I could not fall asleep again."

"That is the trouble with napping sometimes." What was her intent with this conversation? Her gaze continued to dart between Captain Neal and her potato, her story purposeful, as if she expected me to know what she meant by it.

"You will imagine my surprise when I heard footsteps in the corridor in the middle of the night."

Dread pooled in my stomach, twisting in discomfort. I looked at Mr. Gatley, who sat on her other side, but he did not appear to be paying any heed to our conversation. His wife, one seat further, was minding us even less.

"It was shocking for me to discover my friend sneaking down to the kitchens. I followed her because I hoped to partake of whatever treat she was fetching for herself. I did not realize she was going downstairs to meet with you."

A hush fell over the table, and it occurred to me that Miss Gatley had in no way tried to temper the volume of her speech. Her father looked at me sharply over her shoulder. "I say, is this true?"

I looked to Marianne, whose face paled, the color draining from her cheeks.

"Of course not," Mrs. Hutton said. "Marianne would never do something so vulgar. Would you, darling?"

Marianne looked from me to her mother, then to her father. She was the picture of guilt, her eyes wide and round, her skin pale as though bathed in moonlight. "Mama, I meant to tell you earlier—"

"But we did not want to break this news in such a way," I

said quickly, before she could say anything that would condemn us both.

"Isabel," Mr. Gatley hissed at his daughter, "what is the meaning of this?"

"I heard him, Father." She tossed her blonde curls, her voice defiant. "I heard Mr. Bradwell propose marriage to Miss Hutton."

I will marry you. She could not have been close enough to hear me, could she? We were utterly alone, in the near darkness, speaking so softly.

"You thought this would be best discussed during *dinner?*" he whispered. "Foolish child. Now you have forced his hand."

"Marianne," Mr. Hutton said gruffly, "is this true?"

She looked at me and our eyes locked over the table. Her expression was lost, afraid. I wanted to save her. I wanted to marry her. Would it be repulsive for me to save her in this way, or would she be grateful? Her lips parted, and my eyes dropped to them.

We had discussed this before, what we would do if our ruse went too far. I could save her now with an engagement, and she could break it off later, ruining only my reputation and merely bruising her own. If I spoke up now, that did not seal us to one another forever, as Society believed. We would face scandal when the engagement broke, but we would face a worse scandal if we never entered into an engagement at all.

I cleared my throat, holding Marianne's eyes and trying to read her thoughts. I was failing miserably. "We had wanted to do this properly, but apparently now my hands *are* tied. Last night I asked Marianne to marry me."

She visibly swallowed, then gave me a tremulous smile, which she turned on her mother. "Do not be angry with us. I wanted to find a time to speak to you privately before making an announcement."

"Angry?" Mrs. Hutton breathed. Her hands clasped, hovering over her chest. "I am thrilled."

Mr. Hutton looked at me, less sure. "Shall we go shooting tomorrow, lad?"

There was a soft chuckle from Lord Moorington, whose wife remained steadfastly quiet.

"Of course, sir. There is a question I should like to ask you." I emptied the rest of my wine down my throat. I was not off to an auspicious beginning, having secured the woman's hand before requesting permission from her father, and he evidently wanted to amend that slight. "I look forward to it."

Aside from the Huttons' general pleased confusion and Lord and Lady Mooringtons' gentle acceptance of the change, the rest of the party was unhappy. Captain Neal stared at me, his mouth pressed in a firm line, anger dancing in his eyes. The Gatleys hardly concealed their frustrations, and Miss Gatley pouted in the chair beside me.

That was her own fault. She should not have mentioned it if she did not want such a result.

The mood in the room had shifted into heavy discomfort.

"Shaw!" Mr. Hutton called to the butler. "Champagne. We need to celebrate."

The conversation was stilted and uncomfortable until the butler returned, distributing glasses to each of us. We toasted Marianne and myself.

"To new unions."

"It is a shame your mother cannot be here, Mr. Bradwell," Mrs. Hutton said. "It has been years since she joined us for a house party."

"It's been years since she has joined ours as well," Lady Moorington said. "She used to come every summer. Though her children would have been very young, then."

I was heartily relieved my mother was not here, for she would have seen through me at once. "She has trouble in carriages and grows sick. I think she would not hesitate to visit if her body would permit the travel."

Lady Moorington nodded. "We understand. We only miss her."

Mrs. Hutton set down her empty glass. "You will write to her straight away, I presume? I hope she will be overjoyed by this union."

Writing to my mother would make this feel too real. I looked at Marianne, and the concern that edged her brow reached my heart. I feared I had made a mistake.

An hour later we were gathered in the drawing room. Mrs. Hutton stood before the fireplace, prepared to address us. "Now that we almost have the entire house party in attendance"—she looked at Lady Moorington—"I thought it would be great fun if we put up the rug and danced."

Two footmen came forward to roll away the large carpet in the center of the room.

Miss Gatley clapped enthusiastically. "Who shall play?"

"Would you like me to, Mama?" Marianne asked.

"No, darling. You should dance. I will play."

It took only a moment for the footmen to roll up the rug and push the furniture out of the way so there was enough room to dance. Lord Moorington led his wife to the middle of the floor, and Captain Neal asked Miss Gatley to partner him. I lifted my eyebrows to Marianne, crossing the room, and put out my arm. "Will you dance with me?"

She placed her gloved hand on my sleeve. "I will."

"Shall I play a waltz?" Mrs. Hutton asked. I could feel her watching us, and I couldn't help but wonder if she had orchestrated this moment intentionally for my benefit. *Thank you, ma'am.*

Miss Gatley clapped again. "Oh yes, I dearly love to waltz."

My pulse thrummed in anticipation. Marianne smiled happily, infusing me with the confidence that she might be just as glad to dance in my arms as I was to hold her.

Mrs. Hutton pulled out her music and sat at the pianoforte. She warmed up her fingers on the keys while the couples promenaded around the room. Mr. Hutton, Mr. Gatley, and Mrs. Gatley made themselves comfortable on the sofas against the wall and watched us. Mr. Gatley wore an expression of frustration, and I did my best to ignore him. The woman on my arm and her concern was far more pressing.

I bent my head close to Marianne so I could speak without being overheard. "Forgive me."

"For saving me?"

"For putting you in this position."

The song began in earnest, and we proceeded to dance. "I should be thanking you," she said. "I had no notion of what to say."

"Neither did I, but I thought it wise to tell the truth and allow them to draw their own conclusions. I do wonder if your father intends to meet me with the pistols at dawn."

She grinned. "Only if the pistols are meant for hunting."

"Perhaps I can win him over tomorrow."

"You can," she said with confidence. "It should not be difficult. You are joining him for his favorite activity."

I smiled. She seemed to think it simple, but evidently she hadn't caught the flash of surprise in his eyes when the entire drama had unfolded at dinner. "When will we have the opportunity to speak freely, Marianne?"

"After you shoot with my father? I believe the ladies are painting tomorrow, but perhaps we can sneak away before dinner."

"Isn't sneaking what landed us in this mess in the first place?"

"Perhaps. But we are in the mess now, so we might as well take advantage of it." She gave me a saucy smile.

I gripped her hand tighter, moving with the music and hoping she understood my sincerity. "Marianne, I am truly sorry."

She stared at me, her lips parting in surprise.

"So utterly sorry," I repeated.

Her mouth closed. She looked away. "Think nothing of it. We will find a way out of this scrape."

Just as I feared. Marianne did not find this a pleasant situation to be caught in. I tried to cover my disappointment and finished the remainder of the dance, enjoying the feel of her in my arms. The song came to a close and we switched partners. I danced with Lady Moorington, Miss Gatley danced with Lord Moorington, and Marianne danced with Captain Neal. I wished I was close enough to hear their conversation, but Lady Moorington kept me too occupied to eavesdrop.

When we had finished our third dance and exhausted all combinations of partners, we brought the rugs back in and moved the sofas back before the hearth. Games were discussed and people dispersed to join the proper tables.

Marianne's cheeks were flushed, her eyes bright. "I think this entire debacle has given me an idea for the next scene in my book. Would it be terrible if I slipped away to write it?"

I understood this woman so well. How had I not seen earlier that she was my soul's mate?

"Not at all."

"In that case, I'm off for bed." She bade her parents a good night, and I watched her leave.

I wanted to follow and do the same, but that would lead to suspicion I didn't want to expose us to at present. Lady Moorington started a game of whist with Mrs. Gatley, Miss Gatley, and Captain Neal. Mr. Hutton and Lord Moorington were deep in a game of chess at the table beside the window. I wondered how long I would have to sit on the sofa in front of the fire before I could excuse myself to go to sleep.

Mrs. Hutton handed me a glass of port. I swirled the liquid in the cup, staring at the fire, when she sat beside me.

My nerves rose in her presence. Had she seen through me? She watched me take a sip, but gave no hint of her own emotions. "Has your brother James ever told you about the night I found him with Felicity in our library?"

"A little."

"It was clear they had only been dancing. What we did not know was what occurred prior to the dance, though that was truly none of our business. The women with me were terrible gossips, though, and your brother and Felicity never stood a chance." She paused before continuing. "I will never forget how quickly James had been willing to do the right thing."

"For her reputation," I said. James had been forced into marrying a veritable stranger, but he had made the choice to do so. It was ironic I found myself in a similar circumstance.

"And his own," Mrs. Hutton corrected. "Your parents have always carried pride in the Bradwell name."

"Are you wondering if I possess that same pride?"

"That is not a question for me to ask." She gave a soft smile and looked at the fire. "I have always desired for my children to marry for love. I have helped them in selecting partners and was able to watch Adam and Julia both achieve exactly what I wanted for them. I've been fortunate until now."

Until now.

"Marianne, however, has been difficult," she continued. "Time and again I have believed I found the perfect man to catch her interest, but time and again she has found fault with them all."

"Do you think she is selective?"

"I think she does not give her heart away easily. I feel that once she does, it will be irrevocable." Mrs. Hutton watched me, and I did not know exactly what she meant for me to understand. "If you love my daughter, then I am glad to welcome you to our family, Mr. Bradwell." She stood, straightening her skirt.

Did I love Marianne? I was grateful she hadn't posed the question to me, for I did not know how I would answer it at present. Our engagement was not real, and until Marianne indicated that she would like it to be otherwise, I did not feel comfortable discussing my feelings with anyone else.

"I think I will get some sleep," I said.

"Good night, Mr. Bradwell." She gave me a sad smile, and I wondered what she saw in my expression. Guilt? Failure? Or perhaps it was the understanding now dawning on me that once again I have done something my father would not be proud of.

CHAPTER 19

MARIANNE

F *orgive me.* After Henry had saved me from certain ruination, he had asked for my forgiveness. It had taken every last ounce of control I possessed to refrain from going to his room in the night so we could speak plainly to one another. My parents certainly would have taken issue with that.

But now I felt . . . unfinished. I wanted him to explain his apology and how he intended to remove us from this mess. Surely he had a plan.

I sat in the morning room, light streaming through the windows and filtering over the fan I was painting. I dipped my brush in the water and the violet paint again, sweeping it gently over the second panel to continue the flowers.

Miss Gatley sat across from me, painting blue flowers over her fan with extra dedication. Or perhaps she was angry with me for stealing the man she had come here to ensnare and was now hoping to punish me by not looking me in the eye. Indeed, since the moment Henry had announced our engagement, Miss Gatley had not looked at me once.

Mr. Darcy jumped up on the sofa cushion and slid beneath my arms to settle himself on my lap. His short gray fur tickled my skin as he settled in place. "You need to move, sir, or I will not be able to finish this fan."

Mr. Darcy didn't seem to care about what I wanted. He purred softly and made himself comfortable.

"Perhaps it is time for a break," Mama said.

Lady Moorington leaned back and looked shrewdly at her fan. "I should probably cease painting entirely. Mine only grows worse the more I try to improve it."

"Our time might be better spent planning an engagement ball, anyway," Mama said, eyeing me closely. Was she watching for a reaction? To see if I would repulse the offer? Something about her phrasing or her tone was not quite right, but I couldn't identify what it was.

I needed to tread carefully or I would give us up. "It seems a little unnecessary to be planning a ball for the occasion."

"We mothers do love to dote on our children," Lady Moorington said. "You would not take that opportunity away from your dear mama?"

"Never. I only wonder if it is too soon."

"Do you not wish to celebrate your engagement?" Miss Gatley asked, still looking at her fan and applying far too much paint for the panel she was working on.

"Of course I wish to celebrate it." If she thought to entice a confession out of me, she would be sorely disappointed. I looked at my mother. "Name the date, and we shall begin preparations."

Mother nodded. "Friday next? We can invite local Society. If we plan it for the end of our house party, our friends will be able to attend, and your sister will still be here."

"Lovely idea," Lady Moorington said.

I had not seen my sister since yesterday, for she had chosen not to join us for dinner or in the drawing room afterward. "Where is Julia? Did she not wish to paint?"

"She is feeling unwell. I believe she is resting."

Sleeping was all she seemed to do these days.

"Your grandson has an abundance of energy," Mrs. Gatley said meekly.

"He is a sweet boy, but he tires poor Nanny."

"Some children are certainly more tiring than others." Lady Moorington sounded as though she spoke from experience. Given her son's reputation at present, I imagined the stress he heaped on her shoulders was not derived merely from his younger days.

"Speaking of children, when can we expect Daniel?" Mama asked.

Lady Moorington directed her attention to her fan again. "Today, I think. You never can know with him." She gave a smile, but it was clear her nerves were fraying.

"We will be glad of his company whenever he can see fit to join us. He has always been a joy to have around."

I shot Mama a glance, hoping to convey that she was doing it a little too brown, but she ignored me. Her friend's comfort was her first priority at present.

I stood. "I think I will visit Julia now. My fan needs to dry, anyway."

Lady Moorington leaned over to look at my floral design. "It's lovely, dear."

Miss Gatley's frown deepened. She dipped her paintbrush in the water and then into the red paint with far too much enthusiasm, before flicking the brush up and sending a volley of watered-down red paint at me. It sprayed over my face and gown and speckled my fan, causing me to take a sharp intake of breath.

"Isabel!" her mother said quickly.

"Oh dear, did I do that?" Miss Gatley raised her face, but apology was not visible on her countenance. "How clumsy of me."

My fan was ruined. Even watercolors could not be removed

without ruining the entire painting. I clenched my jaw and wetted my brush, swirling water over the red splotches in order to dilute them to a pink that better matched my other colors.

The women in the room remained quiet. I failed to understand why Miss Gatley had targeted me in such a way. If she was angry that I had procured a proposal out of Henry, then she only had herself to blame—it was she who had forced him to follow through on his initial offer.

I looked at Miss Gatley, dropping my brush onto the linen beside my fan again. The red paint dried crustily on my face, but I did not remove my gaze from Miss Gatley until she looked at me. "Not to worry. I was able to save it. But I fear I must go wash up now." I stood, looking at my mother. "And then I think I will visit Julia."

I escaped to my room. The paint wiped easily from my face with a wet cloth. I sat at my writing desk and pulled out my manuscript. I had finished the final pages last night, staying awake far too late in order to write the ending that had come to me following dinner.

A second opinion would do my story well, but Henry was not the man to provide it, surely. He admitted his dislike for romance, as was made more evident every time he sent me pages. His story would do better as it was when I first read it.

I gathered the pages of the entire manuscript together and tied twine around them to keep them in order. Henry had asked time and again to read my story, but it was too frightening. What if he did not like it or thought me an awful writer? Not as clever as the lady who had written *Pride & Prejudice*. Not as imaginative as Jonathan Swift. Not as romantic as Byron. Fear often came in the way of taking risks, but knowing that didn't make my fear any less powerful.

Marbury had accepted my first manuscript without my ever having received a second opinion on it. Surely we could find a publisher for this book as well.

I opened the drawer of the writing desk and slid the manuscript inside. I had held up my side of the bargain. Now it was Henry's turn to hold up his.

Julia reclined on her bed, her face pale, her cheeks chalky.

She blinked at me. "*Engaged*? To Mr. Bradwell? Do you love him?"

That question I most feared, for I didn't know how to answer it. I sat on the edge of her mattress and fiddled with the flowers embroidered on her coverlet. "How does one know when one is in love?"

She leaned back, disappointment forming lines between her eyebrows. "If you were in love, you would know."

That was not what I wanted to hear. I had hoped for a formula, a rule, an explanation—anything that would make me feel secure in my feelings. Henry had given me heart palpitations, swarmed my stomach with butterflies, and rescued me from being stuck both in a lake and on a muddy bank. I wanted to be with him, and when I was away from him I thought of little else. But did I *love* him? I didn't know.

"He must love you, or he would not have offered for you," she said.

I laughed. "He only offered because Miss Gatley forced the situation upon him." And then I had almost forced it upon him the night before. That proved he was a gentleman and nothing else. I widened my eyes at my sister. "Do not tell Mama that."

"Of course I won't."

I bent over the coverlet, burying my face in my hands. The darkness closed around me, and I pushed Henry's image completely from my mind, letting out a groan.

"What of Captain Neal? Did he not come here with the express purpose of courting you?"

"He did," I said, my face still buried in her coverlet. "I am not certain if he'll remain now. He surely must feel duped or tricked. It is the worst sort of rudeness."

"I cannot understand you when you speak that way, Mari. Sit up."

I obeyed. "I must speak with him. I intend to do so. But he went shooting with Papa and Henry."

"Oh dear."

"And now Mama wants to throw an engagement ball at the end of the house party, but I hardly know my own mind."

"That is not even two weeks away."

"I am fully aware of how soon it is, how quick it feels," I said with feeling.

"Henry should write to his mother first, should he not?"

"I'm sure he will, but I haven't had a chance to speak to him since we announced our engagement at dinner last night. It all feels so fast and unsettling." I lowered my voice, infusing it with gravity. "Julia, I am not certain he even desires to marry me, or if he was only trying to save my reputation. The worst part of it is"—I drew in a ragged breath—"after dinner, we put up the rugs and danced and he *apologized*. He asked me to forgive him for saving my reputation and pretending we were engaged. A man in love would not beg apology for finding himself engaged to the woman he cared about."

She did not look convinced. "A man who was not willing to marry you would not have offered himself up as a sacrifice, either."

"A very good man would, and Henry is the best of men. Besides, that is not a very promising way of looking at the situation, you know. A sacrifice?"

Julia smiled. "It sounds to me as though your heart is made up on the matter."

"Because I respect and revere him? Goodness, Julia. That is

not love. I respect Shakespeare and Fanny Burney, but I do not wish to marry either of them."

"I think I know more about it than you," she said, lifting an eyebrow. "Respect is certainly one component of love. Oh, how I wish I had been at dinner to watch this. I want to know for myself how this man looks at you."

"You very well could have been at dinner. I feel as though I have not seen you at all since we arrived in Cheshire. I have spent more time with Frederick than with you these past few days. Are you ill?"

She rubbed her temples. "Yes. I cannot abide even the thought of attending dinner. Gruel has been much more the thing for me."

"Gruel."

"Yes, a very thin recipe. Or rolls. Cook has sent up many rolls these last few days, for they are nearly all I can stomach."

Understanding hit upon me so squarely, I felt unintelligent for not having identified it sooner. The last time Julia had eaten nothing but bits of rolls, she had been pregnant with Frederick. "You're with child?"

She grimaced. "I did not want to say anything until I had the opportunity to tell Mr. Walding. But he is not here yet, and I am miserable." Her eyes filled with unshed tears. "I fear the flooding has been far more extensive than we initially believed when we first received our steward's letter. Perhaps I would have been better returning home instead of coming here."

I sat up and pulled her into a hug before releasing her and leaning back. "Oh dear. Is my movement making you nauseous? Forgive me. I'm so thrilled."

"Yes. Please don't move the bed so much," she said with a watery smile. "I hope I shall feel much more the thing after I am reunited with my husband."

"This is such excellent news. Has Mama figured it out?"

"I am sure she has, though she has yet to say anything about it. Perhaps she is also waiting for Mr. Walding to arrive." Julia's eyes glazed over with fresh tears. "But he is not here, and I feel *so ill.*"

"Oh, my poor Julia. How can I help you?"

"Do not rattle my bed. That is all I ask." She gave a hiccup and stilled, waiting for apparent nausea to pass before speaking again. "Thank you for showing Frederick the duckling. That is all he has talked about since yesterday."

"How? He hardly speaks more than one word at a time."

"You will be quite impressed, I wager, because he *has* formed something of a sentence on the matter. He told me *Anne hold duck.*"

"What a clever boy! I am happy to be included in anything regarding those ducklings. I think they have trumped Mr. Darcy in Frederick's esteem."

"He has not mentioned the cat to me at all today, so you may be correct."

I tilted my head, unable to curb my grin. "I hope this new little one will be able to keep up with your energetic boy."

She sighed. "The only thing concerning me at present is making it through the day. I will worry about this child when he or she is in my arms." Julia leaned back against her pillows again and looked at me through slightly narrowed eyes. "You know, one way to determine how you feel about Mr. Bradwell is to talk to him."

"I agree. But finding the opportunity for private conversations is near impossible with so many people around."

"Impossible? Hardly. Invite him for a ride and lose the groom. Invite him to play chess and move the table to the opposite end of the room from Mama. Invite him to take a walk down to the lake, then slow your steps to put distance between you and your chaperone. You can invite him to fish with you, where you could sit in a boat together in full view of whoever is chaperoning, but there will be a great enough distance for private conversation."

"I think sound travels on water. Surely whoever chaperones us will hear everything we're saying in the boat."

"You are missing my point. It is possible to have a private conversation. I should know, for I finagled quite a few of them before securing a proposal from Mr. Walding." She grinned unrepentantly. "Now that you are engaged, you shouldn't have much trouble. Though sometimes it still requires creativity." She leaned forward and took my hand, squeezing it. "I have faith in you, Mari. You've always been the creative sort."

Indeed. More creative than she knew.

CHAPTER 20

MARIANNE

The men had thus far spent the entirety of the day outside. They hunted in the morning, shot targets at midday, and could be seen fishing the lake in the afternoon. It seemed Henry was making up for the last few days of not joining my father in various exploits by partaking in all of them now.

Or he was avoiding me. I hoped that was not the case.

Captain Neal joined them in each of their activities, but I assumed he was glad for an excuse to be out of the house. Mr. Gatley and Lord Moorington were less devout, but they did come and go at will.

I grew more anxious as the clock advanced and the sun began its descent. By the time I had dressed for dinner, I had not spoken a word to Henry all day. I did not wish to face Miss Gatley and her anger again, nor Captain Neal and his understandable frustration. I was tempted to hide in my room for the rest of the evening, but that would only postpone the inevitable.

Keene dressed my hair and helped me prepare for dinner. "You look radiant, miss."

"Thank you, but I am not quite ready to go down. I think I need a moment alone."

She bobbed a curtsy and disappeared.

Pulling a sheet of paper out of my writing desk, I ripped off a slip at the top, picked up my quill, and dipped it in ink.

Meet me at the willow tree beside the lake tonight. Midnight?

It was far less dangerous now that we were allegedly engaged, but passing notes or meeting in secret was never fully safe. If we were caught together, it would only solidify our situation, which was a frightful thought when I did not know how he felt about it to begin with. But I could not remove Henry's apology from my mind. I wanted an opportunity to speak plainly with him so he could explain the meaning behind his apology and how he felt about our engagement.

I also needed to inform him that my manuscript was ready for publishers. I could likely contrive a way to tell him that piece of information in public—it was a weak excuse to seek out a private conversation with Henry—but I would be lying if I pretended I wasn't eager to be near him again, to speak plainly to him. I valued his insight and conversation.

When the ink dried, I folded the strip of paper and tucked it into my glove, the edges scraping against my soft forearm.

The entire party was already assembled when I reached the drawing room. Everyone except for Daniel, who, it appeared, had not yet arrived. Judging by the disappointment on Lady Moorington's face, he was either not coming at all or he was extremely late.

Henry stood near the chessboard table, listening to my father. I caught his gaze when I looked away from the countess, and my feet directed me toward him without any conscious effort on my part. He was so handsome, his curly hair pushed and pomaded into something of a style, his cravat simply tied, his waistcoat neutral. His clothing was understated but fit him well, and I could not deny that his blue eyes fastened so steadily on me made my heart skip.

I dipped my head in a curtsy when I approached them. "Have you received your fill of hunting, fishing, and shooting?"

Papa smiled guiltily. "You are too gentle a creature to understand, but I fear that is an impossible task, darling." He leaned forward and kissed my temple. "Thank you for lending me your Mr. Bradwell for the day."

My Mr. Bradwell. I liked the sound of that.

It appeared that Henry and my father were somewhat friendly now. He fit in as a country gentleman so easily.

Henry tore his gaze from me. "Indeed, I felt as though I was at home. My older brother James enters very much into your way of thinking, sir. I often spend entire days with him in much the same manner as we did today."

"It is no wonder you are such a good shot."

"I must thank the army for *that*. My fishing leaves something to be desired, though."

Papa clapped him on the back. "We have time to work on that, my boy."

Henry looked swiftly at my father, his cheeks reddening slightly. He appeared pleased by the interaction, but it was hard to tell entirely, and his eyes dropped to the floor. Was he happy with how his day had gone, spending time with my father? He had not been able to do so with his own since he'd died at Waterloo, and I imagined he missed him desperately.

Shaw announced dinner was ready. Henry looked at me. "Will you do me the honor of allowing me to escort you into dinner, Miss Hutton?"

Thank heavens. "I would be delighted." I slipped the piece of paper out of my glove where it could no longer scratch my forearm and gripped it in my hand discreetly.

"I must find your mama," Papa said, kissing my temple again before he left.

Henry bent his arm toward me, and his jacket shifted enough to reveal the small pocket in his waistcoat. That pocket was my aim. I stepped forward to take his arm and pretended to stumble on the carpet, putting my hands out and catching myself against his stomach. I slid the note into the small pocket as his arms went around me, glad he carried no pocket watch to take up the available space there. Henry righted me, holding me by the shoulders until I released his waistcoat.

"How clumsy of me." I spoke loudly for the benefit of anyone who might have witnessed my terrible acting. It was not lost on me that I used the same false words Miss Gatley had used earlier when she flung paint all over my fan.

"Are you well?" Henry asked softly, his head bent as he looked at me with concern.

Grand. Even he was not convinced by my charade.

"I am perfectly well." I lowered my voice. "I slipped a note into your pocket."

A surprised scoff ripped from his throat as he presented his arm to me again. The entire party was on its way to the dining room, but Mr. and Mrs. Gatley had apparently watched the interaction and waited for us to approach.

"Are you well, dear?" Mrs. Gatley asked.

"Yes. I am in new slippers and my foot caught on the edge of the rug."

"How fortunate Mr. Bradwell was standing by."

I looked at him, then lowered my gaze. "Yes, ma'am. Fortunate indeed."

Mr. Gatley made a noncommittal huff and pulled his wife from the room.

Henry lifted his eyebrows lightly at me and leaned forward. "I do not think Mr. Gatley is very pleased with us presently."

"I think he would be quite pleased with *you* if you were to forsake me and break the engagement."

Henry chuckled, the deep sound hitting me in the stomach.

"Then he is destined to remain disappointed, for I have no plan to do any such thing."

My stomach twisted in anticipation. What did he mean by that? I wanted to ask him, but we stepped into the dining room and circled the table to take our seats. We were unfortunate to find that the only two remaining seats placed me beside Captain Neal. I had successfully avoided him all day, as he had spent it in my father's company, and I did not chance to speak to him before dinner. The man was surely angry and with good reason.

I sent him a tremulous smile when I took my seat.

He returned it briefly, but still I could not gauge his mood.

At least I could trust there would be no immature flinging of paint at dinner. If the captain or Miss Gatley aimed a soupy spoon at me, I would merely move.

"Did you enjoy your day, Captain Neal?" I asked. "I judged my father took full advantage of such willing company."

"I did," he said tartly. "It was a good opportunity for me to clear my head and reassess my plans."

"Reassess? You do not intend to leave us, do you?" I could not blame him, but I felt guilt for it all the same.

"I am now less motivated to remain." He looked to Henry before settling a bland smile on me again. "I made it clear that I have limited time at my disposal and a very particular goal. It should come as no surprise to you that, unless circumstances were to change, I now must accomplish that goal elsewhere."

What was I meant to do in this situation? Apologize for becoming engaged to someone else? Did I lead him to believe I was not looking at anyone else? *Was* this my fault?

The first course was brought out and Captain Neal turned his attention to his dinner partner.

"This has been quite an exciting twenty-four hours," Henry said softly. "Especially when one considers all that happened at dinner last night."

I gave a soft snort. "That is putting it mildly."

"I am in general a patient man, but finding it incredibly difficult at present. Can I ask the nature of the . . ." He did not appear to know how to finish his question.

"Of my fall?"

"Yes." His eyes danced. "I find that with you I am inordinately curious."

"If I could answer that now, I would not have needed to resort to ink."

"Touché." He dipped a spoon in his soup and took a bite, then leaned back and looked at me. "Speaking of ink, have you made good progress on the book you were . . . *reading?*"

By reading, I assumed he meant writing. "Yes. I finished it."

His eyebrows rose. "Well done, Miss Hutton. You must be very proud of yourself."

"I am. It was a difficult book to read, but I had a sudden burst of inspir—*energy,* and was able to complete it last night."

He grinned, his smile so wide I was certain of his genuine happiness for me. He understood the difficulties of writing, and of the elation that accompanied finishing a story. It was only my second time reaching this point with a manuscript, but I still felt as though I was lifted into the clouds a bit for having completed it. There was a general catharsis to writing *the end.* I felt more complete for having finished the book.

"Will you lend it to me? I should like to read it."

I gave my full attention to my soup. "I do not think I can."

"You will force me to wait until I can purchase my own copy from a book shop?"

He had a point there. One way or another, if I was to publish this book, he would be able to read it. "I fear you will not enjoy it. What if you hate the book?"

"I doubt that will be the case, but even if it is, it certainly will not end our friendship," he joked.

I tilted my head to the side, holding his gaze.

He dropped his general joking demeanor. "I will love it. I

have loved all of your recommendations so far. They are nothing but an improvement upon what I had previously . . . read."

"This is different." This was not notes on his writing; it was writing of my own. Surely he could see how they were not even close to the same thing.

"I understand that. Of all people, Miss Hutton, I do understand that."

He did, didn't he? I took a sip of my soup and lowered my spoon. I could not commit to letting him read it yet, but maybe I should. Perhaps it was better to know how he felt now than wait until he could read it published.

"If I allow this to happen, you will not let it color your agreement? If you hate it, you will still help me?"

"Gads, Mari," he said, shortening my name. Had he realized he'd done it? It sent a thrill through me, and I prayed no one else had heard him. I supposed it wouldn't matter that he took such liberties with my name, since we were engaged, but the familiarity warmed my chest nonetheless.

"Do you think I would renege on my promise?" He shook his head. "It hardly matters anyway, for I've already done it."

"You have already done what, exactly?"

He folded his napkin and put it in his lap, then leaned toward me under the guise of reaching for his goblet. He lowered his voice to a whisper. "I have already written to publishers on your behalf."

CHAPTER 21
HENRY

If I could capture the look of surprise Marianne wore when I told her I had already written to the publishers, I would keep it forever. Perhaps I would take up painting just so I could try to recreate her expression on canvas. It was so lovely and innocently sweet. I took another sip from my goblet to hide the smile threatening to burst on my face.

"You are in earnest?" she asked breathlessly. "How did you know I was finished?"

"You weren't. At least, not when I posted the letters."

"You must explain that, sir." Marianne laughed, and there was a lightness to her tone and bearing that had been missing earlier. I wanted it to remain always. What heaviness had been plaguing her before?

"While we were in London, you mentioned you were nearly finished. I decided to send letters to a handful of publishers on your behalf so I could gather interest and information."

"Where did you ask them to direct the return mail?"

"I made a note that if a reply was immediate, they could write to me here at Hutton House, and if it was to take them more time, they could write to me at Sedwick Lodge." I took a spoonful of my soup. "My plan was to go there directly after the house party."

"If my mother has her way, you will probably remain here long enough to plan a wedding," Marianne mumbled.

Should I tell her that the prospect of remaining here longer did not sound unpleasant? "I think I ought to visit my own mother first." I gave her a smile, but she looked pained. The heaviness returned to her shoulders. Was it the prospect of wedding me that gave her stress? The idea of marrying a brother-like figure? Someone she was not attracted to? The idea made me ill.

I was eager to pull the slip of paper out of my waistcoat pocket and read what she had written to me. What could she possibly have to say that she couldn't speak out loud? Clearly we managed to have all manner of conversations about things that we likely should not say aloud, though I thought we did a good job of disguising our topics well.

The rest of dinner passed quickly in comfortable conversation. The ladies left us to our port, and Mr. Hutton pulled out his pipe. I watched Marianne leave the room and longed to follow her, though I didn't mind being with the men either. Spending the day with her father had been a boost of something akin to affection I hadn't known I desired. He was attentive and praiseworthy, reminding me of my father in the way he admired my horsemanship and shooting or gave me fishing advice.

One day spent in his company would never replace my father, but if he was to become my father-in-law, I wondered if it would one day feel as if he was filling the void now residing in my heart. I shoved the thought aside. It was far too premature for such melancholy thoughts.

Shaw filled my glass with port, and I sipped at it.

Oakey smoke filled the room. Mr. Gatley had procured a pipe and lit it while Lord Moorington and Captain Neal enjoyed their port. The men discussed our failure at hunting this morning and the need for decently trained hounds.

"You've done well not to let them in the house," Mr. Gatley said. "Spoiled hounds will never do what they're told."

Lord Moorington nodded in agreement. "My man is an excellent trainer. I can lend him to you, but I will need him back in the autumn."

"Are you breeding puppies?" Gatley asked.

"Yes. I like to train them young," he said, emptying his glass.

"What's this I've heard about your matching bays, Gatley?" Mr. Hutton asked.

"Sold them." His voice was gruff, and he motioned to Shaw to refill his glass.

Mr. Hutton puffed at his pipe. "Traded them in for something else?"

"Not yet. I had planned to purchase them again, but things are not working out as I intended." His gaze flicked to me briefly, then away again.

I tossed my gloves on the table and sipped at my port again.

Mr. Gatley had planned to purchase his own horses again? It seemed he had been relying on me to do that by his pointed look. I peered at his clothes, but they looked ordinary—no threadbare elbows or yellowed cravat. I supposed a man could maintain his wardrobe even if he could not stand the expense of additional horses.

Clearly not everything was as it seemed with the Gatleys.

We finished our port and joined the ladies in the drawing room where they were seated on the sofas.

Mrs. Hutton stood when we entered the room. "I hope your day of sport has not tired you too greatly. I had planned a few parlor games for this evening."

"Oh yes," Miss Gatley said. "Blind man's bluff, perhaps? That has always been a favorite of mine."

Captain Neal smiled gallantly. "It has been an age since I've played a game of that sort."

Was he implying that it was meant for children? If so, I would have to agree. But his smile said otherwise. Mrs. Hutton left the room and returned shortly with a small sash, which she carried to the center of the room. "I have a blindfold. Who would like to begin?"

"Perhaps Miss Gatley would like that honor," Marianne said.

Miss Gatley looked at her with a challenge and lifted her chin. "I should enjoy it very much."

Mrs. Hutton tied the blindfold around Miss Gatley's eyes. "Who else is joining us?"

I stood, helping to form a circle around them with Marianne and Captain Neal. Lord and Lady Moorington joined as well, but the Gatleys chose to remain on the sofa beside Mr. Hutton.

Mrs. Hutton gripped Miss Gatley by the shoulders. "I shall spin you five times." She proceeded to do so, then released Miss Gatley's shoulders and gently stepped back to join the circle. Miss Gatley put her hands out and walked forward until she met with Lord Moorington's lapel. She froze, likely recognizing from his girth who it was. "Mr. Bradwell?" she guessed.

"Wrong," Lady Moorington said, laughing.

Miss Gatley retracted her hands and turned the opposite direction of Lady Moorington's voice to find the next person. She tentatively reached out until she made contact with Captain Neal's sleeve, then slid her hands up his arms and touched his face gently. She swiped a finger down the center of his nose, the smile widening on her lips.

"Captain Neal?" she asked.

"Indeed!" He reached forward and lifted her blindfold, and they smiled at one another. Something flashed in his eyes. Perhaps he was noticing her for the first time? She had very clearly orchestrated this entire situation in order to freely touch Captain Neal, for no one would possibly guess after feeling Lord

Moorington's width that it was *me*. I'd yet to decide if she was merely oblivious or clever. Perhaps both.

"Since Captain Neal was correctly identified, he will be our next victim," Mrs. Hutton said.

The captain leaned forward so Miss Gatley could more easily tie the blindfold around his head. She took him to the center of the circle and spun him five times by the shoulders, then stepped back to take her place. He moved forward, coming directly at me, and when his hand rested on my arm, he smiled. "Drat. You are not a handsome young lady."

I couldn't help but laugh along with the rest of the room.

"You must guess," Mrs. Hutton said.

"Bradwell?"

"Well done!" Miss Gatley said.

He lifted the blindfold and handed it to me. I had feared for a moment he was going to call me Moorington simply to have another chance to seek out Marianne, but he surprised me.

I took the blindfold from his outstretched hand. "You do not wish to tie it on for me?"

Neal laughed and took his place back in the circle beside Miss Gatley.

"I can help you," Mrs. Hutton said, coming to my aid. She tied the blindfold and took me to the center of the room, then spun me five times. She had not tied it tightly enough, and if I looked down, I could see her shoes. The trouble was I didn't know which shoes belonged to whom.

Mrs. Hutton took her place, and I put my arms out, stepping cautiously until I came in contact with a sleeve. I looked down and recognized the shoes to be Mrs. Hutton's. I thought I had walked away from her? I gently tripped my fingers up her sleeve, making a thinking sound. "Miss Hutton?"

"Wrong," came a chorus of answers behind me. I dropped my hand and stepped back. Where had Marianne been in relation to her mother? I had thought she was to her mother's left, but only if Mrs. Hutton had returned to the same place. I moved in the direction I thought Marianne was and came upon another lady. A quick feel of her sleeve proved she was Lady Moorington.

"Miss Gatley?" I asked.

"Wrong!"

Marianne, where are you? I backed into what I believed was the center and pivoted. She had been standing directly across from Lady Moorington. I turned what I thought was a half circle and felt for her gently until my hands came in contact with a puffy sleeve. The bottom of the gown was white, the color of Marianne's evening gown. I gently trailed my fingers up her arms until I reached her jaw. Her skin was smooth beneath my fingers, and I was glad I had removed my gloves and left them at the table during our port.

I trailed my fingers gently over Marianne's cheekbones, feeling the slope of her nose and the perfect symmetry of her heart-shaped face. I could hear her breaths turning ragged and I swallowed the lump that had formed in my throat. "Miss Hutton?"

"Yes," she breathed. She reached up and lifted my blindfold. My hands dropped to my sides. Fire flamed in her eyes, sprouting hope in my chest. Surely she must feel something for me beyond that of a sibling relationship if the way she was looking at me now was any indication. I longed to pull her into my arms, and it appeared she would welcome the gesture most ardently.

She blinked, shaking her head a little and wearing a tremulous smile. "I suppose it is my turn."

I took the blindfold from her and put it around her eyes, tying it in the back, then led her by the arms to the center of the circle. I spun her five times, and the room felt like deafening silence. I was loath to release her, but what choice did I have? We were under scrutiny from all angles.

My hands slipped from her shoulders, and I took my place

back in the circle. She started forward until she reached Lady Moorington and guessed the woman's identity immediately. When I glanced up and caught Mrs. Hutton's gaze, she was watching me, her eyes warm.

I looked away quickly, but not before I had registered what I was seeing there. She wanted a love match for her daughter, and judging by the interaction she had just witnessed, she believed she had found it.

I had to agree with her on one side. I did not want any other woman in my life. I wanted Marianne. But what if Marianne did not want me?

The game continued for a little while longer before turning into charades. My mind was so filled with Marianne, it failed to decipher any of the riddles. It was well past midnight when we separated for bed, and Marianne approached me.

"I wondered if you had any interest in seeing the library tomorrow, Mr. Bradwell? There are a few of my father's books I thought might interest you."

"I should like that very much."

"Good. I will take you there after breakfast. You can disregard my previous idea." She looked at my waistcoat pocket with meaning until I nodded.

When I reached my room, I pulled the note from my pocket and unfolded it.

Meet me at the willow tree beside the lake tonight. Midnight?

Well, blast. Had she changed her mind about meeting outside because we were already past midnight, or because my behavior during the game had put her off me? I tossed the note into the fire so it wouldn't be found and scrubbed a hand over my face.

Enough of this back and forth. Tomorrow I would swallow my reservations, bury my fears, and tell Marianne how I felt.

CHAPTER 22
MARIANNE

My breakfast plate glowed in the morning light streaming through the large open windows. Lord Moorington sat across from me, Henry beside him. We made an odd group for breakfast, but the gentlemen carried the conversation well enough.

"My wife is beside herself," Lord Moorington said, spearing a sausage and cutting it in half with more force than necessary. He chewed somewhat angrily. He'd found a pair of willing ears to vent his frustrations to, and he was using us to full advantage. "I care for Daniel, of course, but the way he causes her to worry does give me reason to wish I had the authority to box his ears."

"I do not imagine Daniel would accept a punishment such as that. At least not easily," Henry said.

"Indeed, or I would have thrashed the lad already." Lord Moorington's slight smile belied the gravity of his words, and I doubted very much he would thrash his stepson. He probably did wish to knock sense into the man, though. None of us had enjoyed watching the countess's disappointment grow with each day her son failed to arrive.

"Do you think Daniel will join us at all?" I asked.

"I should hope so. We will pray for a late arrival instead of no arrival at all."

Henry sipped his tea and placed the cup back on the saucer. "Do you recall when we first met, my lord? You were attending a house party at Lady Moorington's house—back when she was still Mrs. Palmer, I believe."

"I do," he said, his round cheeks ruddy. "The Thurstons' carriage had trouble and you let them take refuge in your hunting box while they waited for the carriage to be fixed."

"Yes. Perhaps something like that has befallen Daniel?"

Lord Moorington grimaced. "I do not think a single man traveling in the summer can find himself in quite the same trouble as a family traveling in the snow. But I thank you for the perspective, son. I will do my best to reserve my anger for when it is warranted." He pushed his chair away from the table and stood. "I must see to it that Lady Moorington has received her breakfast." He gave us a sad smile and left.

We ate quietly, listening to his footsteps recede down the corridor. When he was gone, I emptied my teacup and set it on the table. "Are you ready to see the library?"

Henry raised his gaze to me, and it held a warmth, deepening the blue of his eyes. I would have been nervous, but something about his expression put me at ease. We started toward the library.

"Perhaps I said the wrong thing to the earl," Henry said. "He seemed only to want someone to agree with him."

"I cannot think offering the benefit of the doubt is ever in a bad taste."

"We shall hope that Daniel proves me right, then?"

"For Lady Moorington's sake, I do hope so." We reached the library, and I pushed the door wide open, leaving it like that. I stepped inside and crossed to the windows, sliding open the drapes to let sunlight stream inside and highlight the swirling, disturbed dust.

"What a haven," Henry said reverently.

"I knew you would understand."

Long bookcases lined the walls. A narrow ladder attached to a brass rod across the top to make it possible to reach the higher shelves. It was not a large room by any means, but it was packed full of books from the floor to the ceiling.

"Is your father an intellectual?" he asked.

"You would not think so after spending the entire day yesterday with him outside enjoying athletic pursuits, but yes, he has always been fond of reading. He merely has self-control with books, which I did not inherit from him."

"But you did inherit a love of libraries." Henry walked along the shelves, reading the spines as he moved. "I recall the one in your London townhouse to be just as beautifully curated."

"Papa takes great pride in his libraries, but they are personal to him. You will never hear him boast of his books or exhibit them the way he does fishing or his hounds or his horses."

"You praise his love of books, yet you do not believe he would support you in your own pursuits of publishing?" he asked, his attention on the shelves.

I shrugged. "He does not believe women should write, and he does not read novels written by female authors. He has purchased some for me indulgently, but he will not read them himself."

Henry stopped perusing the shelves and looked at me. "That is why you do not want to ask him for help in securing a publisher."

"That is why I asked you. You did not seem to have any problem with a woman writing a book."

"It is true, I did not. I hold no prejudice against female writers."

The lack of levity to his tone made me nervous for a reason I could not identify. I cleared my throat. "When do you think you will receive word from the publishers you've written to?"

"It could be any day now, depending on where they direct the replies. I am surprised I have not received any letters already, but I understand sometimes these decisions take time. Not everyone is willing to take a chance on an unknown, even if she comes highly recommended."

"But you were willing," I said.

He stepped away from the shelves and rested his hands behind his back. "Indeed. I have never thought intellectual pursuits were for men alone. My mother is a brilliant woman, even if she is not a devout reader, and the conversations I have had with my sister-in-law are some of the best intellectual discussions I've participated in."

Could the man be any more perfect? He stepped closer until he was at my side and looked through the window to the lake and the willow tree.

"You changed your mind last night," he said.

"It grew too late."

"I wondered what your reason was." His blue eyes were bright in the sunlight. "I hoped the hour had dissuaded you and not something else—something I said."

"You did not put me off the meeting. I will admit to growing a little wary, but it was the lateness of the hour and the fear that I was being presumptuous above all else."

"You cannot be too presumptuous with me," he said. "I think that would be impossible."

I drew in a breath. "That is a relief, because we have yet to speak about what happened at dinner the other night, and I think a conversation is in order."

"I wholeheartedly agree with you."

"Then shall we meet tonight at the willow tree?"

"Or we can speak now." He dipped his head. "Do not make me wait an entire day, Mari. I do not think I can bear it."

I scoffed lightly. "*You* cannot bear it? I have been an absolute mess of nerves since the engagement announcement."

"Then tell me what I can do to put you at ease," he murmured.

"I suppose the unknown is the most frightening of all. I do not know how you feel about this arrangement, yet it seems to be progressing at an alarming rate. My mother wishes to plan an engagement ball."

"Then let her."

It was what I wanted to hear and simultaneously not enough. "Every step we take to solidify this engagement will make it more difficult to dissolve."

He stepped closer, bending his head to look in my eyes. His messy curls were swept away from his forehead, and I wanted to dig my fingers through them. If he drew any nearer, our chests would be touching. "What if I do not wish for it to be dissolved?"

My heart hammered. I tipped my chin so I could look up at him. "What do you mean?" My voice came out as a whisper, too afraid to voice the question loudly, to give it power.

He swallowed, and I watched his Adam's apple bob. "I enjoy your company, Marianne."

"I enjoy yours as well." But marriages were built on more than enjoying one another's company.

He watched me. "Yes, as a brother."

Had I said that? I believed I had only meant to put him at ease. The way he had traced my face during blind man's bluff last night, the way he spoke to me now, left no room for confusion. This man was attracted to me, at the very least, and I was certainly attracted to him.

"What if our engagement does not need to end?" he asked.

"You would like to forever remain promised to one another? I fail to see the benefit of such an agreement."

"No, you goose. I mean," he said, smiling, "what if we marry? We would be able to write together, to discuss books, to avoid Society if we so chose."

My pulse thrummed. He was everything I'd wanted in a husband, and he desired the very same things I did. Could a man be so perfect for me? Would that I could be so fortunate. "You paint a lovely image, Henry. I fear you are about to say something to ruin it."

"Why must I ruin it?"

"Because nothing ever works out so splendidly, does it?" Every time I had met a gentleman who seemed wonderful, I inevitably learned something that proved we would never suit. Even Captain Neal had an aversion to animals, giving me cause to believe we would never understand one another. Thus far, Henry had yet to reveal his flaw, his final requirement, the thing that would make his suit unattractive, or perhaps make him repulsed by me.

He took my hand gently in his, holding my gaze, and with those connections, my heart as well. "What if it can?"

My heart stalled, forgetting to beat—or perhaps beating so quickly it felt as though it had given up. He leaned closer, and I wondered briefly if I was about to be kissed when I felt my hand rising, and Henry pressed his lips to my knuckles. "I care for you, Marianne. I enjoy your company. And I do *not* in any way see you as a sister."

"I must now admit that I feel the same."

He stilled. "You are in earnest?"

"Yes. I in no way see you as a sister, either."

Henry laughed, and the tension dissipated instantly. His smile was just as glorious as his affection, and his eyes danced. "Please tell me you will not complete your thought there."

"No, I won't. In truth, I do not see you as a sibling in any form. I never have."

He held my hand to his chest, letting me feel its quick rise and fall. "Then you will permit me to tell you how ardently I esteem you? I want no other woman in my life, Marianne. I only want you."

Heat flooded my chest, and I pressed my other palm to Henry's heart. It beat rapidly, giving me a pulse of confidence. His breathing grew rushed, and my lungs attempted to mimic his. Leaning up on tiptoe, I reached to press my lips to his—

A screech tore through the room and Henry pulled back quickly, shouting. "What the *devil*—"

A ball of gray fur caught my eye. "No, Mr. Darcy! Bad kitty!" I reached to pull the cat from Henry's leg, but his claws were out and he scratched my forearm.

"Are you hurt?" Henry asked.

"That hardly signifies! I do not know what has gotten into him." I crouched down and soothed my angry tone. "Mr. Darcy, come here now."

The cat looked at me. We all seemed to hold our breath for a moment before he released Henry's leg, climbed to the floor, and ambled to my side.

"What is it?" Mama said, rushing into the room, her chest heaving. She looked from me to Henry.

"Mr. Darcy attacked Henry," I said. Undoubtedly protecting my honor, though I did not add that bit of information.

"How odd." Mama looked at the cat with alarm. "He's never done such a thing before."

"Does he often spend time in the library?" Henry asked, bending to inspect his leg.

"In London he does. I did not know he'd found the library here."

Henry straightened. "Let me see your arm."

"It is only a scratch."

He took my forearm and turned it, inspecting the long, red mark. "You ought to have that wrapped."

"It will heal."

Mama reached us. "I apologize, Mr. Bradwell. It is unlike Mr. Darcy. He has never attacked anyone before."

Though, in Mr. Darcy's defense, I had never tried to kiss another man in front of him, either.

Henry eyed the cat warily. "I forgive him. Perhaps he only needs to grow accustomed to me."

"Perhaps," I said, though I was not convinced. Was this to be our future? My cat attacking each time Henry tried to draw close to me?

"That will happen in time," Mama said. "While I have you both, can I receive your opinions? I want to send invitations out today for the ball. Mr. Bradwell, do you think your mother would like an invitation?"

"I think it would give her a great shock. Perhaps I should ride home and deliver it myself."

"Must you?" I asked, the words slipping through my lips without consent.

He looked down at me, and I could not mistake the affection there. "I think I must. My mother deserves to hear this from me. Perhaps I can persuade her to join us here. I do not think it will take me above two days to reach Chelton."

"Likely not." Mama's brow pinched. "We can change the date of the ball if that is easier for you, Mr. Bradwell."

"Please, you must call me Henry. We are to be family, after all."

She nodded.

"The date you selected will be perfectly fine. I will return in five days at the most, and I hope to bring my mother with me."

"You will extend the invitation to your entire household, I hope?"

"Benedict and Thea are enjoying their honeymoon now, but I

will be certain to include everyone in the invitation." He wiped his hand down his waistcoat. "If you will excuse me, I must pack my things. It would be best if I was on my way shortly."

"Of course," Mama said, stepping back to let him pass.

Henry gave me a briefly searching look. "I would enjoy having a new book to read on the journey. Could I take the one you recently finished?"

He wanted to read my manuscript? No. He couldn't. Not yet. I was still deciding whether or not it was ready to be consumed by another person. That person could not be someone whose opinion I cared for so deeply. "I do not think it is ready."

He gave a nod, but disappointment flashed in his eyes. "Very well. I do hope you will trust me with it someday."

"Someday," I said quietly, guilt slithering through me.

Henry bowed softly to each of us before leaving the room.

Mama took my arm and inspected the scratch. If she thought our conversation was odd, she kept it to herself. "Do you need a plaster for it?"

"No. It will heal."

She dropped my arm. "Did I interrupt a moment?"

"Mr. Darcy interrupted a moment," I muttered. "*You* made Henry leave the estate entirely."

"To bring his family here. If he is going to tell his mother of you, I think you can safely believe he is smitten, darling."

"You doubted him?" I asked, searching the shelves for my blasted cat.

"Not anymore." Mama moved to leave but stopped at the door. "When you are finished here, will you come to the morning room and help me address invitations?"

"Of course."

She hesitated. "For what it is worth, I am sorry for chasing him away."

"It is not your fault."

She left the room, and I located Mr. Darcy and gave him a

quiet scolding. "You will learn to love him, because otherwise you will no longer be permitted into the house."

Meow?

I rolled my eyes and picked up my cat, petting his back as I made my way upstairs. "My arm does not feel nice, you know."

Meow.

The worst part was that I didn't even get my kiss.

CHAPTER 23

HENRY

The trip home to Chelton was far too fast for my liking. I would have enjoyed an extra two days in the saddle merely to allow more time to determine what I would say to my family. I was generally a quiet man, and this news was bound to inspire a mountain of questions.

Our large family estate came into view in front of me as the sun descended behind me, the world falling into darkness. My chest soothed and tightened in tandem. It always did my heart good to return to Chelton, but the task ahead of me made this a bittersweet arrival. I left my horse in the stable and crossed the gravel drive to the back door. I should have cleaned my face at least before going in search of my mother, but I knew her well. She would want to know of my arrival the moment it occurred.

I found my family in the drawing room. James and Felicity were deep in a game of chess and Mother sat on the sofa nearby, speaking to them. She looked up, and her eyes widened when they fell upon me. "Henry?"

I gave a small tip of my head. "Good evening, Mother."

She came toward me with her hand out. "We did not know to expect you."

I laid a kiss over her knuckles. "You won't wish to come any closer. I have been in the saddle for two days."

Mother smiled indulgently.

"Only two days?" James asked. "Where did you come from?"

"A house party."

James laughed, then seemed to sense that I was serious. "Gads, a house party? You?"

"It is astonishing how popular a Bradwell man can become when his brothers are both newly married."

Felicity moved a piece on the chessboard, then leaned back and watched me with a discerning eye. "We were with you in London a few months ago, if you recall. I remember the mamas who trailed after you, and Ben was not married yet. Do not underestimate yourself."

"It is nice to see you as well, Felicity."

She grinned. "Welcome home. Actually, your timing is lovely because I've recently acquired a new book I think you will enjoy. Have you read the latest Dalton Henry novel?"

My stomach twisted uncomfortably. "I have. Either way, I'm afraid I'll have no time for reading. This is a brief call."

Mother took her seat on the sofa again. "Whatever for?"

With their three sets of eyes watching me curiously, I found the words more difficult to choose. Declaring my feelings for Marianne had been frightening and took a great deal of bravery, but even that seemed easier than announcing to my family I had fallen in love.

My heart pulsed, jumping erratically at the thought. Love? That was what I attributed to Marianne. I wanted to be at Hutton House, and I was eager to introduce her to my mother. If nothing else so far proved my feelings, these impulses certainly did.

"You are beginning to make me nervous," Mother said.

I shook off my rambling, distracting thoughts and straightened my shoulders. "I am engaged."

The room was so quiet I could have dropped my handkerchief and I would have heard it hit the floor.

"You?" James asked. "Engaged?"

"That is not what surprises me, but I am astonished at the speed." Felicity shook her head. "Not that I am one to judge the swiftness of an engagement, but it is shocking."

I smiled. "I was not found alone in the library with her, so you needn't fear." I paused. "Well, we *were* found alone in the library, but that was after we were engaged."

My mother had remained silent through this but seemed to regain her bearings. "Who is the woman?"

I faced her. "Marianne Hutton. The youngest Hutton girl."

"Yes, I know who Marianne is." Mother sat on the edge of her sofa, her brows lifted. "She was still carrying around a doll when last I saw her."

"I think we need to hear more about this library incident," James said, grinning.

I leaned forward, bracing my arms on the back of the sofa. "I think I will retire for the evening before I drop to sleep in this very room."

"How unkind to leave such information with us and then run away," James said, nearly pouting.

Was it unkind? I was only tired. I rubbed a hand over my eyes. "What would you like to know?"

Mother watched me closely. "How did you meet her?"

"She is a Hutton, Mother. I have known her most of my life."

"We saw her in the park," James said. "While we were still in Town. That had not been the first time you'd seen her recently, if I took your measure correctly."

If I was not careful, I would be required to explain our run-in at the publisher's office, and that was not something I cared to tell them. Each of my family members watched me with interest, their expressions open and curious, but in no way disapproving. I could tell them anything now, for I had their full

215

attention. It would be so simple to speak to Felicity. *About that author you wished to share with me, Dalton Henry, I must confess . . .*

My heart thundered, my hands growing shaky. I glanced to the mantel and could envision Father standing there, watching us with curiosity, observing this conversation. Telling Mother and James of my books would be akin to telling Father, and I did not know how to live through becoming such a disappointment to them all.

The silence began to stretch too long. I blinked, directing my attention to James again. "We became reacquainted in Town. When I returned after Ben's wedding, I escorted her to the opera and various drives in the park, as a gentleman does when he is courting a young lady."

"Yes, but you must own that we did not expect this from you."

"I did not expect it of me either."

"For what it's worth," Felicity said, "I had my suspicions. I did not think you would return to London so soon without purpose."

"But London is not a two-day ride from Chelton. Whose house party were you attending?" James asked.

"The Huttons'. We made our engagement plain to the party, and Mrs. Hutton would like to throw an engagement ball." I looked at my mother and saw the lines tighten around her eyes. "I was hoping you would be there, but I do understand—"

"I will come."

The entirety of the room was silent again. I tried to read my mother's expression, but I failed to interpret it. "We can have another ball here and introduce Marianne to Bakewell society."

"No. I will come. Two days of travel, you said?"

"Or longer, if you want to take a slower pace."

"Two days is all I think I could manage. When must we leave?"

I looked at James, but he shrugged. My mother had not traveled anywhere in years. It was a great burden on her—she could hardly make it to the nearest village without losing the contents of her stomach. She grew inordinately ill, and I hated to put her in that position. But if she chose to accompany me, I would not pretend to be disappointed, either.

"Will one day of preparation be enough? We can leave the day after next."

Mother nodded. "That will be sufficient."

"In that case, I am off to bed." I circled the sofa and took my mother's hand, pressing a kiss to the back of it. "Thank you."

She smiled sweetly, but I could see the nerves displayed in fine wrinkles on her forehead.

I took myself up to my room. It held a chill despite the fire freshly blazing in the hearth. My small satchel was waiting on the chest against the wall, and I opened it and removed my sleep shirt. The servants at Chelton were efficient, and it was very clear why I'd had no notion of how to clean the mud from my clothes. How absurd that I should have thought myself capable.

Though I would never complain about that night with Marianne or the events it led to. Had I not met her down in the kitchen then, we might not have become engaged.

By the time I was ready for bed and nestled in my chilly blankets, I lay awake, my eyes alert. A story idea had bounced around in my mind since the moment Mr. Darcy had attacked me and saved Marianne from a premature kiss. It plagued me now, nudging like a battering ram to my brain.

I slid out of bed, lit a candle from the burning fire, and carried it to my writing desk. Everything was as I had left it, so it only took a minute to prepare all the things I would need— quill, knife, inkstand, paper.

I cut the tip of the feather so it would be fresh and dipped it in the ink. Without thinking, I pressed the quill to the paper and began to write.

The sun had nearly reached its zenith when my eyes opened the next day. It had nearly been sunrise when I finally put away the manuscript pages and went to sleep. I could not help it. The story had flowed from my quill with the smooth tranquility of the river that ran in front of our house. My neck burned when I recalled the nature of the story, but I vowed to never show it to another living soul.

I had never intended on writing a romantic story, but it was streaming through my ink, and I did not intend to stop it. I was eager to return to my desk now, but my mother was likely waiting with a dozen questions about the nature of my relationship with Marianne and how it had reached an engagement.

I dressed quickly, missing Felton. I'd not heard from him since his departure in London, and I hoped all was well with his father. I tucked my newly written pages in the desk drawer before I went down for breakfast.

It was well past breakfast time, but a tray was sent for me, and I went in search of my mother, locating her in the parlor with Felicity. They sat at the round table, a handful of papers spread out between them. The image looked all too familiar.

"The benefit of having three sons married within a year is that I already have my list made up of who ought to be notified," Mother said. "We only need to adjust it slightly."

I pulled out the chair across from them and sat. "So I have done you a favor in the expeditious nature of my engagement."

"Hmm." She looked at the clock on the mantel. "Did you sleep well?"

"As a matter of fact, I did. Once I managed to fall asleep, that is. I thought you would be packing."

"The maids are doing that for me. Does Mrs. Hutton expect me to join you?"

"She made me promise to extend the invitation to the

entirety of our household. She would like you to remain at Hutton House for as long as you are comfortable." I looked at Felicity. "All of you."

My sister-in-law smiled. "That will be wonderful. Marianne is a friend of mine, and I look forward to renewing our acquaintance."

"She is not the only person of note at Hutton House currently. Your aunt is there with her new husband."

Felicity looked up from the list she'd been perusing. "Lord and Lady Moorington?"

"Indeed, Daniel is meant to be there also, but he had not yet arrived when I left."

She laughed. "A house party in which his mother is in attendance? I think it will be a miracle if he arrives at all."

I had begun to wonder the same thing. "Will you and James join us?"

"We would be happy to. Shall we finalize this list first?" She turned the sheets of paper around so I could read them.

So many names numbered the pages, they blurred before me, growing overwhelming. I spun the pages back around toward the women. "I will leave these things to you and Marianne to decide. I care for nothing but the bride."

Felicity grinned.

I cleared my throat. "Where is James?"

"Riding," Mother said, dipping her quill to add another name to the bottom of the page.

I stood as a footman carried the tray inside and set it on the table. I took a slice of bread and chunk of cold ham from the plate and smiled. "I think I will go find him. Good day, ladies." I dipped my head, then tore a bite from the bread as I left the room.

It was easy to find James racing down his favorite hill, and pushing my horse to a gallop in order to catch up with him was an invigorating bit of exercise.

"Marriage then, eh?" James asked when I pulled up beside him. We kicked the horses up the hill at a walk. The sun beat down on our backs, and the breeze was fresh.

"I love her."

He sent me an affectionate smile, one typically reserved for when we greeted each other after extremely long absences. "Love will change you, Hen."

"For the better?" My writing had already suffered such a change. I hoped *that* particular alteration was temporary, though.

"If she is already giving you the desire to be a better man, then she is the one for you."

"Our entire relationship has been nothing but Marianne helping me to improve." I rubbed the back of my neck, scared to voice aloud the thing that had silently plagued me since Marianne refused to allow me to read her novel. I'd understood her hesitation before, but after I had declared my feelings for her, I'd expected that to change. I tried not to give the concern any consequence, but I did not know how to accept that she could love me while failing to be vulnerable with me.

"What is it?" James asked. "I can see something is bothering you."

"I am not sure she trusts me."

James's dark brow bent into a frown, and he pulled his horse to a stop. I turned around and slowed so I could rest beside him. We had reached the top of the hill, so we looked out over the countryside, our home, and the river that ran past it beneath a stone bridge.

"What makes you believe that? Trust is an important part of marriage."

"I believe she values me well enough. Indeed, she knows I have my uses."

James's eyebrows rose. "Perhaps I do not want to hear the details of your library incident, after all."

I chuckled. "It is not like that. I have yet to kiss the woman."

James was quiet for a moment. "You've not kissed her, yet you are engaged?"

I lifted one eyebrow at my brother. "Did you kiss Felicity prior to your engagement?"

"No." His lips flattened. "I did not kiss her until we were married. Carry on."

"Marianne has helped me with numerous things, but every time I offer my assistance, she hesitates, and fails to allow me to return the help."

"She must care for you if she accepted your proposal."

"We were forced into it." I held the reins with one hand and rubbed the back of my neck with the other. "I offered to carry full responsibility for a dissolvement if that was what she wished. She chose to marry me."

"Miss Hutton cares for you, then, but you fear she is afraid to trust you."

"Evidently."

"Do you recall when Benedict was in a similar situation and you offered him advice?"

I straightened in the saddle. My horse was growing antsy, but I didn't allow it. I cast my mind back to a few months previous when we were in London together.

"He did not know how to prove he was worthy of Thea, and you told him to let her win, to be patient, to trust in her affection for him. You cannot force Miss Hutton to trust you, but perhaps you can prove you are worthy of it. Either way, you need to be patient."

He referred to an entirely different situation, but the principles applied. "I think you are correct, and that is what I need to do. But how do I accomplish it?"

"You've always been the wise one," James said, turning his horse back toward Chelton. "I am certain you will figure it out."

CHAPTER 24

MARIANNE

Tomorrow would mark a week since Henry had left us to travel to Chelton and tell his mother our news, and I was increasingly eager for his return. Nothing about our relationship felt real or settled to me, and his absence only exacerbated this foreign unease. To say nothing of the fact that with him gone, every activity we partook of seemed to be an opportunity for Miss Gatley to prove to Captain Neal I was an inferior specimen, and that he would do well to cast his eye in her direction.

To aid her in securing a husband and showing Captain Neal his visit to Hutton house was not entirely wasted, I allowed myself to bear the brunt of her antics.

Today's ruse was more difficult, however, for forcing me to feign a lack of skill where I typically excelled. In that sense, it was taking *more* skill for me to shoot terribly enough to score worse than Miss Gatley.

We were all gathered in the back garden. Mother had archery targets set up, and most of the guests opted to sit and watch with lemonade and tarts, but Miss Gatley, Captain Neal, and I stood with bows and arrows in the midst of a match.

I had a feeling Miss Gatley was pretending to be extraordinarily ignorant based on the way she required such extensive help from the captain. Since he didn't seem to mind, I vowed to quit being so annoyed on his behalf.

Miss Gatley lined up her arrow and pulled back the string. She idled in that position and looked at Captain Neal. "Like this?"

"Move your fingers up a bit—here, I'll show you." He adjusted her hold on the arrow, moving her wrist and lingering on her hand. Perhaps there was a budding romance between them after all.

She released the arrow, and it bumped into the target before falling to the grass below.

"That is an improvement! Thank you, Captain." She beamed up at him.

"I am happy to assist with your archery any time you wish," he said gallantly.

I was rather proud of myself for refraining from rolling my eyes.

Miss Gatley turned her gaze on me. "It is your turn now."

I stepped forward to take my shot. I needed three pitiful arrows if I wanted to score less than Miss Gatley—which I did want, very much. If I lost this round, Miss Gatley and Captain Neal would face one another, and I would be free to eat a tart and sit far enough away to avoid hearing their flirting.

I shot wide the first time, missing the target completely. I nocked my next arrow and gave a pitiful pull on the string, so it failed to reach the target.

"Oh, dear," Miss Gatley said. Was she worried my abysmal shooting would call upon Captain Neal for assistance?

I nocked the final arrow and pointed it too high, shooting quickly before the captain could come to the same conclusion. The arrow arched in the sky and fell straight down, lodging into the grass. I lowered my bow. "Drat. I suppose it is not my day for shooting well."

"Anymore, you mean?" Captain Neal asked, his discerning eye locked on me. "You shot rather well when you were practicing this morning."

A blush raced up my neck, and I could feel it warming my cheeks. I bent my head to hide my reddened face and focused on unfastening my leather wrist protector. "Good luck to you both."

After removing my archery equipment and placing it on the table, I took a glass of lemonade from my mother and drank it. The other two flirted more than they shot, and their round took an inordinate amount of time.

"They make a handsome couple," Lady Moorington said politely.

Mr. Gatley gave a grim smile. "If one approves of the navy."

"Do you not?" the earl asked.

Mr. Gatley gave a guttural sound. "I do not approve of my daughter having a husband who does not live in England."

Lady Moorington looked at the man in question. "Surely Captain Neal will not live on ships forever. For the time being, he can certainly take his wife with him."

"There is much money to be had in his line of work," Lord Moorington said. "Prize ships and whatnot."

"Perhaps, but Captain Neal has not found himself lucky in that regard, has he?" Mr. Gatley said with some bitterness.

I looked at my father, but he seemed to find more interest in his tarts than he did the conversation. Mama caught my eye and gave me a small shake of her head. It was best not to engage in such a vulgar topic as money from the war and prize ships, especially when we were discussing his daughter's prospects.

Happy to let the matter drop, I eagerly turned my thoughts to my book. I had rewritten a portion of the story in the last few days and only had a handful of pages left. It would soon be ready to provide to any publisher who responded to Henry favorably.

"This heat is growing to be too much for me," I said cautiously.

"You must be overly warm from standing in the sun so long, dear," Lady Moorington said, twisting her parasol above her head.

"Indeed. I think I will rest inside before dinner."

Mother shot me a smile, as if she knew resting was not foremost on my mind. I had developed a reputation in my home for sneaking away to read, but when no one spoke it aloud, it was much better. I'd rather pretend I did not prefer my fictional friends to the present company. "We will see you in a few hours, then."

I stood and dipped my head to the remaining party before walking into the house. I shot a glance at the archers over my shoulder and found Captain Neal watching me leave, Miss Gatley watching him. I slipped through the French doors and made my way to the library to obtain more ink, which my father kept in here. After retrieving a small bottle, I made my way toward my bedchamber.

I pulled up abruptly when I turned the corner and found a man waiting in the dimly lit corridor.

My eyes lit upon his azul waistcoat, disappointment settling in my stomach. In that brief moment before recognizing Captain Neal, I had hoped Henry returned to me. I placed a smile on my face. "Is there anything I can do for you?"

He rested his hands casually behind his back. "Are you unwell? I watched you leave, and it worried me."

"Only tired. I hoped to rest before dinner."

He glanced at the bottle of ink in my hands. "Do you intend to write a letter first?"

"I had some correspondence to see to, but I am not sure I'm up for it at present." I wished I had the ability to develop a yawn at will. I was afraid I looked much too awake and alert to sell my excuse of exhaustion.

He watched me for a moment longer, and I had a niggling feeling something was not quite right. What *was* he doing here? His chamber was down in the opposite wing.

I tried to make my voice sound light to hide my wariness. "Who won the competition?"

"You likely would have, had you remained."

"I was a miserable shot in the last round."

He took a step closer. "That was intentional, was it not?"

My cheeks started to warm again. "I do not know what you mean."

He gave me a smile, tilting his head to the side in a way that highlighted the bend in his once-broken nose. He knew I was fully aware of what he implied. "Miss Gatley is sweet-tempered and pretty enough, but we both know she was displaying a great deal of artifice. How are any of us to know who would have won if both of you had done your best?"

The edge to his words worried me. I tried to keep my tone light to balance it. "I think it is a common practice among women to dilute their skill in order to obtain the attention of a handsome gentleman. We are offered so few opportunities together. Can you blame Miss Gatley for making the most of any moment offered?"

I was not, in general, a supporter of falseness to capture a man, but I felt a kinship to Miss Gatley—likely due to the dilution of my own skill today—and could not allow her to be so maligned. She was merely trying to grow closer to Captain Neal. Where was the harm in that?

"Ah, and that is what confused me, Miss Hutton." He took another step closer, but I stood my ground. "Is that why you pretended to lack any skill at archery as well? To give me an opportunity to draw close to you?"

Where were all the servants, and why was the house so quiet? I gave a sharp laugh. How could the captain have interpreted my actions in such a way? It had not been a cry for attention, but the opposite. "No, of course not. I was doing my best to give you and Miss Gatley time together. I thought I was doing you both a favor."

Irritation flashed in his eyes. "The person I came to Hutton House for was not Miss Gatley."

I had hoped we would be able to avoid having this conversation. With Captain Neal's general apathy toward me since Henry had announced our engagement, I had believed that was possible. Evidently, he wanted to clear the air between us. I dragged in a sustaining breath. "I apologize. Had I any indication that I would . . . that things would turn out the way they did, I would have . . ."

What? Told him he wasn't needed at Hutton House? There was no proper way to end that sentence.

Captain Neal looked at me through narrowed eyes. "Is a marriage with Mr. Bradwell what you desire? Engagements can be broken."

A chill swept through me. "Indeed, when both parties wish it."

"Even when only one party wishes it, it is sometimes for the best. Generally the woman's reputation is not badly harmed when she is shortly married to another."

Good heavens. Was he implying what I thought he was?

Captain Neal took another step closer. He still held his hands behind his back. "If you desired it, you would not need to remain engaged—"

"I am afraid you've mistaken my meaning, Captain. I am pleased to be engaged to Mr. Bradwell. I am only sorry if it has caused you any grief, for that was not my intention. I did not know Mr. Bradwell would return my affection."

A muscle jumped in his jaw. "So you admit you cared for him before you left London?"

"That is not what I meant." I searched for something to say to lessen the brunt of my feelings. He was angry, and he had every right to dislike me, but to speak so aggressively was alarming. I tried to redirect the conversation. "Miss Gatley is lovely—"

"She is nothing but a fortune hunter."

That gave me a start. "That's impossible. Mr. Bradwell is not in possession of a fortune, and he was her intended beau."

"Perhaps you do not know him as well as you believe. Mr. Gatley has dug himself a hole and he is relying on his daughter to free him of it." He gave a small shake of his head. "Forgive me, Miss Hutton. That is not what I wished to discuss with you. I only wanted to inform you that you are not required to fulfill any obligation to Mr. Bradwell."

"I am . . . flattered, Captain."

"Flattery means little to me," he said quietly, a sharp edge to his voice that left me feeling cold. "You gave me reason to believe I would end this house party engaged. You further lifted my expectations with the note you left in my chamber." His voice dropped to a frightening whisper. "I hope you consider the implications of the situation before you make your final decision."

"That letter had not been—"

"You cannot change the narrative now, Miss Hutton. You have treated me poorly, and I expected more from you."

He walked away without giving me a chance to reply, his exit leaving me with equal parts concern and relief. It felt as though he'd stepped into my chamber, opened all drawers, trunks, and cupboards, then left again. Nothing was complete, shut away, or tied up neatly. It was an angry, dangling sentence without end.

I had given him cause to believe we could potentially find ourselves engaged, that was true. But to put such store in a possibility? He seemed to imply we had as good as made a declaration, which was not true. Was I required to honor his misassumptions? *Had* I given him leave to believe I was more settled on his suit than I'd realized? The note had been fairly condemning, but all I had written was that I was eager to further our acquaintance.

My eyes squeezed closed. I was not faultless in this situation. Though the note had not been meant for Captain Neal, he did not allow me to correct his assumption that it was. I should have corrected it straight away.

I went to my room and set up my ink stand, pulling out the pages so I could complete my final alterations. But I couldn't focus on the novel. Captain Neal's desperate attempt to break my engagement had ruined my equilibrium.

Mr. Darcy slipped off my bed and ambled toward me. His gray striped fur stood on end as he stretched, then lay flat again.

"Good day, sir. I did not know you were there."

He walked past my legs, drawing his tail down my shin.

The sound of everyone returning to the house traveled up the staircase and corridors to my room. Perhaps if I could not focus, I would find a quiet corner of the library to read instead.

I put away the manuscript, hiding it in the drawer, and looked out the window, surprised to find most of the party still gathered on the lawn—everyone except Captain Neal. If they were outside, who was making all the noise in the entryway? I picked up Mr. Darcy, cradling him to my chest, and stepped from my room to nearly collide with Mrs. Shaw as she walked by. I was startled to find her leading a small group of people, and I pulled too hard on my door handle, slamming it closed in surprise.

"Miss Hutton!" Mrs. Shaw said, grasping her chest.

Mr. Darcy leapt from my arms again, dashing away to find refuge elsewhere.

"I am beginning to think he is not fond of me," Henry said.

A smile spread over my lips. His voice brought a welcome infusion of warmth, and I couldn't help but grin at the sight of him disheveled from his travel and all the more handsome for it.

"Welcome back, Mr. Bradwell." I took in the remainder of

the party—James and Felicity, and a woman who must have been Mrs. Bradwell, her face an alarming shade of white. "Welcome to you all. Is there anything I can do for you?"

"I was showing them to their rooms, ma'am," Mrs. Shaw said. "They want to rest before dinner."

"Of course." I curtseyed while the housekeeper led them away, but Henry remained beside me.

He took my hand, squeezing my fingers softly. "Good day, Miss Hutton."

"It is now," I said.

Henry grinned, lifted my knuckles to lay a kiss on them, then left to follow his family and see them settled. My heart relaxed. Captain Neal's dissatisfaction aside, I did not regret my choice.

CHAPTER 25

MARIANNE

I did not see Henry again until we had all gathered for dinner. His mother was unwell and opted to take a tray in her room, but the rest of the party dined with us. After Henry's explanation of Mrs. Bradwell's carriage illness, I imagined she needed time to recover.

Mother had tables brought into the drawing room for whist after dinner and two games were made up. I sat with Julia—who felt well enough to join us in the drawing room once we finished eating—and Felicity on the sofa near the fire, choosing to forego whist so we could visit.

"We are pleased you could join us," I said to Felicity. Our friendship had been borne in ballrooms a few Seasons previous and from the mutual acquaintance of our mothers, but we had never been close enough to write. Now I hoped we could come to be like sisters, for she would soon become my sister-in-law.

"I'm not usually fond of social functions, but this was an invitation I could not refuse. It does my heart glad to see Henry has made a connection."

It did my heart glad as well, but that went without saying. "How has marriage suited you?"

Felicity glanced to where her husband was playing whist, teamed up with Henry. "It suits me very well. I highly recommend matrimony when one's husband is so kind."

Julia shifted on the cushion beside me. "Agreed, as I have said to my sister many times. Though it helps when you are in love."

"Then I think I shall quite enjoy it," I said, sneaking a look at Henry. He was so handsome, even with his smile subdued. His gaze flicked up and caught mine, and I was suddenly suspended, held in place.

"Yes, I think she is most definitely in love," Julia said, grinning.

My attention snapped away from Henry, and I tried not to blush.

Captain Neal entered the drawing room. I had not realized until that moment he never joined us after the gentlemen had had their port. Had he been packing his trunk? We might all be more comfortable if he chose to return early to London—or perhaps that was just me. After our troubling conversation in the corridor earlier, I felt uneasy around him. He had not been pleased since the moment my engagement was announced, but his mood seemed more erratic now, more dark, his frustration directed at me.

It was just my luck when he came to sit directly across from me on the other sofa. "Good evening, ladies."

"Are you interested in playing whist, Captain?" I asked. "One of the games will be finishing soon."

"Not this evening." He looked at the tables of players and back to me. "I have decided to keep my distance from a certain person, lest I give anyone a false expectation of my intentions."

It was a pointed comment. I straightened my shoulders. He could not make me feel worse for my behavior. Had I not already apologized?

"Indeed, I think it is best if I leave altogether." He held my gaze. "Do not try to dissuade me, for I have made up my mind. My man is already preparing my things for departure."

"I am sorry you'll be leaving us," Julia said. "Are you to return to your ship?"

"Not directly. I have other business that needs my attention first." He looked at me and away again.

Julia shot me a questioning smile. I was glad I wasn't alone in finding his behavior strange. Some men licked their wounds for so long after being rejected that they were only serving to worsen the injury. Captain Neal appeared to be one of those men.

The games of whist came to an end and the partners shuffled about. Felicity went to take Henry's place so she could partner with her husband, and Henry offered me his hand. "Would you like to play a game of chess with me?"

I did not wish to flaunt my engagement, so I subdued my smile. I'd not seen him in almost a week and dearly wished for some conversation. Captain Neal's eyes were glued to the fire, resolutely ignoring us.

"I would enjoy that, Mr. Bradwell. Thank you." I allowed him to help me rise, then reclaimed my hand.

We moved to the chess table, which was blessedly at the opposite end of the room from whist, and took our seats, pulling the pieces from our drawers in order to set up the game.

"Was your travel comfortable?" I asked.

"For everyone except my mother, yes."

"I admit, it was a great surprise to see her."

"It was an even greater surprise when she expressed her desire to join me on my return journey. I cannot say I am upset, even if I do not know her chief motives. She has not left Chelton in some years. I think being with some of her old friends will do her good."

Henry had given me the white side of the board, so I moved

my pawn. "And the reception of your news? How did they take it?"

"Thrilled, as expected. My mother was more difficult to read, but if I am happy, she will be happy." He dipped his chin and looked at me. "I *am* happy."

A smile spread over my lips that I could not dim, regardless of my efforts. "Do not cause me to smile."

"Whyever not?" he asked, laughing.

I tempered my joy—or at least I attempted to make it less visible. "I do not wish to parade our happiness in front of Captain Neal. He is very unhappy with the way this house party has ended for him."

Henry looked over at the sofa, his brow furrowing. "Has he spoken to you about it?"

I felt a moment's temptation to share the thread of fear Captain Neal had sewn in my gut. But he would be leaving shortly, as he had mentioned, and his dissatisfaction was no cause for true alarm. "A conversation was needed, and it was had."

All levity left his expression. "Nothing too inappropriate?"

"I think his pride has been wounded. He feels coming here was a waste of time, that I raised his expectations unnecessarily."

Henry sat back, crossing his arms over his chest. It was not a posture I had seen from him often. His expression was thoughtful and the position amplified the muscle on his arms I had seldom seen.

"Cease your displeasure," I said. "If anything, he has just cause for feeling that way after being duped."

"No one has been duped."

"Was that not what we set out to do from the beginning?"

He gave a flicker of a smile. "I suppose that's a fair assessment, but your injury to Neal was not intentional, and very slight in my opinion." He leaned forward and moved a pawn.

"Now, speaking of what we set out to do from the beginning, you will be pleased to learn I have heard back from one publisher. The letter was waiting in my room when I returned."

My heart raced. His smile indicated he had heard good things. "What did they say?"

"I think you ought to wait and see if Johansson replies before we write back to this publisher, but if they do not, then this will be a good option. They are very interested to see what you have."

I beamed. "You've done it."

"Not quite, but we are one step closer." He cleared his throat and dropped his gaze to the chess pieces. "It would be easier for me to sell the manuscript if I had read it."

Fear coiled in my belly.

His attention remained on the game. "You need not allow me to, of course, but I greatly wish to. I vow it will in no way alter our arrangement. When I find it to be so wonderful that it shall put me out of business, I will still proceed to sell it."

I gave a soft chuckle, but still I felt wary. It was one thing to deliver it to an unknown publisher, but to have someone read it whom I knew personally? Whom I cared about? His rejection would be a deeper wound than I was prepared for. I moved a piece on the chessboard merely to give myself something to do. Had it been a white or a black piece? I did not know.

"You need not decide now."

"It is frightening, Henry. What if you hate it? What if you think I am a silly girl for writing a love story. What if—"

"Then I am a silly girl, too, for I have been writing a love story of my own."

I scoffed. "If you are referring to the pirate tale I have been assisting you with, I do not think you can truthfully call that a story about love."

"No. I know very well it is not. I fear the entire novel needs to find its way to the fire." He cleared his throat and moved a pawn. "I refer to a new story I've begun."

"You have not," I said, disbelieving.

"Indeed, I have."

"May I read it?"

He lifted his gaze. "May I read yours?"

Stalemate.

Henry leaned closer. "If you cannot trust me with this, how can you trust me in anything?"

He was right to ask, but it was still daunting. "It is frightening to make myself so vulnerable."

"I understand. I have done the same. In fact, I repeatedly make myself vulnerable while you pick apart every page I give you."

I laughed quietly, but there was no humor in the sound. "That is unfair. I had no such criticisms for the first version of the novel I read. Part of me wonders if the criticisms are easy to find, because I think it was perfect in its original state."

He gave me a boyish smile. "Sometimes I wonder if you say those things with the express purpose of puffing me up."

"Trust me, that was never the case. I deeply wanted to despise your writing in the beginning. I was vastly disappointed to discover how very talented you are."

Henry let out a loud from-the-belly laugh, gathering attention from others in the room. I glanced over and found Captain Neal watching us, irritation splashed across his face. It was not kind to display my relationship in such a forward manner. There would be plenty of time for laughter after he left tomorrow. I leaned back in my chair and subdued my tone. "I am glad you returned, Henry."

He looked up from the knight pinched between his fingers. "As am I."

CHAPTER 26

HENRY

Marianne lost the game. It was not difficult to see why, when she paid no attention to what she moved or where it went. Once she moved my rook, and I had to put it back and tell her to go again.

"I think I will go to sleep," she said.

"Sleep?" I questioned.

She gave a guilty smile that didn't seem in the least bit earnest. "I've nearly finished with my alterations. Will you bring me more pages now that you've returned?"

Would I? I didn't know if it was worth the effort anymore. I agreed with Marianne—my pirate story was much better before I had tried to change it. "I'm half-tempted to cease rewriting that awful story altogether."

"It is not awful," she said, her voice high. "Neither do I think it is doing what you want it to."

I agreed with her. It had been a struggle to write and had taken far more consideration to add the romantic storyline. I should have listened to my heart instead of my brain and put my foot down with Marbury.

"Good night, Miss Hutton. I hope you will trust me soon."

She gave me a funny look, mostly guilt and nervousness, then curtsied and left for bed, her mother close behind her.

Lord and Lady Moorington had already gone up to sleep. Mr. Hutton and Mr. Gatley stayed at their table with glasses of amber liquid on the other side of the room. I had moved to sit beside my brother on the sofa when a servant came in and gave a note to Captain Neal. He unfolded the paper, reading it quickly before shoving it in his pocket. The strange thing was that it had not been sealed, so it must have come from someone in the house.

Who would be writing him a note? I looked over my shoulder and found Miss Gatley on the sofa beside Felicity, chatting about London.

Surely Marianne had not sent the note. But it would be like her to apologize, and she had never been averse to sending me notes.

A thread of inky black jealousy coerced its way through my stomach, and I moved to push it out. How absurd. I had only just been speaking to her about our relationship, and I was fairly confident in it.

Captain Neal stood. "I will take my leave of you all now, for I will be gone when you wake."

Miss Gatley looked up quickly. "You're leaving us?"

"Unfortunately, yes." With barely a smile in her direction, he strode from the room.

The room grew heavy, and the rest of the occupants left shortly after, until only James and I remained.

"Do you want me to leave as well so you can go find a book?" James asked.

I rubbed a hand over my forehead. "I do enjoy your company more than reading, you know."

"Sometimes?"

I grinned. "Sometimes."

He poured us both a glass of brandy from the cart and

handed one to me. "You did not tell me the Gatleys were here. I had to discover that at dinner."

"I did not realize it was worth noting."

"The man tried to push his daughter at Benedict just a few months ago, but I ended his efforts before it could become a problem." He swirled his glass, taking a sip.

"I thought you were on friendly terms with him."

James looked up. "Friendly? That isn't quite right. He had too many questions about Chelton and who inherited Sedwick Lodge. I did not reveal anything. It was all too imposing, but I thought we were rid of him."

"Is he trouble? It was suggested to me he was a fortune hunter."

"That might be a safe assessment. He'd known far too much about our family, and when I complained about it to my valet, he told me Gatley's servant had been asking too many questions."

So Gatley used his servants to gather information. He could not have done so about me, surely? Felton was not even here. Though I'd seen firsthand how people spoke too freely, forgetting who might be listening while they attended to their chores. "Do you think Captain Neal has been warned?"

"If he's leaving in the morning, it hardly matters."

We both emptied our glasses, and James set his on the small table at the end of the sofa. "Any progress with your Miss Hutton?"

"As far as obtaining her trust? Not yet."

James lowered his voice. "Your conversation looked serious."

"I had hoped we were making inroads, but we shall see. As loath as I am to admit it, I think your advice to have patience is the most applicable. But it is deuced difficult."

James grinned. "My advice is always applicable. Speaking of your upcoming marriage, have you made any plans for how you intend to provide for your wife? Are you to live at Sedwick?"

"I believe so. The house is a little out of the way, but it will suit us both very well."

"There isn't much good soil unless you clear part of the trees." He leaned back, lost in thought. "I do not know how you can use the property to turn a profit otherwise. Do you have any interest in sheep?"

This would have been a conversation with my father, had he been here. It was only natural for James to mention it, but I didn't know how to tell him that he need not worry for my finances. "I have a little money put by, so I am not entirely concerned with that dilemma."

"Money? From what?" His face cleared. "Oh, when you sold out? I did not consider that. Are you considering joining the army again?"

Guilt crept into my chest. He had never outright asked me this before, and usually when the conversation strayed to my plans for the future, I was able to bring it round to something else. But the other day, when I had simply told Marianne how I felt instead of putting it off and hiding behind my nerves, I had felt a burden lift from my shoulders. Perhaps plain speaking now would lift a similar burden.

"No, I have no plans to return. I . . . in all honesty, I did not care for it. I know Mother has always wanted me to consider returning, but I do not think I can."

"Mother? Are you joking?" James shook his head. "She would be thrilled to hear you are done with the military for good."

Shock ripple through my stomach. "What do you mean?"

"It is a dangerous occupation. Mother would be happy if we all remained in Chelton for the rest of our days, wives and all. She does not want you on the Continent."

A smile flickered on my lips, because I could see the truth in his words. "But the family name—"

"Yes, yes, the all-important family name. It has caused too

much grief in my life. I have given this a great deal of thought in the last year, coming to the conclusion that we can respect the legacy left for us while also creating a new one for our children." He rubbed his chin. "You know, I always wanted to join the army too, but Father wouldn't allow it. He said one son is enough, and even then, he struggled to approve of your joining up directly out of Eton."

My body froze. The blood ceased pumping, my heart ceased beating. I could not believe what I was hearing. "We cannot be remembering the same man."

"We are. He was proud of the army and proud of his accomplishments, but I think it was a relief only one son followed in his footsteps."

I did not know how to take this skewed opinion of my father. It certainly wasn't what I thought. "You weren't there, James."

Soberness fell over his expression, leaching into the rest of the room. "No I wasn't, even though I wanted to be. I'll never understand what you went through."

He'd *wanted* to join the army? "I thought I had saved you from such a fate."

"You were doing me a favor, but I didn't think so at the time. I was forced to remain in university while you got to go off and fight the frogs."

"There was no glory in war." I swallowed the lump in my throat. "Father was glad to have me there. He introduced me to dozens of men. His *military son*, his *legacy*."

"Yet you sold out?"

"When he was no longer there, I had no reason to remain. He was not alive to be disappointed in my choice."

The silence in the room was heavy and thick. "You've carried his disappointment with you ever since, have you not?"

I looked up sharply. "Am I that obvious?"

"No. To be honest, I thought you never wanted to speak

about it because of the awful things you had witnessed. Now I can see you couldn't bear to for other reasons."

"You are correct on both counts. Since coming home, I have found refuge in stories and worlds of make-believe. I'm not plagued with awful nightmares, as some of my friends have been, but the evils of war do not leave anyone without scars."

He looked enlightened. "Which is why you read so often?"

"Yes." I swallowed. "Read . . . and write."

It was quiet, my pulse thudding in my ears. It made me nervous to admit the truth, but I needed to be honest with James. If I could not speak the truth to my family, how could I expect Marianne to be so vulnerable with me?

He narrowed his eyes. "Writing? Like Byron?"

"I am not a poet. I write novels."

"When? How?"

"With a quill. Often in the library."

He leaned back, appraising me. "All that time you spend reading isn't really reading?"

"Much of it is, but not all."

He gave me an appraising look. "Well, are they any good?"

"Felicity seems to think so."

James looked wounded. "You have told my wife, yet you haven't told me?"

"No." I grimaced. "She tried to recommend one of my own books to me when I arrived at Chelton."

His wounded expression shifted to shock. "You are *published* and you did not think to tell us?"

"I did not know how it would be received, and then the books did so well. Time passed, and there never seemed to be a good moment for it."

James's dark eyebrows drew together. "You could have trusted us."

"It is not about trust. It is about the anxiety that accompanied even just the thought of having this conversation. I knew I would have to admit I was never returning to the army when I explained my chosen occupation. I was afraid to do that."

"There are other ways of honoring our family name, Henry. You do not have to do it the same way Father did. I think the way you are doing it now is wonderful."

I cringed. "Yes, well, I have not used my real name on my published books, so I am not truly leaving a Bradwell legacy through the novels, either."

"What do you publish under?"

"Dalton Henry."

James laughed. "In a sense you still honored your name."

I felt lighter, as though I'd tossed another boulder from my shoulder, just as I had thought. He'd accepted my news so readily, and it was something of a relief—surprising as it was—to discover Father had worried for my safety. He had been proud of me, I know he had, but I wondered if he would be proud of my current accomplishments too. Like James said, I was still honoring my name but in a different way. I did not consider it that way before, but I saw it now.

I was tempted to tell him of Marianne's writing and how it connected us, but that was her secret to share. Perhaps I was due another conversation with her. Maybe in the kitchen later tonight, or the library . . . we were already engaged, and ever since Mr. Darcy had gotten in the way of our kiss, I had wanted to do little else.

Perhaps I would write her a clandestine note of my own.

CHAPTER 27
MARIANNE

I crossed my final T and put the quill away, leaning back in my seat and looking at the last page of my novel. I was truly finished, and I felt confident in the story. It wasn't *Pride and Prejudice* or *Evelina* by any means, but for those seeking a similar story, it would hold its own.

I waited for the ink to dry, then stacked the pages together. I wanted badly for Henry to read it and love it, but feared the opposite occurring. I knew he would hold up his end of our bargain regardless, but could he truly champion a work if he did not believe in it?

How would I ever know unless I tried? I could not have faith or trust in him unless I first offered him my faith and trust. There was no safe way to figure out ahead of time whether it would be worth the risk. That was the point of trust after all, was it not?

A white rectangle on the wooden planked floor caught my eye, and I crossed the room to pick it up. Someone had slid a note under the door.

It wasn't sealed, so I unfolded it and read six beautiful, hastily scrawled words.

Meet me at the willow tree.

My gaze immediately sought the manuscript sitting on my desk. I was not dressed to go outside, but that was easily remedied. Fortune had smiled upon me, presenting an opportunity to give Henry my manuscript, to show him I trusted him. I tossed the note in the fire so it wouldn't be found and dressed quickly, if a little haphazardly. I let my plait hang loosely over my shoulder and pulled my cloak on, fastening it at the neck. I hardly paid attention to what I was wearing, but it was dark outside, so Henry would hardly notice it.

The house was still and quiet when I collected my novel and slipped out of my room, shutting the door behind me. I tiptoed downstairs, letting myself out the front door. It was unlocked, so Henry must already be waiting for me. The manuscript tucked beneath my arm, I quietly took the steps down to the gravel. The sound of horses nickering caught my attention, and I found a carriage waiting in the shadows to my right, the horses unsettled and impatient.

"What in heaven's name—"

Hands came around me from behind, one wrapping my waist and the other shoving a balled up cloth over my mouth, muffling my screams. The manuscript fell from my arms, the carefully penned pages scattering over the gravel.

I screamed, trying to lurch away, but the sound was too muffled, too quiet to be heard from the house. My feet were lifted in the air as I was carried, kicking and wriggling, to the carriage. The realization that something very wrong was about to happen dug like a dagger in my stomach.

An unfamiliar servant opened the door to the carriage and I was thrown inside, my captor following to keep his cloth over my mouth, but a brief respite allowed me to gulp air and scream as loud as I could.

"Quiet!" Captain Neal commanded, throwing the bunched

cloth over my mouth again. "I will not hurt you, but you must be quiet."

The cloth held a sour odor, making me gag. I kicked out, trying to land a hit with my elbow and free myself from his strong hold. The carriage started rolling forward and panic grew in my stomach. My efforts to free myself were bound by a steely arm.

"I do not wish to quarrel," Captain Neal said, slightly out of breath.

Then unhand me.

"I cannot remove the handkerchief until I know you will not bring attention upon us. Will you speak civilly?"

Had I any other choice? My mind worked as swiftly as it could to find a way out of this wreck of a situation. Fool that I was, I had burned Captain Neal's note. No one would be coming after me soon, so it was up to me to find a way to free myself. I relaxed as best I could until he took my actions as acquiescence and lessened his hold, removing the handkerchief.

I gulped in a breath of fresh air and slipped over on the bench as far from the captain as I could. "Help!"

He looked out the window. "They will not hear you now."

It appeared he was correct; we were too far from the house. "What is the meaning of this madness?"

"Madness?"

"I do not know another word for snatching a woman in the night and taking her—" The realization of his probable destination settled upon me, and I sucked in a breath. "Where are we going?"

"Do not concern yourself with those particulars, yet."

"*Where?*"

He cleared his throat. "Gretna Green."

Shock rippled through me. The very gall of the man! I scoffed. "I will not marry you."

"Do you believe you have a choice?"

"Yes, I most certainly do."

He leaned back, content we were far enough from Hutton House to avoid discovery if I was to scream. "If you did not wish to marry me, you should not have led me to believe that would be the outcome of this house party."

"I assure you, the depth of what you believe I promised was most unconsciously achieved. I have done nothing to encourage you more than any other gentlemen."

"You cannot toy with a man's expectations and expect no repercussions," he said, his voice low and even. "Your initial acceptance of my courtship is proof you would find contentment in a relationship with me. I am not a ridiculous man, Marianne. I take time to make decisions. I weighed you against the other women in Town and found most of them wanting. You are acceptable."

What a compliment.

It explained why it took him so long to show his interest in me. He had been whittling down his options. "Why must you marry at all right now?"

He straightened in the seat. "I have never made my desire for a family a secret from you. I am not young anymore, and I do not wish to be an old man raising children. You are very attentive to your nephew, young and robust. You will make a fine mother."

I did not enjoy being described by my marriageable attributes. He made me feel like cattle. "What about a *wife*? Do you honestly believe I will make a good wife to a man who forces it upon me?"

"As I said, you were once willing to marry me, or you would not have accepted my courtship. This does provide a measure of awkwardness, I will admit. But we will overcome that in time."

"Overcome *abduction*?" The man was truly mad.

"If this is so abhorrent, then you should not have encouraged me. I need a"—he cleared his throat—"wife. I need children. I have no other family left. The Neal line is completely gone. I have seen many storms in recent months, as I have shared with you, and my recent brush with death reminded me of my mortality. If I do not produce children now, there will be *nothing* left of me on this earth if the next storm takes me away."

I stared in his direction. The storms he was constantly talking about had affected him more deeply than he had let on. I recalled his recent fright, but never did it occur to me he had been relying on me so heavily. "You wish to secure your bloodline?"

"It is not a ridiculous notion."

"No, the sentiment is not, but how can you rejoice in creating a family in this manner?"

"All will be well," he said comfortably. "In time, all will be well."

He sounded like an utter lunatic. He must have been, if he believed this was his only option for securing a wife. "Why did you choose the willow tree?"

"We've met there before, if you'll recall our race that first morning. It is also the first thing one sees when they walk through your front door, Miss Hutton."

So it was merely a coincidence. An unfortunate, frustrating coincidence. I had read those familiar words and didn't refine upon the odd handwriting. What I had believed to be a quickly written note from Henry had been someone else's handwriting entirely. I feel like a fool.

I tried to analyze the door handle, but it was difficult to see in the dark and I was unfamiliar with this carriage. At the speed we were going, if I was to open the door and jump out, I could not guarantee a safe landing. Especially not if we were driving along a stone wall or near a ravine.

"I understand your hesitation, but you will see this is for the best."

"It is best to take me from a man I love and force me to

marry you instead? I am not a ship, Captain Neal, and we are not on the ocean. You cannot merely take me simply because you won the battle and are more powerful."

He was silent for a minute. How could he imagine I would view this the same way a navy man would, where they overpower prize ships and claim their reward? It was absurd.

"We shall reach Scotland swiftly if we do not stop to sleep."

That was how he had planned to keep me from escaping at the inns? He would not let me into them?

"We will change horses, of course, but it is best to have this matter settled quickly. It will be a long journey back to Plymouth when our wedding is complete. I have been notified I need to report back earlier than expected, so we have little time to lose."

I'd heard stories of women who were forced into marriages. Scotland had made it far too easy to accomplish, in my opinion. I feared what Captain Neal would do to make it legal. An image flashed in my mind of him leading me onto a ship, crossing the planked gangway to my doom.

I slashed it from my mind. I would find a way to escape before we reached that point. Surely we would need to change horses often enough I could alert someone nearby to my situation. If the carriage slowed, I could take him by surprise or leap from the doorway. While I was busy planning ways to escape, Captain Neal produced a thin rope, foiling every idea I had.

He lifted my ankles and began to wind the rope around them. "Forgive me, but I do not wish to take any chances. I've already lost you once after feeling content and secure." When he finished tying my feet, he tied my wrists together behind my back.

Jumping from the carriage or taking the captain by surprise had just become far more difficult. I would not despair. There would be a way out of this situation. I only needed to put my mind to the task.

I leaned my head back against the squabs, turning away from him.

"You will not hate me forever," he said with quiet confidence.

Oh, he was very much mistaken.

CHAPTER 28
HENRY

The scream that slipped through my open window had first pricked my ears with awareness, and then my body followed. I wondered if Mr. Darcy had gotten in a quarrel with a barn cat, but I'd never seen him stoop to such levels as going outside. I put away my pen, for it was growing late and I needed to cease writing for the night. I stretched and went to the window. My body went cold.

A carriage was making its way down the lane away from the house, and it belonged to Captain Neal. I recognized it from his arrival. He had evidently borrowed it from an aunt—it was clearly outmoded. But why would he be leaving so late at night, and why had his departure sounded like a scream?

Unease swept through me. I dressed quickly, picked up my candle, and made my way to Neal's room. It would be better to ascertain he was the man who had left before I fell into a panic. I knocked at the door, but no answer came, so I let myself inside. The room was empty. He had indeed left.

But the scream. The scream implied he had not left alone.

My heart started racing. There were very few women in this house who would have screamed while leaving with him late at night. I ran down the corridor, turning toward the family rooms, and knocked softly at Marianne's door, but she did not answer. I squeezed my eyes closed, knocking softly again, but still no answer. When I opened the door, it gave willingly, so she had not latched it from inside. The room was dark, but I lifted my candle, and my stomach sank to the floor when I found it empty.

Surely she was merely in the kitchen attempting to make herself tea or . . . but the *scream*.

I found my way to James's room, glad I had been with him when Mrs. Shaw showed him where they were sleeping. I knocked quietly and pushed at the door, but it was latched. It took louder knocking to rouse James and have him come to the door.

"What is it?" he asked sleepily.

"I'm not entirely certain. Captain Neal left a few minutes ago, and I heard a scream come from his carriage before they left."

"They?"

"A man could not make that noise, and Marianne's room is empty."

Alertness entered James's gaze. "I'll meet you at the stables."

I handed him my candle to make his dressing expeditious, then turned and ran. The task of reaching the stables and saddling two horses should not have taken very long, but felt like it took ages. Every minute was a lifetime.

Questions plagued me as I worked. Had she wanted to go with him? Had she desired this? He had received a note in the drawing room last night from someone in the house. Had they designed to leave together?

But the scream. It always came back to that moment.

If I was mistaken, and she had willingly left, she could tell me from her own lips.

I gathered the reins from both saddled horses and led them out of the stables toward the front of the house. I was antsy to be on my way. Every minute was precious time drawing them farther away from us.

The starlight and the lantern I'd lit in the stables shone bright enough to light my path, and I moved to stand directly in front of the doors. Something on the ground caught my attention, and I realized it was paper strewn about.

"What the devil?"

I bent to gather the sheets of paper, bringing the lantern close enough to read. It was Marianne's hand, which I knew well from her copious notes on my manuscript and her letters. I made out a few lines before looking down at the volume of papers. Was this her novel?

The front door closed with a thud. I looked up to find James buttoning his coat as he came hastily down the steps.

"What is all that?" he asked.

"Proof Marianne was taken against her will."

He crouched to help me pick up the scattered pages. "How so?"

"She wrote these. If she had gone willingly, they would not be scattered about now."

We compiled the pages, gathering all of them from what we could see, and I ran up the stairs to leave them inside. James was in the saddle when I returned, and I jumped up before turning my horse and taking off.

"Do you know what direction they've gone?"

"I have my suspicions," I said, anger coursing through my body.

"To Scotland it is." James kicked his horse to keep time with mine, and we tore across the open road.

CHAPTER 29
MARIANNE

The carriage was moving at an alarming rate, and I feared we would break an axle or lose a wheel on the dark road at this speed. I had known people who died in carriage accidents, and it was not something to be taken lightly.

"Should we not slow down?" The pocked road jostled me unnecessarily. If he was so certain of his infallibility, he didn't need to be traveling so quickly.

The captain didn't respond, which led me to believe he was thinking over my point. I had no idea where we were, but a good deal of the road north of Cheshire was not well managed. We hit a particularly large rut and gained so much air that I left the seat for a moment before crashing back down. With my hands tied behind my back, I had no ability to soften the jostling.

"If you refuse to slow the carriage, then at least untie me."

"I cannot."

"Will you tie my hands in front at least? I fear I will break my wrists in all this jostling."

He seemed to consider my dilemma on a held breath before moving forward and sighing simultaneously. Moving my cloak out of the way, he untied my hands, holding them in a vise-like

KASEY STOCKTON

grip as he moved them to rest on my lap and tied them again. It was a vast improvement, and I did my best not to be grateful to him. The man had still tied me up.

Though now I just might be able to find my way free when we stopped at the next inn to change horses. It was my only chance. At the rate we were traveling, by the time my parents found me missing in the morning, I would be halfway to Scotland already.

If I could slow us down, though, that would give my father time to catch up to us. Anything would help.

"We are traveling at a dangerous speed, Captain. It will do you no use to steal a bride if she is dead before the ceremony."

He ran a hand over his eyes. "Perhaps we ought to—"

The wheel hit another bump and we rocked to the side, swaying as the carriage tried to find traction again. Captain Neal's arm flashed out across me, holding me to his side, while his other arm braced us against the wall.

We tipped dramatically one way before going the other, then dropping to the side. There was a loud snap, and the carriage slid as if falling down a hill, jolting us with it. Captain Neal's body softened my blow, but my head came down hard against his shoulder like a whip crack when we finally landed.

I rolled off him when the carriage settled on its side, my shoulders crunching into broken glass. Water seeped into my gown, and I realized with alarming awareness we had landed in a stream of some type. The overturned carriage was now filling with water.

"Hurry, Captain, we must move quickly."

He did not respond. It was too dark to see his face or the depth of the water seeping into the carriage.

"Captain!" I yelled. "You need to remove these ropes."

Still no response. His nautical knots would be impossible to untie on my own, but I could cut them. The water was now to my ankles. I rooted around for broken glass from one of the windows, selecting a large chunk. I bent over and wedged it between my shoes to hold it in place. Sawing my rope back and forth, I worked away at the fibers. The glass dislodged a handful of times and I had to search the rising water to wedge it back between my feet and continue.

It took far longer than I expected for the rope to fray. Cold water flowed at a slow, steady pace through the broken window, soaking my gown and feet and increasingly wetting my hands. I slipped in my haste to cut the rope and the glass tore through my sleeve, slicing my skin.

I cried out, but did not cease my attempts to cut the rope. Finally the last bit broke and I unraveled it from around my wrists. I turned back to Captain Neal, but he still did not move. "Wake," I cried. "We need to find a way out of here."

I bent in half, working at the knot he'd used to bind my feet. Water rose to my shins, making the rope slippery. My numb fingers could not find a secure enough grasp on the tight knot.

The water was beginning to rush through the broken window at an alarming rate.

"Help!" I yelled. Where was the coachman? I would never be able to lift Captain Neal from this water on my own. The glint of the moonlight on the water showed how high it was rising. I abandoned my task. Escaping this death box was my utmost priority. I turned, taking the captain by the shoulders, but when I shook his arms, his head lolled forward. Had he hit it hard enough to make himself unconscious? I pressed my fingers to his throat, feeling for a heartbeat, but found nothing. It could have been my own chilly numbness. I shoved him, pulling at his coat until he was sitting up, his head high above the water.

I had to seek help. My strength was not sufficient to remove this large, sodden man on my own. The river inside the carriage had ceased rising, but it reached halfway up his chest where he was propped against the wall. I hoped we had found ourselves at the level of the river outside too. If that was the case, Captain

Neal's head would stay above water until I could return with assistance.

I tried to stand. My cloak dragged in the water, so I fumbled with the tie until it came free and sunk to the watery floor. The door was located above my head, the other door pressed to the ground. I reached up and unlatched the door, then pushed up. It easily gave way, opening to allow more moonlight in. I stood, bracing my hands on either side of the door to lift myself out.

That proved more difficult than it sounded. My arms did not have enough strength to lift my body. I braced my hands again, hopping with my tied feet until they perched on the edge of the squabs. The carriage rocked with my efforts, and I jumped again, pushing up as hard as I could until my bottom rested on the edge of the doorway and I could maneuver myself to the top of the carriage.

"Help!" I called. Where was the coachman? Had he been thrown into this river as well? I searched the dark water, but it was deceptively calm beyond the upheaval of my overturned carriage. There was not a sound or soul in sight beyond the rippling water or the wind whispering through the trees. The earth was far too calm for the chaos I had been enduring.

I swung my legs around until they hung from the side of the carriage. Holding onto the opening, I rolled to my stomach and lowered myself until my feet landed on the mossy, rocky riverbed. The water was moving too quickly, and until I could untie my ankles, I would not be able to make it to the banks. I shivered, calling out for help to an empty road. I avoided looking into the carriage and the unresponsive man inside. Would rousing him be my only hope? That was a dismal thought, for I feared he was past rousing.

The sound of thundering hoofbeats lifted my hopes with each steady beat against the packed dirt road.

"Help!" I yelled as loudly as I could, more scream than word slipping from my tongue, again and again, so I would not lose this opportunity for assistance. "Help!"

Shadowed men on horseback passed on the road, shortly visible through the trees.

"Help!" I screamed again, pleading for them to hear me.

They did.

The horses returned, and when the first man looked my way, down through the broken trees to the water-laden carriage, he leapt from his horse and crashed down the riverbank.

"Mari?" Henry called.

"Yes!" My heart swooped up, lodging in my throat. Sweet relief poured through me and though I was beginning to lose feeling in my feet, I was warmed.

He came down the bank with a lantern in one hand, splashing into the river with no hesitation, his free arm reaching toward me.

"I cannot walk. My ankles are bound together."

The lantern lit his face, anger flashing across it. "Where is he?"

"Inside."

Henry's gaze dropped to the carriage where the river now rushed through the broken windows. He trudged through water up to his knees, taking slow steps to avoid slipping on the mossy rocks. When he reached me, he set the lantern on the carriage and bent, sliding his arm under my knees and his other around my back, lifting me smoothly out of the water. I grabbed the lantern and clung to his neck, burying my forehead against his thundering pulse as he carefully made his way out of the river and onto the bank.

"I tried to untie my ankles, but my fingers were numb from the water."

He set me down gently. "It is cold. May I?"

I nodded. James took the lantern and held it close while Henry bent at my feet and worked the knot free. He unwound the rope and tossed it away. I leaned forward to rub at the tender skin. My wrist smarted from the cut it received from the glass, and exhaustion fell over me like a heavy blanket of dense fog.

"Captain Neal hit his head when we crashed and has yet to rouse. I . . . I did not find a pulse, but my hands were numb, so I do not know if he is—"

Henry looked at me sharply. "He's unconscious?"

James started toward the water. "We will see to him."

Henry slid his hand around my neck, his thumb brushing along my cheek, and bent to press a kiss to the top of my head. Then he left me on the grassy slope.

I watched them trudge through the water again. Henry waited outside while James climbed inside and took Captain Neal under the arms, pulling him up enough that they could pass him through the doorway. They worked together to lift him out, carry him across the water, and lay him on the grass. Henry bent over Captain Neal's heart, his gaze on the lantern sitting on the earth between us. He lifted his face to his brother, who was wringing water from his coat. "He's alive."

"We need a doctor."

"Where are we?" Henry asked.

"I haven't the faintest."

They went silent.

"We rode too long for me to have any notion of our location," I said. I knew the river, but we could be in a number of different places that butted along the waterway. "If we can travel to the nearest town, I might know where we are and who to contact."

The brothers shared a look. Henry gazed back at me. "I think you deserve to return home."

"We cannot leave him here."

"Can we not?" Henry asked, though I knew he was jesting.

"I am well enough," I said. "I will stay with him while you ride for a doctor—"

"No," James said. "Help me mount him on my horse and we will all ride out together. It will be easier to tend to him at Hutton House."

"And far faster to go straight there and send for a doctor than to try and locate one in the middle of the night," Henry added.

James looked at me. "Did you have anything of importance in the carriage?"

I thought of my manuscript littering the gravel in front of my house. "No."

"Then we need not worry about it until tomorrow."

"And the coachman?" I asked.

"Blast," James muttered. He took the lantern and ran down the bank, searching. Henry joined him, and they searched the surrounding grounds before returning to my side. "It is too dark," Henry said.

James's face looked grim. "We cannot postpone taking Captain Neal to a doctor any longer. We will return to search for the coachman at first light."

I stood on shaky legs while the Bradwell brothers lifted the unconscious navy captain and draped him over the front of James's saddle. Henry took me by the waist and lifted me onto the front of his before mounting behind me. His arms went around my waist to take the reins and I leaned into him, grateful for the warmth his body provided. He dropped his mouth near my ear. "Let us get you home."

"In your arms, I am already there."

CHAPTER 30
HENRY

I had never seen red before, nor had my vision ever blurred purely from anger. When I found Marianne shivering in the river, unable to move for the rope binding her legs together, I could have breathed fire from my nose. It was fortunate for me Captain Neal was already unconscious, or I could have put him in that state myself.

We reached Hutton House in the dark. I helped Marianne down from the horse and put my arm around her to lead her up the steps into the house. We rang for the servants near the door, but given the hour, it would likely take some time for them to wake.

"Leave me," she said, looking over my shoulder to where James was climbing down from his horse in front of the house. "James needs your help more than I do."

"Where should we put the blackguard?"

"His bedchamber will do," she said calmly. "I can direct you there."

My mouth flattened, my jaw clenching every time I thought of the man. "I know where it is. You can go up to your room if you'd like. I'll have the doctor see to you when he arrives."

"Send him my way *after* he sees the captain, please."

I wanted to reach out and pull her toward me again. "You are the kindest soul."

"Hardly. I do not wish to have that man's death on my conscience."

"Very well." She made a good point. The captain was failing and needed to be seen as soon as possible. "We'll see to it the doctor is shown to him straight away."

Marianne smiled, taking my hand in her cold one. "Thank you, Henry." Her voice wobbled, and I could not imagine the fear that had kept her captive all evening.

Convention be hanged. I tugged Marianne toward me, wrapping my arms around her back and pulling her tightly against my chest.

She sucked in a breath that caught. My heart squeezed with affection for her and relief to have her safely home again. Her hands slid around my waist beneath my coat and grasped the back of my shirt in her fists. I did not care for anything at present but this woman.

Leaning back slightly, I waited for her to tilt her chin back and look up at me. It was dim in the entryway, for James had the lantern outside, but I could still feel her steadiness and see the shape of her lips in the borrowed moonlight. I leaned down, hoping Mr. Darcy was not lurking nearby to foil my advances, and pressed my lips to Marianne's. Heat slid from her lips to mine, sweeping through me like a fierce warm wind. My senses came alive, burning within me.

Marianne responded, clutching the fabric of my shirt so tightly I felt the pressure on my chest. Or perhaps that was her heart hammering against mine. I tilted my head and deepened the kiss, letting her feel my relief at having her returned home safe and whole.

A throat cleared in the doorway, and I broke away from her to see my brother standing there, raising the lantern to illuminate us and grinning. "If you are nearly finished, I could use some help with the cad out here."

Marianne buried her face in my chest, then released me and stepped back. I hoped her mortification was not a sign of regret, but she gave me a sweet smile that put my fears to rest. "Good night, gentlemen."

"Good night," we chorused back. I watched her make her way slowly up the stairs before turning and walking through the doorway, past James.

"It is only fair," he said, catching up to me, light from the lantern swinging as he walked.

"In what way?"

"I recall you interrupting my first kiss with Felicity."

I stilled, looking back at him over my shoulder. "When? Oh . . . when you were out riding?"

"And you fetched me home to see Cousin Matthew. Yes."

My lips flattened. "It would seem we were both interrupted because of disreputable, sorry excuses for men."

We stood in front of the horse together, discussing the best way to carry Neal, when Shaw stepped outside. "Did you ring, sir?"

"Yes." I approached the butler. "This man needs a doctor, and with haste. We will carry him to the room he was previously occupying, if that suits?"

He looked at the captain. "It suits."

"Miss Hutton also needs to be seen to, though her injuries are not as severe. She could use a hot bath and her maid."

"Right away." He left to see to the orders.

James and I took Captain Neal from the horse and carried him inside.

"I checked his pulse while you were checking Miss Hutton's," James said. "He is still alive."

"Good. I am eager to see him stripped of his military title and thrown in gaol."

269

"One thing at a time, brother."

A groom was sent to fetch the doctor. A valet and a footman were roused to change Neal's clothes and watch him until the doctor arrived. James and I exchanged our sodden clothes for dry, as well, and returned to the corridor to be available should we be needed.

Mrs. Hutton was sent to attend to her daughter while the maid heated water for a bath, and Mr. Hutton met us in the corridor outside Captain Neal's room.

He frowned. "Thank you, gentlemen. It seems a paltry offering, but I know not what else to say."

I cringed. "It is not finished yet."

A valet opened the door and carried out the soiled clothing, and we found a maid kneeling before the hearth, starting the fire, while another pulled blankets over the invalid.

"What ails him?" Mr. Hutton asked.

"Marianne mentioned he hit his head when the carriage crashed into the river." I could not even say the words without offering up a prayer of gratitude that she had come out of the accident mostly unscathed. "He has not been conscious yet."

Mr. Hutton's jaw tightened. "How far did they reach?"

"We do not know," James said. "I believe we followed them for just over half an hour when we came upon the wreck. It is fortunate they were not much farther."

Mr. Hutton huffed. "You can go rest. I will see to it the doctor finds the captain."

"He needs to see to Marianne's arm, as well. She's cut it, but she can wait," I said.

He nodded.

"If you need assistance to make certain the captain does not escape—"

"That won't be necessary," Mr. Hutton said, clapping me on the shoulder. "I will sooner hang than let the scoundrel from my sight."

We left the disgruntled father to his post.

"I think I'll be off to bed, then," James said. "I can lead the men to the river at first light to search for the coachman."

"That is only a few hours away."

"Yes. I'll manage. I'll take a few men if they can be spared. I assume you would prefer to remain here."

"Marianne will sleep late, I hope. I'll join you in the search."

James nodded. "Good night, Hen."

I was grateful to have had him by my side this evening. We parted, and I traveled back down the corridor, hovering outside of Marianne's door. Sooner or later a maid was sure to come or go, so I did not fear needing to wait long. As it turned out, it was a quarter of an hour before anyone felt the need to open the door, and it was Mrs. Hutton.

She startled to find me leaning against the opposite wall, but closed the door behind herself and came to meet me, adjusting the cap over her head. "She is sleeping now."

"The doctor has been sent for."

She nodded. "I'll wake her when he is ready to see to her arm. I've wrapped it as best as I could so it does not inhibit her sleep."

Silence sat between us for a long moment. When Mrs. Hutton spoke again, there were tears gathering in her eyes and coloring her voice. "Thank you, Henry."

I dipped my head.

Mrs. Hutton embraced me, and I returned the motherly hug. She stepped back and wiped her eyes. "I cannot ever thank you enough."

"I am only grateful I was awake to hear her leave."

"Providence," she said.

"Undoubtedly."

"Now, you must retire. I am certain you are exhausted."

"I wanted to assure myself that Marianne was well first."

"She is well."

It gladdened my heart, though there was no end, not yet. We still had to manage Neal, take him before a magistrate, locate the lost coachman and the horses that had pulled the carriage, and clear the wreck from the river. I went to my room with both a heavy heart and the comfort of relief. All of that lay ahead of us, but Marianne was safe.

CHAPTER 31
MARIANNE

I slept through the doctor's ministrations. The physical exertion of last night could not be wholly blamed for the fatigue plaguing me, but paired with the fear of wondering if I was ever going to see Henry or my family again, my weariness was complete. Captain Neal belonged in Bedlam. The man was mad.

By the time Keene helped me dress for the day and leave my room, a bandage on my arm protecting my cut, it was past noon and I was wary of the state in which I would find our guests. Did they all know of my late night adventure? Neither of my parents had yet to ask me what cause I had to walk outside alone after midnight, and a reckoning awaited me. The reprieve my traumatic evening had provided would not last forever.

I knew I needed to face my mistakes and foolish choices, but that was never an enjoyable exercise.

The sound of commotion in the entryway reached my ears before I descended the stairs. Servants carried trunks through the open door, sunlight shining on the marble floor and the bustle of the evacuation. Miss Gatley stood nearby, tying her bonnet strings under her chin.

When I reached her, she did not even feign happiness to see me.

"You are leaving?" I asked.

"My father insists."

The sounds of servants heaving trunks and buckling them to the boot of the Gatley carriage outside filled the space between us. If she was unaware of what occurred last night, it would be best not to bring it to her attention. But I was eager to know how thoroughly I ought to guard myself against speculation and gossip from the *ton*.

"You will miss the ball."

Miss Gatley pulled on her gloves. "I think we are to attend another house party in Sussex. Do not take great offense at our departure. I am in need of a husband, and there are none to be had here."

The desperation of her actions struck me. "Can you not remain for the sake of enjoying our company?" I liked to think that if our weapons were dropped, if we were no longer fighting for attention from the gentlemen, we could have become friends.

A look of longing passed over Miss Gatley's face, but it departed as soon as it had arrived. She cleared her throat softly, straightening an already straight glove. "I have little choice in the matter."

"Might we speak plainly with one another?"

"You may," she granted. Did that mean she would not do so in return?

"If you are in such dire need of a husband, why did you reveal my meeting with Henry? Surely keeping that secret would have aided you. In the least, it would have provided you with more time."

The last trunk was carried outside. The door remained open to the distant sounds of packing and impatient horses.

"Despite my present circumstances, I do not *want* to marry for a fortune."

"A blessed thing, that, for Henry does not possess one. Your efforts regarding him were fruitless to begin with."

She looked at me oddly. "You may not be properly informed about his situation."

I thought the same for her, but I did not say so.

Miss Gatley peered at me. "He inherited a goodly sum, along with a house, when his father died. It is not anything to be smirked at." She looked away. "My father's servant heard it from Henry's valet only a few months ago. It hardly matters now, anyway."

A goodly sum? To say nothing for the income he has undoubtedly accumulated with his successful career thus far— though no one else knew of that portion.

Miss Gatley sighed, weariness bending her shoulders the slightest bit. "The Warburtons are having a house party and there are said to be three eligible gentlemen in attendance. I believe that was always Father's contingency plan."

I weighed my words, and her impending departure loosened my tongue. "If you are not happy, why are you submitting to the scheme?"

Miss Gatley chewed her words. "He is my father, and he has asked this of me. What else can I do?"

"You disrupted his intentions for Henry—"

"I am willing to help my father, but I will not marry just anyone. Especially not a man who is besotted with someone else."

Footsteps clicked their way across the marble floor, precluding me from replying to her bold statement. I did not think he had loved me then, but the idea he might have done so sent a volley of pleasure through me regardless. Mrs. Gatley came forward, led by Mama.

"We are sad to see you leave," Mama said. "I hope you will join us again."

Mrs. Gatley dipped her head and, taking her daughter's arm, they quietly left. I stood at Mama's shoulder and watched them load into their carriage—Mr. Gatley already waiting inside—and leave.

"Were they aware of the situation?" I asked, afraid to look at Mama, fearing what I would find on her countenance.

"No. They had made their minds up already. It was not spoken of, but I believe they are under the impression Captain Neal left of his own accord."

"We will not be able to keep his presence here a secret."

"No, but their departure has bought us a little time before we become the subject of gossip." She took my arm, gently forcing me to face her. "I am afraid the captain is not in good health. Dr. Mathers believes he will not survive the day."

An odd sense of disquiet slipped through me. "Has a magistrate been informed?"

"Yes. Papa visited him this morning. Both of the Bradwell men left at sunrise to manage the carriage and coachman, and Papa intended to meet with them after he dealt with Captain Neal."

"Have they returned?"

"Not yet." She drew in a shaky breath. "You need to consider what choice you would like to make. If Captain Neal does not last the day, he need not be arrested at all. We can bury the situation before it ever reaches Society, but then the man will not be stripped of his standing in the navy."

"You think they would do that?" I asked. I wasn't familiar with military protocol.

"Certainly. A dishonorable discharge at the least."

"Or we preserve his memory and our reputation."

"Indeed."

How could I make such a decision? It would affect far more

than me. My family, Henry, his family name by association. I was an engaged woman, but not yet married, and the stain it could paint over us would not be pleasant. "If he survives, though . . ."

"Then it is an unnecessary question, darling. He will be arrested and tried."

I nodded. "I will wait."

"Shall we pass the afternoon more comfortably? The rest of our guests are gathered in the drawing room. Even Julia has joined us. I thought we could net purses today. Our hands will be glad of the busywork, I should think."

"Indeed." I drew my uninjured arm through Mama's and allowed her to lead me to the drawing room. "Let us better occupy our hands and our minds."

CHAPTER 32

HENRY

I pulled the limp handkerchief from my pocket and swiped it over my perspiring forehead. It had been unhappy news to discover the coachman had been pulled from the water earlier this morning by a local man. An unnecessary loss of life.

The carriage itself had proved an altogether frustrating matter, but it was now pulled from the water. A handful of the Huttons' servants were dismantling it and filling a wagon with the pieces, since it had been damaged beyond repair.

Mr. Hutton and Lord Moorington remained to see the local constable about the coachman's body, but James and I started for home, leaving the last of the work to the servants. We had done a fair amount, and I was eager to return to Marianne.

"Shall we stop?" James asked when we reached a small, unfamiliar town. He nodded toward the public house.

My belly rumbled in response.

He grinned at me. "I will consider that my answer."

Eager as I was to be at Hutton House, I understood the importance of not falling from my horse in fatigue. Little sleep last night and manual labor this morning combined to make me ravenous. "Can we be quick about it, though?"

"Yes. I realize how desperate you must be to see Miss Hutton."

We left our horses and let ourselves into the pub. Taking seats at a table against the wall, we requested two meals from the serving girl. The taproom was mostly empty, save for a handful of men drinking at the other end of the room. Another man sat near us, his head bent forward as he snored against the table.

"That is pitiful," James said, leaning closer and lowering his voice. He nodded his head toward the other men. "To think they find satisfaction in this way of life."

"I understand you cannot abide idleness, but there is something to be said for slowing down at times."

"Felicity taught me that much. But sleeping the day away in a public house? And not even in one of the rooms upstairs? I do pity *him*."

Steaming hot pies were brought to us, and I dug in, not caring what kind of meat they contained. The aroma was rich and it served to satiate my hunger.

"It is too bad Benedict and Thea are enjoying their honeymoon," James said around a mouthful. "When we regale him with the adventure later, he will be sorry to have missed it."

"I do wonder if he has had enough adventure of late."

"Perhaps it is I who missed his extra set of helping hands at the river this morning."

"I missed him as well." I laughed, taking another bite.

The sleeping man near us roused, rubbing his face before raising his body from its slumped position. His back was to me, and he lifted his cup to his lips, making a disappointed sound to find it empty.

He tapped the cup a few times against the table, then turned, stretching his back.

James lowered his fork. "Daniel Palmer?"

I knew that name. I looked over sharply. This was Lady Moorington's son?

Mr. Palmer looked over his shoulder warily. Purple shadows fell under his bloodshot eyes. His hair was in disarray and his clothing rumpled so excessively that I had not initially noticed he was a gentleman.

"What the devil are you doing here?" James asked.

He gave us a lazy smile. "Avoiding my mother."

"Yes, she knows," I said, before I could think better of it.

He looked surprised.

"We've been at Hutton House," James explained. "Your mother and stepfather have been guests there as well."

"Ah, you're attending the house party? That is my destination," Mr. Palmer said. It was very clear he was doing anything *but* making his way to Hutton House.

"You can accompany us the rest of the way. We are happy to wait while you gather your things." James cleared his throat. "Or refresh your hair."

Daniel stared at him for too long. Perhaps he did not like to be pushed into action, but he had come this far. It was ridiculous not to come the rest of the way.

He eyed us warily. "I try to avoid these situations, because my mother tends to use them as opportunities for matchmaking. So, as you can see, I have had trouble convincing myself to make it all the way." He rubbed a hand over his face. "Who else is in residence?"

"It is a veritable family reunion for you," James said. "Your cousin Felicity and my mother are both there."

"The Huttons, of course," I added. "And their eldest daughter, Mrs. Walding."

"Miss Hutton is not yet married, yes?" Mr. Palmer asked.

"Indeed, though she soon will be." I couldn't help my smile. "She has recently agreed to become my wife."

Mr. Palmer relaxed. "Happy news."

"Thank you." I was certain he meant it was happy for him that she would not be thrust upon him as a potential bride. Especially if his mother had been participating in some unwelcome matchmaking of her own.

James took a swig of his ale and set the cup down again. "The Gatleys were recently in residence, but they will likely be gone by the time we return."

"It is a small house party," I said. "I am afraid there are no young ladies to throw your cap at."

Mr. Palmer shook his head, his posture relaxing further. "That is a relief. My cap would like to remain firmly on my head." He stood, brushing down the front of his waist coat. "I will ride the rest of the way with you. I can be down in a quarter hour."

"Take all the time you need," I said, fairly certain it would take more than fifteen minutes to make the man presentable.

He left, trudging up the stairs and disappearing from sight.

"That was fortuitous," James muttered.

"I think his dear mama will be glad to have him."

"How long do you think he has been hiding out here?"

I considered the comfortable way he had been sleeping and then went off to his bedchamber. "He was expected over a week ago, so I dare say he has been hiding out for at least that long."

"I do not envy the man. Felicity has remarked he has not been quite the same since his father died. I have seen grief waste people away. I hope it does not happen to him."

We waited nearly half an hour for Daniel to reappear, enough time for us to order and share another meat pie. He carried his trunk and stepped into the room, looking like an entirely different man. His face was fresher, shaved, and his hair damp, clean, and in order. His eyes were red, but they had cleared somewhat, and his clothing was fresh. He looked every bit the gentleman—though a very tired, slightly ill-looking gentleman.

"I suppose it is time," he said.

I didn't understand his apprehension. His mother seemed perfectly lovely and eager to see him again. It was an emotion I knew intimately, as I desired to see Marianne just as greatly.

Only another half hour and she would be in my sights again.

CHAPTER 33
MARIANNE

"Your grandson is a delight," Mrs. Bradwell said, smiling at Frederick while he lined his wooden animals up on the floor.

"You have found him in a calmer moment," Julia promised, but she smiled indulgently at her son.

Mama looked at Frederick. "All grandchildren seem perfectly delightful, do they not?"

"Indeed. I am eager for one of my own."

Felicity did not say anything, and I wondered if she would prefer a change in conversation. Mr. Darcy came to her rescue by coming out from beneath the sofa and stretching his back.

Frederick looked up from his wooden elephant, his eager gaze falling on the cat at once. Oh, dear. Mrs. Bradwell was about to see just how *un*delightful Frederick could sometimes make himself.

"Kitty!"

Mr. Darcy froze mid-step and looked back at Frederick.

"Gentle, darling," Julia warned.

Frederick waddled over to my nervous cat and picked him up, squeezing him with love and deep affection. "Kitty!"

Mr. Darcy accepted the embrace gracefully. I stood, crossing toward them and kneeling before my nephew. "We do not wish to squeeze Mr. Darcy too hard, or he will not want hugs in the future." I gently pried his arms free and took the cat into my lap, stroking his back. "Shall we pet him softly?"

Frederick knelt, laying his head on Mr. Darcy's back and hugging him again. "Soft kitty," he said quietly.

Mr. Darcy did not rebuff this advance. Perhaps the cat could grow more accepting of Henry, for clearly he was adaptable. Even just a few weeks ago he would not have permitted such public affection from anyone.

"You have a way with children," Mrs. Bradwell said.

I looked up at her. She would soon become my mother-in-law, and her approval sent a splash of pride through me.

The door opened and Shaw stepped inside. He held a stack of papers in his hand that looked oddly familiar, and my heart leapt to my throat when I recognized the dirt-smeared paper.

He held my manuscript.

I jumped to my feet before he could request Mama's attention. Mr. Darcy sprang from my lap and ran to the edge of the room. Frederick ran after him.

"I believe that belongs to me," I said, my voice shaky.

Mr. Shaw looked from the papers in his hands to me, nodding.

I gave an uncomfortable laugh, accepting them. "I wondered where that had gotten to." I thought perhaps they had run away on the wind or something equally depressing. I was glad they were here, even if they were most likely ruined and would need rewriting.

"Those are yours?" Mama asked, her eyebrows shooting to her forehead. "But . . . it is a novel."

My throat constricted, my body freezing. She had found them first? My secret sat bare and open in my hands. Every pair of eyes in the room turned to face me. Julia, Mama, Felicity, Mrs.

Bradwell, Lady Moorington. There were an abundance of people here, and any reply died on my tongue.

"You mean to tell us you wrote a novel?" Julia asked.

Did I? Could I pass this off as an extremely long letter? I glanced down to the stack of papers in my hands. That was quite the missive.

Mama shook her head. "Mari? I do not understand."

"It is not something I wished to be widely known," I said weakly.

She seemed to sense the audience was putting me off, but at this point, it would be better to explain to everyone. The secret was revealed, and in a way, everyone in the room was family now, or would soon be. Even Lady Moorington would become family, my sister-in-law's aunt, and Mrs. Bradwell, my husband's mother.

My *husband*. Even thinking that sent a thrill through me. My heart was eager to see him again. Were he here now, he would have supported me whether or not I chose to tell them of my authorship. That realization only served to remind me that I had a choice. I had decided long ago I could not share this information with anyone for fear they would not understand, they would judge or disapprove. But that was simply a coward's way of not being forced to put my trust in the people I loved.

Just like with Henry, I could not trust my mother, sister, or father without first putting my trust in them.

I cleared my throat. "Yes. I wrote a novel. Actually, I've written two."

Surprised, blank stares returned to me, so I did the only thing I could think of: I filled the silence.

"I intended to publish under my initials. A publisher in London bought the first book three years ago, but—"

"*Three* years?" Mama expostulated. "Good heavens, darling, why keep the secret for so long?"

"Because I was frightened you would not approve, or that

you would not enjoy my stories. And I feared it would displease Papa."

I could see she understood, and she said nothing further.

"I hoped if I could publish my novels and find a way to support myself with them, I need not marry for security, but could find a match for love."

"All I have ever wanted for you to find was a love match," Mama said quietly.

"I know." I smiled. "And that is what I have."

Julia scoffed. "I cannot believe you've written a novel—*two* novels," she corrected herself. "Can we read them?"

"Hopefully you will be able to do that soon." I looked down at the mess of papers in my hands, the mud and condensation having blurred some of the words. "I am afraid this was scattered outside. I need to return these pages to their rightful order, and I fear I'll need to rewrite a good deal of them. If you will excuse me?" I looked to my mother, who nodded, her smile glowing. I could feel her pride radiating, and it gave me courage.

"That is wonderful," Lady Moorington said. "I will be first in line at Hatchards when your book reaches their shelves."

"It might not have my name on it."

"Your secret is safe with us," Mrs. Bradwell said.

I let out a breath, very relieved. Keeping my alternate identity a secret for so long had been taxing. I did not wish for all of England to know I authored these books, at least not yet, but having my family aware of the situation would surely make it easier and take some of the strain of hiding it away.

Mr. Darcy made an uncomfortable sound on the other side of the room.

"Oh, Frederick, leave him alone," Julia said.

I crossed the room and picked up my cat, to my nephew's dismay. "I think Mr. Darcy needs to help me."

"Want kitty."

"Kitty will return later, but Kitty needs a nap."

Julia stood. "Frederick needs a nap as well."

———

I took the better part of the afternoon to organize the novel into the correct order. There were only half a dozen pages that were ruined beyond legibility, and I rewrote them to the best of my memory. I would need to rewrite the entire novel before sending it to any publisher if I wanted them to take me seriously. At least I could offer this to Henry to read first.

Keene helped me dress for dinner. "Have the men returned?" I asked.

"Oh, yes. They returned over an hour ago."

"That is a blessed relief."

"They brought Mr. Palmer with them as well."

I looked up at that. "Mr. Palmer? What do you mean they *brought* him?"

"He arrived with them. I heard something about the Mr. Bradwells finding him in a pub."

Oh, dear. That was not promising.

"Can you do me a favor, Keene?"

She stopped gathering my day dress from the edge of the bed and looked up at me. "Of course, miss."

"I hoped to have a private word with Henry before dinner. Would you ask him to meet me in the library?"

She grinned, and I could not help but find it contagious. "Right away, miss."

I picked up my manuscript, checked my hair in the mirror, and took myself down to the library. My heart raced. I was eager to see him again.

Blessedly, the man did not make me wait long.

The door creaked open, and Henry stepped inside, closing it

behind himself. "We should have secured an engagement from the very beginning. It provides much more privacy, does it not?" His low voice was comforting.

I leaned back to sit against the desk, hiding the manuscript resting behind me. I could not help the smile that stretched across my face, for seeing him brought so much joy to my heart.

He carried papers in with him. He set them on the desk beside me as his arms went around my waist, pulling me in for a hug, his temple resting against the top of my head. He inhaled slowly, his arms tightening around me.

I breathed in, comfortable and safe. "I am glad to have you here."

"Did they tell you about the coachman?"

"No."

"A farmer found him." His tone was enough to understand the man had not been found alive, and I did not wish to know more details than that.

"I fear there will be a similar outcome with Captain Neal."

Henry scoffed. "I had hoped the man would stay alive long enough to answer for his actions."

"And here, I do not even wish to speak of him." I leaned back and Henry loosened his hold, but did not release me.

"Then we will not speak of him," he said resolutely.

"I brought you something."

"I bought you something as well."

"The next chapter?"

He smiled, revealing his perfect, slightly uneven teeth. "No, I brought the first chapter of my new book."

My heart stuttered. "I thought you did not wish for me to read it."

"I think it must be about you, with how easily it flows from my quill, so you have every right to it."

My heart galloped. "A love story."

"Precisely."

"In that case . . ." I turned around and picked up the dirt-smudged novel, my pulse racing. "I was trying to bring this to you last night when Captain Neal stepped in."

"Outside?"

"I had received a note telling me to meet at the willow tree. I read it so quickly, I did not see anything amiss with the handwriting. The meeting place was the same I had written you to meet, so I tossed the note in the fire and went."

"Do not tell me that blackguard has a similar hand to me."

"It was messy, but I think you must, for I did not question who wrote it."

Henry looked down at the papers I held. "You will allow me to read your novel?"

"I want you to. I made the decision yesterday. My mother also knows of it, but I've yet to tell my father."

He took the papers and handed me his.

"Shall we feign exhaustion and return to our rooms to read?" I asked.

"I fear now that everyone knows of our writing, they will see directly through that excuse."

"Everyone? Who have you told?"

He flipped through the first few pages before setting his attention on me again. "James. He was a great support. Now I must tell my mother."

"Well, she knows about me. All the women in the house do."

A smile played on his lips, drawing my attention there. "Look at us, unable to keep a secret."

"I think we did a marvelous job of it until now, and I do not think trusting others with those private, important things means we have failed. I find great success in it."

"I could not have said so better myself." He leaned down to kiss me, trapping the pages between us as he drew me closer, his lips finding mine. Mr. Darcy leaped onto the desk behind me and Henry backed up, but the cat didn't attack. He curled up and sat on the pages Henry had brought me instead.

"I think you've gained Mr. Darcy's approval," I said.

Henry kissed me again. "I love you," he whispered in my ear with a gentleness that embodied the man he was.

"I love you, too."

CHAPTER 34

MARIANNE

Daniel Palmer's addition to our house party had done nothing but send Lady Moorington into a fit of pleasure and Lord Moorington into a pique. I applauded the earl's skill for hiding his irritation, though. Aside from the clenched-jaw smiles and constantly furrowed brow, he seemed perfectly at ease.

We were making our way toward the drawing room after dinner when Keene opened the servant's door nestled into the wall, her wide eyes looking from Shaw to me.

The butler left his post at the drawing room door and spoke to her sternly. She replied in a whisper, and he looked directly at Papa. Something was happening, and I was nearly positive it had to do with Captain Neal.

"I am afraid Neal has awoken," Shaw relayed to us.

"The doctor?"

"The doctor has been sent for," Keene said.

Papa nodded. "I will see to him."

I moved to follow him, and Henry's hand shot out to grab mine. He looked concerned, but he needn't worry. I gave him a reassuring squeeze, and he released me.

"I will walk with you, Papa. I would like to know of his condition."

My father offered me his arm and led me up the stairs. When we reached the corridor, he hesitated. "We are not sure what state we will find him in."

"I have no wish to see or speak to Captain Neal."

He looked relieved. "I wondered if you were hoping to hold him to account."

"Not tonight, at any rate. Though his poor health is of his own doing, and that might be punishment enough."

"Indeed," he agreed, but he looked troubled by my statement.

I was certain he did not think it my place to hold Neal to account, just as it was not my place to write books, to meet with a publisher, to do those things women were not welcome to. I drew in a breath. "It was my foolishness that took me outside last night, and I accept it. The man wronged me, and I would like to see that he is unable to treat any other young woman in the same manner."

Papa looked at me, his brow furrowing. "You chose to walk outside last night?"

Oh, dear. Had he not known? I swallowed. "I was under the impression Henry was meeting me."

The disturbed look that crossed his face caused me to explain quickly.

"Only so I might give him something. It was not—that is, I needed to . . ." I drew in a breath. "A book. I wrote a book, and I wanted Henry to read it."

Papa was very still. "You wrote a book?"

"Two books. One of them is with a publisher, but they will not send it to print, likely because they discovered I was a woman. Henry is helping me find a new publisher without revealing that bit about me."

Papa was silent, the moment stretching between us. I could

hear sounds from the drawing room near the base of the stairs, but it was perfectly isolated where we stood. He watched me for a moment, his head tipping to the side in confusion. "Why have you not told us?"

"I did not think you would be pleased."

He shook his head slowly and drew me in for an embrace. "I am impressed, dear, and not at all surprised. I only wish you would have known you could ask me for assistance. You did not need to do it on your own."

Shock rippled through me like the small waves on our lake. "You are in support of it? But I am a woman. You do not read books written by women."

"Yes, because they do not appeal to me. Not because they are authored by women. I would be glad to read *your* book, regardless."

Had I so terribly misjudged him? My father truly respected what I had accomplished?

He stepped back, pride shining in his eyes, and I knew at once I had mistaken him before. Or perhaps he didn't value women as authors before now, but he would value me, and I could prove his previous opinion wrong.

"If I wait here, will you tell me how he fares?" I asked, drawn by a sudden curiosity.

"Of course." He let himself into the room, and I waited in the corridor, listening to the hum of unintelligible voices on the other side of the door. A quarter hour must have passed by the time he returned to me.

The grimace he wore was not promising. "I'm afraid he does not have long for this world."

"Did he speak to you?"

Papa shook his head.

"He has no family to inform," I said.

"Pity."

The doctor arrived and followed Papa back into the room. I

made my escape to join the party, finding them playing charades again in the drawing room.

I sat on an empty chair near my mother and watched as Henry smiled at me from across the room. There was a great deal of work to do before I could submit my novel, but I knew with his help it would find the correct publisher.

Daniel Palmer gave a riddle to the group. "What must be broken to be used?"

"A clock?" Mama asked.

Lord Moorington snapped his fingers. "An egg."

Daniel's gaze only briefly flashed to his stepfather in an acknowledgment he'd heard. "Yes."

"You have arrived just in time, you know," Lady Moorington said.

"Oh?" Daniel retook his seat, looking at his mother.

"Yes. We are to have a ball at the end of the week to celebrate the engagement."

"Oh," he said again, devoid of emotion. He ran a hand through his dark hair. "How grand."

"Do not fear," James said. "My wife does not dance. You can partner her as often as you wish and sit out for the entire evening."

Lord Moorington coughed. "He will do his duty. He is a Palmer man."

"Yes, my lord," Daniel said, though I detected sarcasm in his tone.

As for me, I could not wait to dance with Henry again.

CHAPTER 35

HENRY

When we returned from a ride the following morning, Shaw held a salver to me containing two letters. I took them and thanked him, flipping them over to discover the sender. I looked up and caught Marianne's gaze.

"Is it them?" she asked breathlessly.

"Yes." I took her hand. She gathered her habit in her other hand to keep it from dragging. "We shall read them together."

We walked down the corridor, past the drawing room where our mothers were gossiping, toward the open doors that led to the ballroom. Two men were painting designs on the floor in preparation for the ball to be held in two days' time, while a maid was fixing fresh candles into the lowered chandelier to be lit that evening. I pulled Marianne's hand until we reached the far wall, where light poured through the long windows and flooded us with warmth.

I looked at her. "Would you like to open them?"

"No. I can hardly stand the suspense." She watched me, waiting.

I was quick to rip them open and scan the words, then

handed her each letter to read herself. "Three publishers with interest, Mari. *Three*. You shall have your pick."

"You will advise me?"

"Of course." I smiled. "I knew they would want it. No more need to bother with Marbury."

"For either of us, perhaps?" she said.

I looked into her deep brown eyes. "What do you mean?"

"When we select a publisher and send them my manuscript, you ought to send yours as well. The original story, before you changed it."

The adventure story that was without romance, she meant. "Leave Marbury? He has done so much for me."

"Which you ought to be grateful for, of course, but you and I both know the story you wrote first was best. If Marbury does not want it, you ought to find someone else who does." She took my hand. "It is not disloyalty. It is remaining true to yourself. You may tell him of your plan first and allow him the opportunity to change his mind."

"I do not think he will."

She shrugged. "Then do as you wish, and find someone to publish the story you meant to tell. You do not need to change yourself to please others. You—and your words—are perfect the way they are."

I leaned forward and kissed her, heedless of the servants working around us or anyone else who might happen to pass by. The only thing I cared for in this moment was this woman. "Perhaps I will."

She grinned, then unfolded the letters and read them again.

Footsteps clicked down the corridor, leading someone toward us. I looked up to find Mrs. Hutton in the doorway, a worried expression on her brow. "That will be enough for now," she said to the servants. They ceased their efforts, facing her with confusion. "Cook has tea prepared in the kitchen. You may resume afterwards."

"Mama?" Marianne rose, crossing the gleaming, polished floor and avoiding the fresh paint, and I followed her. The maid at the chandelier and the men painting the floor all put aside their tools and filed from the room, leaving us alone. "What is the meaning of this?"

"Captain Neal has died."

Marianne gave a short intake of breath.

I, for one, was not surprised, though it certainly threw a pall over my mood.

"However unpleasant our relationship was with the man, I worry our celebration would not be in good taste." She reached forward, taking both me and Marianne by the forearms. "Though I dearly wish we do not need to cancel."

"Must we?" I asked. "The man was a blackguard who attempted to force Mari into marriage. We shall not celebrate his death, but I do not imagine anyone thinks the house needs to go into mourning, either."

"No, we certainly did not plan on doing so." Mrs. Hutton dropped our arms and clasped her hands together, her brow furrowed in concentration. "It is true that we would not wear black for him. It is a pity . . . but I think you are correct. By Friday, it should not be considered inconsiderate."

"Has Papa located any family?" Marianne asked.

"No. It seems the captain was telling the truth. Papa has written to the naval office and will see to it the proper channels are informed." She drew in a long breath and shook her head. "If you are certain you do not want him dishonorably discharged post—"

"I don't. He will soon be forgotten, and as that was his deepest fear, I think it is punishment enough without raking us through the mud of gossip."

Mrs. Hutton nodded in agreement. "I suppose we will proceed as planned for now."

"I think it is appropriate," Marianne said.

Mrs. Hutton turned to me, her smile losing its worried edge. "I am so glad to welcome you to our family, Henry." She squeezed my hand and left.

Marianne

My gown for the ball was superb. Sky blue with white embroidery throughout, it fit like a dream and made me feel like a princess when I entered the ballroom. Keene had gone to great effort to curl my hair into ringlets, gathering it in a flattering design high on my head and accentuating my bare neck. The room sparkled with the dancing flames of hundreds of candles and the excited energy of the guests who had already arrived.

I took my place beside Mama near the door. "Has Henry come downstairs yet?"

"Yes." She glanced over my shoulder. "Here he comes."

I looked to find him approaching and my heart nearly gave out. He wore a bottle green coat over black breeches, his curly brown hair rich in color and effortlessly mussed, his attention riveted on me. His gaze was direct and left no question as to the object of his thoughts.

Was it considered ill-mannered to sneak away with one's affianced during an engagement ball for a moment alone?

"He is handsome," Mama said quietly.

I swallowed. There would be no sneaking away while we were being watched so closely. "Indeed, he is."

Henry bowed to each of us. I offered him my hand, and he lifted it to place a kiss on my gloved knuckles.

"Are you prepared to meet the entire county? I do not believe my mother spared any paper when sending out invitations."

"More than just our county," Mama said. "Be prepared for the top half of England to congratulate you."

Henry bore the teasing easily. "I welcome it. The greater the crowd, the longer I will be permitted to stand at Marianne's side this evening under the guise of welcoming your friends."

Mama gave a little chuckle. "You are quite the charmer."

"My brother has earned that descriptor in our family," Henry said. "Though Marianne has a habit of bringing it out in me."

Mama looked at me with tenderness. "I do think you've made the right choice in husbands, darling."

I could not have agreed more.

With Henry standing at my side, we welcomed every acquaintance who lived within a reasonable distance until our ballroom was a veritable crush. By country ball standards, we had exceeded even my expectations, and I knew my mother's propensity for overindulging in her guest list. By the time Henry was able to lead me onto the dance floor, it was late in the evening. He guided me through a boulanger until it was time for me to move on to the next partner. By the time the dance had finished and I ended up back in Henry's arms, I was quite ready for the waltz that came next.

As it turned out, so was he. He pulled me close, moving through the motions, his gaze set on mine.

"I have had a little time to read this week," he said quietly.

"Oh? Have you found anything in my father's library to interest you?"

"No. I haven't had time to look there. I've been busy with your novel, my dear."

My heart leaped to my throat. "How far into the story have you read?"

"The entire thing."

Speech evaded me. I found I could not lift my eyes to see the expression he wore. His tone was playful and kind, but I feared the disinterest or boredom I would find in him.

"I loved it, Mari."

"You cannot mean that." I looked up sharply, the warmth of his blue eyes verifying his honesty.

"I was not surprised to love it. How could I not, when I love the woman who penned it?"

My body erupted with gentle butterflies, unforced and unbidden. "I would like to kiss you right now."

The blue of his eyes deepened. "I can make that a possibility."

When the music drew to a close, Henry took my hand and placed it on his bent arm. He smiled genially, leading me toward the terrace at a sedate pace. For the depth of my pounding heart, I was not feeling enough urgency from Henry. His slow steps and gentle way of moving through the crowds were not indicative of a man who wanted to kiss me as badly as I wanted to kiss him.

We stepped through the open doors and into the warm night, the breeze a soft reprieve from the stuffiness in the ballroom. Couples gathered in groups, their faces lit by the torches placed around the veranda. Henry pulled me softly toward the edge. "There is no privacy out here."

"There is the morning room through there," I said, pointing to a door on the opposite end of the veranda.

Henry tugged me along, stopping to greet a friend before moving toward the morning room door again.

"We will be seen," I whispered when he tried to open the door.

He looked down at me and pushed the door open. "We are already engaged."

My heart dove into the room, and my feet followed. Henry's hands were around my waist before the door closed all the way. He spun me so my back nestled flush against the wall, then leaned down, pressing his lips to mine in a long, slow kiss.

Henry leaned back and rested his forehead against mine, his breath ragged.

"I love you."

"I love you, too," he said, and then he leaned down and kissed me again.

EPILOGUE

MARIANNE

Two Years Later

My fingers drummed on my knees, my eyes flicking to the closed door through the carriage window. I wished I'd brought Keene, if only to keep me company. The wait was dragging, growing excruciating. How long had he been in there? Thirty minutes? It felt like ages.

"Where is he?" I muttered, leaning forward to better see through the window.

The door to Marbury's publishing office opened, and I leaned back in my seat quickly. I did not wish to be caught peeking.

Henry closed the door behind himself and came to the carriage, climbing inside and rapping the ceiling with his knuckles.

"Well?" I asked, more breath than legible speech.

A slow smile spread over his lips.

I squealed. "You did it?" I bounced in my seat and the motion of the carriage threw me against Henry. He caught me.

305

"Careful!" he admonished, his gaze dropping while his eyebrows pulled together.

"The baby is fine," I said, brushing off his concern. "I need details, Henry, and you are not providing them quickly enough."

He reached over and brushed a stray hair from my forehead. "Marbury sold the manuscript back to me. I have it in writing."

"How much did it take? A hundred pounds?"

His smile was victorious. "Ten."

I was robbed of speech.

Henry reached into his pocket and pulled out the signed contract, handing it to me. "Your novel is yours again, my love."

"You mean it?"

"I do. We can take it directly to Johansson now, if you'd like."

"Of course. I already told him he could have it if I ever managed to buy my rights back."

The carriage pulled to a stop, and Henry let himself out before turning to assist me down. "What are we doing?" I looked up to find Hatchard's green-trimmed window display. A small gasp slipped from my throat. "Did you know of this?"

Henry's grin could not have been wider. He pulled me toward the window and my fingers rested on the glass. My book, *A Patient Widow* by M.H.B., sat directly in the center of the display, surrounded by flowers folded of paper in an intricate design.

"I was tipped off. Turns out Felton is good for some things."

"That foolish man," I muttered, my smile wide. "Still trying to earn your forgiveness after the Gatley fiasco? It was over two years ago."

"I've told him he cannot prove he has changed by providing me with information, but he can't seem to help himself."

"You adore him anyway."

Henry made a noncommittal sound, though I knew it was

the case. He wasn't holding a grudge any longer. He'd forgiven his valet rather quickly, if I recalled correctly.

"Shall we go inside?" Henry held the door and I went into Hatchards to browse. We found both of our books on the shelves, glad to see very few remaining. When we reached the counter, four new books between the two of us, I stood aside so Henry could pay. I rested my hand on my rounded belly and felt the baby kick. He or she was just as happy to be in a bookstore as their parents were, it seemed.

"Lovely window display," Henry said.

"Have you read *A Patient Widow?*" the clerk asked, taking Henry's money.

"I have," he said, shooting me an amused smile. "We both have."

"Isn't it lovely?" she gushed. "I was half in love with Mr. Dalton myself."

Henry laughed. "Who wouldn't be? He was the perfect hero."

"Have you heard the rumor that the author named him after the adventure novelist?"

"You don't say?" Henry asked. "How interesting."

"I don't believe it," the clerk continued, wrapping the purchases in thick brown paper. She handed Henry our stack of books wrapped and tied with twine. "But I suppose you never know. Have a lovely day!"

"Thank you." Henry tucked the books under one arm and offered me his other. "What a fanciful rumor."

I grinned, stepping outside and letting the warm sunlight wash over my head. "Fanciful indeed." I drew in a steady breath. "I cannot believe we finally have the rights back."

We traveled down the street toward our waiting carriage. "Do you want to know the best part of buying back your manuscript?"

"What?"

307

Henry leaned down and pressed a kiss to the top of my head. "The look on Marbury's face when I told him that M.H. was the same M.H.B. who published *A Patient Widow*—the most popular novel in England."

I choked, laughter spilling from my chest. "You did not!"

He looked down at me with affection. "I couldn't help myself. It is safe to say he will be regretting his choices for the rest of his life."

Satisfaction pooled warmly in my stomach. I let Henry hand me up into the carriage. "I can't say I regret his choices. If he'd published me, we never would have had an agreement."

Henry settled himself beside me on the narrow bench. "True, my love. Thank you, Marbury."

"And books. We cannot forget the important role they play."

He leaned over and kissed me while the carriage rolled forward to convey us home. "Thank heavens for books."

AUTHOR'S NOTE

When researching the publishing process during the Regency era, I stumbled upon information about our dear Jane Austen and the rocky road she traveled to publishing. Her struggle was long-lasting, and her gender created walls and pitfalls we do not face as authoresses today. I decided, as an homage to Miss Austen, to include aspects of her process in my book. Marianne is, in a sense, my Jane Austen character.

Like Marianne, Jane sold her first manuscript for ten pounds. It was also not published, and they refused to sell it back. Jane's brother (who managed most of her affairs and communicated with her publishers) visited the publisher years later and bought back the manuscript for the same ten pounds. Upon leaving the man's office, he could not help himself and revealed it was a book by the same author who had written *Sense and Sensibility*, which was a success by this point. I imagine that publisher kicked himself for the rest of his life.

Jane also would make edits on her manuscripts by writing out the new sentences and pinning them to her paper with sewing pins. She did not publish under her own name, initially, but by "A Lady," and while her books gained popularity while she was alive, she did not become well known until later. Though I've read mixed reports about how popular she became, I think being invited to visit the Prince Regent because he is such a fan of her books likely meant she had reached some level of fame by that point.

Jane Austen is to be thanked for writing the best love story of all time, in my humble opinion, and I loved adding bits of her history to this story. As far as Mr. Darcy the cat is concerned, well, I just couldn't help myself.

A NOBLE INHERITANCE

They say reformed rakes make the best husbands...

Lady Verity wants nothing more than to provide a safe home for her sister, whose simple-mindedness is often misunderstood. When Lady Verity's father and husband both die, passing their house to a stranger, she vows to do whatever she must to ensure her sister's safety. The new earl has a reputation for being a rake, and Lady Verity is prepared to make him an offer he cannot refuse.

Daniel Palmer has run from his past for years, hiding from his failures and inadequacies by burying himself in cards, drink, and women. When a distant cousin and his heir both die, leaving Daniel with a title, house, and responsibilities he does not want, Daniel's impulse is to run. But his mother has different plans, and she invites the previous earl's widow and her two daughters to Arden Castle so they can become acquainted on neutral territory.

When the countess and her daughters arrive, Daniel quickly learns that Lady Verity is hiding something from him. But as he grows closer to the truth, he learns that not everything is as it seems, and sometimes the greatest sacrifices lead to the finest rewards.

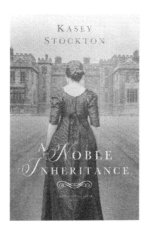

ACKNOWLEDGMENTS

Every book takes a village, and this one was no different. I'm so grateful for all of the eyes I have on my manuscripts, for my author friends who help brainstorm and problem solve with me, and the kind souls who are willing to read not-so-good drafts to give me feedback and help my stories improve. Just like Henry in the book, I have found A LOT of value in trusted friends' feedback, and I know it only improves my craft.

So thank you to my sweet beta readers: Brooke Losee, Nancy Madsen, Heidi Stott, Maren Sommer, Rebekah Isert, Martha Keyes, Kerry Perry, Jessica Boone, and Kelsy Hinton for your time and your feedback. Your feedback is uplifting and helpful, and I appreciate the cheerleading, too.

Thank you Karie Crawford for your polish and your editing expertise! And to Stefanie Saw for such a gorgeous cover. Thank you to my ARC team for your willingness to help me promote this book, and all the lovely bookstagrammers who post kind reviews. The world is a better place with your beautiful photos in it. You do spread joy.

Thank you Jon for doing so many dishes (I know I say that a lot, but he really deserves a medal for everything he does for me). I lucked out with you and I think we make the best team ever. #goteam

Thanks to my kids for your patience and support. Thanks to my family for still reading my books. Thanks to my friends for being kind enough to listen to me talk about books so much.

And finally, thank you to my Heavenly Father for blessing me with the best job ever.

Before you go, I want to thank you for reading my story. I hope you fell in love with Henry like Marianne and I did.

ABOUT THE AUTHOR

Kasey Stockton is a staunch lover of all things romantic. She doesn't discriminate between genres and enjoys a wide variety of happily ever afters. Drawn to the Regency period at a young age when gifted a copy of *Sense and Sensibility* by her grandmother, Kasey initially began writing Regency romances. She has since written in a variety of genres, but all of her titles fall under clean romance. A native of northern California, she now resides in Texas with her own prince charming and their three children. When not reading, writing, or binge-watching chick flicks, she enjoys running, cutting hair, and anything chocolate.

Made in United States
Orlando, FL
30 September 2023

37437112R00193